THE WOMEN
BEHIND THE DOOR

Fiction

The Commitments

The Snapper

The Van

Paddy Clarke Ha Ha Ha

The Woman Who Walked Into Doors

A Star Called Henry

Oh, Play That Thing

Paula Spencer

The Deportees

The Dead Republic

Bullfighting

Two Pints

The Guts

Two More Pints

Smile

Charlie Savage

Two for the Road

Love

The Complete Two Pints

Life Without Children

Non-Fiction

Rory & Ita

The Second Half

(with Roy Keane)

Kellie

(with Kellie Harrington)

For Children

The Giggler Treatment

Rover Saves Christmas

The Meanwhile Adventures

Wilderness

Her Mother's Face

A Greyhound of a Girl

Brilliant

Rover and the Big Fat Baby

THE WOMEN
BEHIND THE DOOR

Roddy Doyle

VIKING

VIKING

An imprint of Penguin Random House LLC
penguinrandomhouse.com

Published simultaneously in hardcover in Great Britain by Jonathan Cape,
an imprint of Penguin Random House Ltd., London, in 2024

First published in the United States by Viking, 2024

Grateful acknowledgment is made for permission to reprint lyrics from
"Crazy World" by Aslan (Dignam/Downey/Jewell/McGuinness/McGuiness).
Reprinted by kind permission of Elevate Music Productions Limited.

ISBN 9780593831687 (hardcover)
ISBN 9780593831694 (ebook)

Printed in the United States of America
1st Printing

For Dan Franklin

One

7 May 2021

She's just back from getting her jab. She's filling the kettle. She isn't sure why. She doesn't really want tea. Any tea – Barry's, chamomile, peppermint. It's just the habit. She gives out to herself sometimes, for making tea that she won't be drinking. But then she thinks – she knows: the tea has replaced the alcohol. She's keeping her hands and her head busy. Better a cup in her hand than a glass, although – she doesn't need to remember – she'd have drunk her gin or her vodka out of a coal bucket. There were often no glasses in the house and that never stopped her.

She has about seven boxes of different kinds of tea. Nicola, her eldest, brought most of them into the house. Paula would swear that one of them, the sage tea, has been there for over a decade, shoved into the corner beside the toaster. It can stay there. She's never going to drink something that is supposed to be shoved up the turkey's arse. She can't remember what it tastes like. She remembers she hated it – she hated the idea of it.

She fills the mug – 'Glamorous Granny', a present from one of the grandkids. Her hand hovers over the boxes and dives into the chamomile. It has calming properties, Nicola told her.

—So does death, hon, said Paula.

—You're gas.

—Am I not calm enough for you, Nicola?

—You're useless, said Nicola. —It's good for premenstrual tension as well, by the way.

—Now she fuckin' tells me.

It's been strange watching her children grow old. She loves being with Nicola, being out anywhere with her. She loves watching people look at her, women and men. This incredible woman – the way she dresses and carries herself, the way Nicola looks straight back at the world. She's my daughter, Paula wants to shout. Believe it or not. She came out of me. At her lowest ebb, Paula can look at Nicola and think to herself, Not everything's been a disaster. And believe it. She's a goddess, Nicola is. She's a goddess but she's going through the change. Paula has a menopausal daughter.

—I drank through mine, she told Nicola, the last time they spoke.

Poor Nicola.

She brings the tea with her, in to the telly. She won't be drinking it, even if it is good for the calmness. The steam will keep her company. And she's perfectly calm. She's even a bit elated. She's had a great day.

She turns on the telly. There's always the delay, when the screen stays black and she half-expects nothing to happen. But there it is now – she'll get another night out of it. She expects everything she has to break. Everything in the house that has a switch or a button. Every friendship, every relationship. Her family.

But it really has been a great day.

She registered for the vaccination about ten days ago, when she heard on the radio that all people over sixty-five could do it. She was pleased with herself that she'd managed it, all the online stuff, especially when she got the text with the six-figure code to verify her application. She looked at it just the once and could remember it long enough to type the numbers into the boxes – and it worked. She'd been going to text Nicola, to tell her. But she hadn't. She was registered – she could see that. It was there on the screen of her phone. She'd be getting a text with the date and time and the venue within four to seven days. But she'd still expected it to go wrong.

She won't be drinking the tea and she isn't really looking at the telly. She's turned the sound down – she can barely hear it. Her other daughter, Leanne, told her that she holds the remote control like it's a wand and Voldemort is coming at her.

—Which one is Voldemort?

—Ralph Fiennes.

—Well, in that case. He can come at me any time he wants.

—He's not the way he normally is.

—Doesn't matter.

—His face is all squashed, said Leanne – they were laughing. —He doesn't have a proper nose.

—I can get past that, hon, don't worry.

It's the time of day when she puts on the telly. She wants the company, but she isn't particularly loyal to any programme. She just wants to sit in front of it.

When the text arrived she was nervous. She doesn't like getting messages from people or numbers she doesn't know. The kids have all warned her – and so has her oldest granddaughter – not to answer or click anything. But she wouldn't anyway. She has a bank account and a card, and a few direct debits that she sorted, herself. She holds the card sometimes and feels proud. She's come a long way. And she doesn't want some creep in the arse-end of Russia cleaning out her account or robbing her identity. Paula was married to a thief and it took her years to get her identity back. No one else is going to rob it. Not if Paula can help it.

But this text looked legit. 'COVID-19 vaccine dose 1 appointment: Paula Spencer, age 66 years. When: Friday 7 May 11.05 a.m. Where: Helix Theatre Vaccination Centre (CVC). Helix Theatre DCU, Collins Avenue, Glasnevin, Dublin 9.

Vaccine: AstraZeneca. Read the patient information leaflet.'
She wasn't expected to respond or click. She just had to turn up.

She has a good friend, Mary, who's the same age as Paula; there's only three weeks between them. They'd half-planned on having a joint birthday party when they both hit sixty-five last year but the Covid had put a stop to that. She'd phoned Mary when she got the HSE text.

—I got me appointment.

—So did I.

—Friday.

—Same here, yeah.

—The Helix.

—Brilliant. We'll make a day of it.

The Helix is 3.2K from where Paula is sitting. She checked it on Google Maps when she got the text and she was wondering how she'd get there. But another friend of theirs, Mandy – she moved into a house down the road from Paula about ten years ago – she drove them. She's a good bit younger than Paula and Mary – she still has two of her kids in school. She hasn't even registered yet but she went along with them for the crack.

—We shouldn't be doing this, sure we shouldn't? said Mary, when Mandy was reversing the car onto the road. —Three of us in the car.

—No harm with the windows open, said Mandy.

She'd turned, so she could see out the back window. She was wearing a leopard-print mask and her glasses were cloudy. She was looking straight at Paula but she didn't seem to know it.

—I can't see a fuckin' thing – are you back there, Paula?

—You're staring at me, chicken.

—Well, tell me if I'm going to hit anything, will you.

She backed the car through the gate but put her foot on the brake, and took her mask off.

—Covid or car crash – which d'yis prefer, girls?

—Covid, please.

—Same here.

—Grand, said Mandy, and she hung the mask off the rear-view mirror.

They started laughing. They were giddy, like kids. If Paula hadn't known better she'd have said that she felt a bit drunk. But she did know better.

—Come here, said Paula.

She leaned forward, as much as her seat belt would let her.

—Why are you coming with us?

—I'll give you a hint, said Mandy. —I'm driving the car.

—Mary has a car, said Paula.

—I asked her, said Mary. —I was worried I wouldn't be up to the driving after the jab.

—And I wanted a few hours away from the kids, said Mandy.

—They're in school.

—Their photographs, said Mandy. —Their clothes, their dinner. Every little fuckin' thing about them. D'you remember that weekend we had in Kilkenny last year – no, the year before last?

—I do, yeah.

—Well, this is it for me, said Mandy. —This is me long weekend.

—Okay.

—Jesus, said Mary. —It feels like longer than – what is it?

—Twenty-one months, said Paula.

—Since we were in Kilkenny?

—That's right.

—Jesus, said Mary. —It feels like another life.

—Doesn't it?

It's hard to imagine it now, the way life was before the lockdowns. But it did feel a bit familiar to Paula when it started. She's always had to be careful. Since she gave up the drinking and stayed that way. She's had to be careful about where she goes, how long she stays. Careful about her friends. Careful about her mood. Very careful with the money. It took her years to make this – living carefully – a source of pride.

She's sitting alone in front of the telly with a mug of tea that she isn't drinking. And that's exactly what she was doing the day Leo Varadkar strolled up to the microphone and shut the country down, more than a year ago. For the first time in her life she'd felt ready. Up for it. Prepared, and ahead of the rest. She's been living with restrictions for years.

She'd been to the Helix before, with her man friend, Joe. Opera stuff, mostly. Arias – songs just, not a whole opera. The first few times she went with him, she kept imagining her husband sitting on the other side of her. *What the fuck are we doing here, Paula? You're not here, Charlo, you're dead. Fair enough – but seriously? Paula – this shite?* And she'd agreed with Charlo; it was kind of dreary. But it was nice, and the theatre itself was lovely. And she'd a box of Maltesers on her lap. *It wasn't always fuckin' Maltesers that you wanted on your lap – sure it wasn't, Paula? Fuck off, Charlo.*

She's doing that a lot, talking to Charlo. But she's the one in charge. He only says what she wants him to. No surprises – it never gets nasty. He's half her age, but so is she when she's talking to him.

—Strange place to have a theatre, isn't it? said Mandy when they were going up the ramp into the car park, directed by two kids in masks and the high-vis gear.

—No charge for the parking, said Mary. —We'll come here again, girls.

—What's strange about it? Paula asked.

She was feeling a bit protective.

—Well, it's not fuckin' Broadway, is it? said Mandy. —It's nearly Ballymun.

—There's a theatre in Ballymun, said Mary. —My John's kids were in a show in it – the Axis.

—A theatre in Ballymun makes sense, said Mandy. —In the

centre, like. Ballymun has a centre – a middle to it, like. But this isn't even Ballymun. Where are we?

—Glasnevin.

—Whitehall – I think.

—D'yis see what I mean? We're kind of on the edge of nowhere. We're not sure where we are.

—It's a university, said Paula.

—Look, I'm sure it's grand, said Mandy. —But it's a weird location – is all I'm saying. You wouldn't go to *Les Mis* here, would you?

They were out of the car, checking they'd their masks and the other things they needed.

—'Course I would, said Paula.

—Me too, said Mary. —I've been to loads of things here.

—*The Wizard of Oz*, said Paula. —I went with Nicola and her gang – here.

—Was there a show of *The Wizard of Oz*?

—The film.

—Why did you go to a film in a theatre? Mary asked.

They were following the signs to the Vaccination Centre.

—There was an orchestra playing the music, said Paula.

—Oh, that must've been brilliant.

—It was.

She was glad she'd remembered *The Wizard of Oz*. She hadn't wanted to mention the times she'd been here with Joe. The girls didn't really get Joe, what Paula was doing with him, how the arrangement worked. Nothing had ever been said but their faces changed, they kind of looked away, shutters came down, when Joe came up in the chat. Truth be told, Paula wasn't sure what she did with him either. Especially now when she hardly saw him.

They were out of the car park itself, the bare cement box, and they were looking through the glass down at the entrance to the theatre.

—How do we get down there?

—Stairs or lift.

—I've a stairs at home, said Mary. —We'll give the lift a go.

A man stepped out when the lift doors opened. He'd a big face that his mask didn't come close to covering.

—Is this it, is it? he asked.

He was looking around for a man to give him the answer, Paula guessed. But there were no men.

He looked at Mary.

—Is this what? she said.

—The vaccinating?

—This is the car park.

—Still – is it? I thought I'd got out.

—It's over there, look it.

Mandy pointed at the glass, and at the theatre outside and the marquee in front of it, and the queue that Paula now noticed seemed to stretch out onto Collins Avenue.

—I thought I was over there, said the man. —Jesus.

He retreated back into the lift and stood in its centre.

—Stairs, girls, Paula whispered.

They were still laughing when they got out into the air and saw that the queue wasn't too bad and that it was moving at a fair clip. They looked back and saw the big man in there, at ground level, behind the glass, still trying to find his way out.

—God love him, said Paula. —He's anxious.

—He's just fuckin' thick.

The HSE text had told Paula not to turn up more than five minutes early. She checked the time on her phone. She was bang on, and pleased. Mary was a quarter of an hour late.

—There's no way they're going to send me home, she said. —My sister, Jenny – her chap. Seamus. He turned up a day late and they still let him in. The priority is to get all of us vaccinated – it's not school.

The queue was moving forward, women and men alone, a few feet between them, as Paula and the others fixed their masks on and walked to the back.

—This isn't too bad.

—No, it's grand.

—Here's Big Mush – look it.

—Ah stop.

—His tongue's hanging out from under his mask.

—Fuckin' stop.

The man with the face passed them on his way to the back. He still didn't look happy. He wasn't convinced it was the right queue.

—Seriously, though, Mandy, said Paula. —You shouldn't be here.

—Where's the harm?

Paula wanted Mary to herself. That was the truth of it. Just for a little while. Just the two of them. Something they could share, with none of the rivalry or complications.

—They'll kick up when they find you, said Paula. —A young one in with all the oul' ones.

—Mind you, said Mary. —Come here.

She'd lowered her voice. Paula had to bring her ear close to Mary's mouth.

—We're not doing too badly, girls, said Mary. —The state of some of these ones.

Paula burst out laughing behind her mask. She'd been thinking the same thing. As far as she could see, she was the only one on her side of the queue that wasn't lopsided. Everyone ahead of her was leaning to the left or the right, or on the verge of falling forward. Mary's laughing had made her glasses steam up. It was like Paula could see the laughter, how it filled the lenses, then faded.

—They're all sharing the one big tracksuit – look it, said Mary. —The men – Jesus.

There was a lot of grey, alright.

—Shut up, for fuck sake, said Paula. —They'll hear you.

—I doubt it, said Mary. —They're deaf as well, I'm betting.

—The women, but, said Mandy. —There's a bit of colour at least.

She was looking around her, head up – gawking – like a big anxious girl searching for her friends.

—Jesus, though, girls, said Mary. —Is this the queue for the hip replacements or wha'?

The leaflet said that there might be after-effects but, so far, nothing; Paula's feeling grand. Sore arm, bruising, dizziness, bit of a fever – none of that, although she's only home. Joe had his first jab a few weeks ago. He's a good bit older than Paula. But he was fine, he told her – he phoned her the day after. And she met him a few days after that, at the seafront. They walked to the roundabout at the end of the Causeway Road and back to his car, where he'd parked it on Watermill Road. The plaster's still on her arm, where she got the injection, so she can't see if there's a bruise. But she's not sore there or anything. And there was a time when her arm and the rest of her body would have been covered in bruises.

Joe was fine, he told her.

—Not a bother, he said. —Nothing untoward.

Fuckin' untoward – Paula? Get lost – fuck off, Charlo.

She hasn't seen Joe since, although they've spoken on the phone and he texted her five minutes after she came out of the Helix. He'd been right; the whole thing had taken fifty minutes, in and out. He hasn't spent a night in her bed and she hasn't slept in his since March last year. Fourteen months. He kissed her at Christmas. That was all. Lips to cheek. No other contact. They haven't held hands. He hasn't put his arm across her back. She could phone him now. She might. But she's happy here in her bubble. It's been a great day. Tomorrow might not be.

The queue had moved quickly, up to the marquee in front of the theatre doors, where they'd been divided into different lines and a girl with a high-vis vest had come at them with a clipboard and a marker. She wanted to know what time they were supposed to be there at. Paula told her her time and waited to be told she was wrong, even though she knew she was right, as the girl looked for her name on the list on her clipboard. She watched the girl as she found Paula's name and ran the yellow marker across it. She'd passed. The girl didn't react when Mary told her her time, and she wasn't interested in Mary's excuse – she wasn't listening. She just flipped back a few pages and found Mary's name.

—Grand, she said, and she went across the name with the yellow marker. —And d'yis have your photo IDs, ladies?

—I do, said Paula, and she went for her shirt pocket.

—No, said the girl. —For inside. They'll want to see it inside.

—Oh, said Paula. —Grand.

Mandy was gone – Paula hadn't noticed. Then she saw her back over at the car-park door, and waved. It was just Paula and Mary.

—I'm quite excited now, Paula, said Mary. —I have to say.

—Me too, yeah, said Paula.

—A good-looking doctor giving me a jab – lovely way to spend the morning.

—You're a fuckin' sewer, you are.

—*Pandemic Passion*, said Mary. —You'd watch that one – go on. Or read it.

—Okay.

—Even at our age.

—Specially.

—Bang on, hon. *Covid Nights*.

—On Netflix – brilliant.

—*Lockdown Lingerie*.

—Who's in that one?

—Me.

—In your jammies.

—Me good ones, yeah, said Mary. —D'you like me new cardigan, by the way?

—Is it new? said Paula. —It's gorgeous.

She'd decided a few years ago that she hated cardigans. She'd looked at herself one day – one night – in the mirror of a ladies' toilet she was cleaning, in the Ulster Bank beside Tara Street station. She was wearing a cardigan and because she'd been bending and standing, bending and standing, it was bunched around her waist like a flat bicycle tyre. It was a present from Leanne but she didn't care – she never wore it again. Or any other cardigan.

—Dunnes, said Mary. —I'm delighted with it, so I am.

—It looks great on you.

—Yeah, said Mary. —Well – you know yourself, hon. If you have the figure for it. Fuckin' flaunt it, yeah? Am I right?

—You're dead right.

—Me, you and Naomi Campbell. We know.

—We do, alright, said Paula. —Is Naomi here, is she?

—She's always late, that bitch, said Mary. —I'll look out for one for you.

She patted her cardigan.

—One of those.

—There's no need, said Paula.

—No bother, said Mary. —Different colour, but – not that you know anything about colour, Paula.

—Ah, feck off.

—We can't be looking like twins.

—No.

—Do twins still look like each other when they get to our age, do they?

—I don't know, said Paula.

—That'd be a bit weird, said Mary.

She glanced around, like she was on the lookout for some elderly twins.

—I don't look like me sister, she said. —Thank Christ. She's a ringer for me father – bald an' all.

—Stop.

Paula was loving this. She felt like she was in school, in the queue to get into the class. With her best friend, both of them cuddled in their own secret language. They were sent inside to the foyer by a man with a walkie-talkie who didn't make eye contact or speak to them. He just waved them on like they were sheep or cars.

—He won't be in the film, said Mary.

—No way.

—Fat fuck.

Something – something about being under a low roof – Mary's words immediately sounded hollow and very loud. They burst out laughing – Paula could feel her mask digging into her. There were people all around them, literally, even if they were all trying to keep the two metres apart – and not all of them were. But they couldn't stop laughing. They'd look at each other and start again.

—I wonder has anyone fainted because they laughed with a mask on.

—It wouldn't surprise me.

A nicer man pointed Paula to a hatch. A young lad – she could see him smiling behind his mask. He even spoke to her.

—Number 10 now – just across there, thanks.

It was strange – not nice – seeing the theatre like this. Like a scene from a war or some sort of natural disaster, a flood or a fire. Or like a church turned into a hardware shop or a brothel. The row of hatches looked temporary, dropped into the foyer in a hurry. But the girl behind the glass was lovely, and patient when Paula was rooting for her passport.

—No hurry.

—I'm a bit nervous, said Paula.

It was true, she realised. Alone, she was nervous. More than excited.

—It'll be grand, the girl told her. —I got it done, like. There's nothing to it and it's not sore at all, like.

—Thanks.

—And you'll get a badge.

The girl was smiling.

—Brilliant, said Paula.

She laughed again, although this time she didn't want to.

The girl slid the passport back to her, and a leaflet.

—You're to read that.

—Lovely, said Paula. —Is it any good, is it?

She laughed, and saw the girl looking past her.

—Thanks again.

She followed the arrows on the floor through the door of what used to be the theatre. She went through the same door, she thought, when she was with Nicola and her kids and her son John Paul's youngest, when they were going in to see *The Wizard of Oz*. That must have been ten years ago – even more. She remembered – Nicola was going out to the toilet with her little one, Lily, during the intermission, and she'd whispered to Paula as she squeezed past her.

—We're separating.

She remembered her heart thumping, like her heart had made sense of what Nicola had said before Paula's head caught up with it. They'd gone to McDonald's in Artane after the film and Paula got the chance to ask her.

—Are you okay?

She was hoping it was the right question to ask, before all the other things she wanted to know.

—Yeah, said Nicola. —I'm grand – thanks. I'm alright.

—Good. Grand. What made – why did you tell me – in the theatre, like?

—The Tin Man.

—What?

—His face.

—Tony doesn't look like the Tin Man, love.

—A bit.

—No.

—The expression.

The heads were close together. They were leaning into each other. Paula was loving the intimacy. Although she liked Tony, Nicola's husband.

—How long are yis married?

Nicola sighed, pushed the air out of herself.

—Doesn't matter.

—Does he know?

—What?

—Does he actually know that you're leaving him?

—I'm not leaving, I'm not going anywhere. And yeah, 'course he does. He thinks I'm seeing someone.

Nicola lifted herself up a bit, away from Paula, so she could look at her.

—I'm not.

—No.

—He just can't imagine there'd be any other reason, said Nicola. —That he might be involved, like.

She settled herself back in beside Paula.

—There's nothing wrong, said Nicola. —With Tony. He's nice and – same as ever. But –.

—What?

—I don't want to feel him against my back any more. Do you know what I mean?

—I think so, said Paula. —Yeah.

She wasn't sure that she did understand but that didn't matter. She was doing it right, she thought. She was listening. She wasn't judging. She thought Nicola was probably crazy but she was keeping it to herself. Letting her talk. Letting her trust Paula. Nicola had been Paula's mother for years, the roles reversed since Nicola was fifteen, younger, since she saw Paula smashing the frying pan down on her father's head and bully-ing him out of the house. This was different, though. Paula was the mother again and it was just great. And terrifying.

They hadn't separated. They must have talked – worked something out. Nicola never mentioned it again. And Paula never asked.

Mary was ahead of her in the queue now. There were two women between them, and a man. It was the poor eejit who couldn't find his way out of the car park earlier. She hoped Mary wouldn't look back and see him as well, the mask stretched across the big face. It would set them off again. And he'd know – or he'd guess that they were laughing about him.

17

He'd assume it. He was that kind of man. Everything about him was defeated – he was lost in his body. She watched him climbing the steps to the stage – his huge back, the meaty legs, hoisting up his jeans when he got onto the second step. A woman at the top of the steps pointed him at one of the aisles, and he was gone.

She was going up the steps herself now. She wondered would she have known she was on the stage, if she hadn't been here before. It must have been huge, much bigger than it looked from the seats. All the vaccination booths were up here. She saw a '39', and a '38'. There was space on the stage for the whole operation. She was less nervous now. There was no sign of Mary. She felt alone. She felt good. She waited – she smiled at the woman. A woman her own age, Paula thought. A volunteer, probably. She was looking down one of the aisles. She looked at Paula.

—27, she said.

She didn't point.

Paula saw the number, down what she thought was the middle aisle – where the crisps and the biscuits would have been if she'd been in her local Centra. There was a tall man at the booth, waiting for her, holding the curtain back. In his late thirties, she guessed. The cut of a doctor about him. But he looked at her, and he smiled, and he stepped back a bit to make sure that she had plenty of room to get past him. He'd a nice blue shirt on him, and serious glasses.

The booth was as narrow as a toilet you'd get in a pub – a little bit wider maybe but the same basic shape. But there was a table and two chairs in it and he was standing at the chair that was furthest from the curtain. She hadn't noticed him going past her. He was looking at her. He'd said something but she hadn't heard him. That happened to her sometimes – she didn't hear. When she was anxious, or afraid she'd be stupid.

—You can sit down, he said – again, she thought.

She sat.

—Thanks.

She noticed – he waited till she sat before he did. He was well reared. She couldn't believe it – she could feel a blush trying to take off, bubbling away under her skin. She'd thought that part of herself was dead; she hoped it was. She'd have hated to be sitting there with her face going all red. But it was hilarious too. She was never too far from the teenager. It was mortifying, but brilliant.

She listened carefully, and answered when she needed to – her date of birth, her health. Grand. Allergies. None. Underlying conditions. None either – she'd keep them to herself. *Urinary incontinence, Doctor, but nothing too mad. And I'm a bit lonely, sometimes. And I kind of wake up in the hall at home sometimes – become aware of where I am, like – and I haven't a clue why I'm there. But grand.*

He was standing again. He was waiting for her to roll up her sleeve. She was wearing a shirt – it was a shirt; it wasn't a blouse – that Leanne had given her. Jeans and a plaid cotton shirt. She was Dolly Parton. But she couldn't get the sleeve up far enough. She had to unbutton the shirt and lower it off her shoulder. Wait till she told Mary. No – she wasn't going to be telling Mary. There were things she kept to herself – and for herself.

—I'm administering Covid-19 vaccine AstraZeneca, he said. —You understand?

—Yeah, she said. —Fire away.

He laughed quietly. She heard it through his mask.

—There'll be a stinging sensation, more than likely.

—Not a bother, she said.

She didn't look. He was right – it hurt. But if he'd seen the state of her skin, years ago – but never that long ago – when she was her husband's beloved punchbag, he wouldn't have mentioned the sting that the needle might give her. He'd have said nothing. But maybe she was wrong. Maybe if he'd been a doctor in A&E – he'd have been a child, if he'd even been alive, the last time Charlo put her into hospital – he'd have been the one doctor who looked at the bruises and asked her where she got them. He was definitely nice. She'd made him laugh – he'd been happy to.

She pulled the shirt back over her shoulder and buttoned up. She watched him filling in the card. It was her vaccination record. She recognised it. Joe had sent her a photo of his.

He held the card out to her.

—Bring this with you when you're called for your second dose.

He smiled. His mask moved with his face.

—Paula.

He was flirting with her. The scamp. Half her age. She nearly ran across the stage to the steps on the other side. To get away from her silly self. She had to sit in the foyer – it still looked like the foyer – for ten minutes. To make sure she didn't feel faint, she supposed. Or sick. Mary was there ahead of her, sitting close to the stairs. There was an empty seat beside her.

—How was that?

—Fuckin' agony, said Mary in a way that made Paula laugh.

—Same here, she said.

—D'you know what, though, Paula?

—What?

—I feel fuckin' great, said Mary.

—Yeah.

—Elated.

—Yeah.

—That's the word, yeah?

—It'll do, said Paula.

She'd half-expected that she'd feel happy. And secure – or, more secure. Not this, though. Elated. Like the minutes after sex. Floating on the afters of the orgasm.

They said nothing for a while, and Paula wondered if Mary felt the same way she did. She sometimes forgot that Mary was a woman. Mary was a comedian. She wasn't just funny but she was a clown, really, always on the go. She was a bitch, Paula, thinking that way. She was blessed having someone she could think of as her best friend, at her age. Growing old with this one beside her.

—What was yours like?

The voice – the sound so near – gave her a fright.

—Jesus –.

She laughed.

—Sorry – I was miles away. What did you say, Mare?

She didn't know why she was asking, because she'd heard what Mary had said. She just wanted the time – to pull herself together.

—What was your jabber like? said Mary.

—My jabber?

—You know what I mean.

—Well, what was *your* jabber like?

—A ride, said Mary. —The Lone Ranger, he was.

They laughed. Paula had no real idea why it was funny. It just was.

—What about your one? Mary asked her.

Paula shook her head.

—No, she said. —Nothing to write home about.

—A man, but?

—Yeah.

She sees her phone light up, on the couch beside her leg. She's had it on silent since this morning, when she got into the queue at the Helix. She keeps it on silent a lot of the time; she hates the buzzy stuff.

She picks up the phone. She brings it closer to her face – her glasses are in the kitchen. It's Nicola – she knew it would be. She's given up waiting for Paula to answer her texts. Paula lets the call ring out. She'll phone Nicola in a minute. That way it'll feel like her decision.

She's sick of her kids. She's just a bit sick of them. She can think that – no one's going to stop her. She's alone in the house and she loves it. Leanne was the last to leave – finally. Paula has lived on her own since – it's five years now, a bit more. It's not good watching her children growing old. Catching up with her. It's not right – for them or for her. It only makes sense when they go off, and come back to visit. When their lives belong to themselves. She's lonely sometimes – she'll admit that to anyone. But it's nothing to do with being alone in the house. It's a lot to do with death. She thinks. Her husband – her ex-husband. Husband – they were never divorced; he got himself killed before divorce came into the country. Her sister, Carmel. Her important people are dead. Joe suggested once – half-suggested it in that fuckin' polite way of his. That she should move in with him. Not him in with her. She was the one who was expected to up sticks. *It might be something to think about.* He could fuck off, so he could. She didn't want to live in an apartment and she didn't want him living here. She didn't want to live with him, anywhere. She can't remember now when he said it. Before the Covid. A year and a half. Two years. Five. She doesn't know. Time doesn't work the way it used to.

She's happy enough. She likes that one – happy enough. It doesn't mean she's happy. She's not sure what that might feel like. But she knows she's happy enough. I'm happy enough – it means leave me alone.

She looks at the clock on the phone. It's nearly six.

She points the remote at the telly, so the sound goes up. She'll turn it down when she phones Nicola. It'll give Nicola the idea that she's busy, she's been doing something productive. Even if it's only watching the telly. She scrolls down through the news channels and stops at CNN. That'll sound serious enough. She watched CNN earlier in the year, when those lads in their Halloween costumes tried to take over the Capitol place in Washington. When it looked like the start of a civil war or something. Her Jack – her youngest – lives over there, in Chicago. She texted him to tell him she was watching. He texted back, and she texted back. And watching what happened that night, and what didn't happen, and knowing that Jack was watching it at the same time. It was brilliant. Thrilling. She didn't surrender till three in the morning. And even then she slept here, on the couch. She'd brought the duvet down from Leanne's old bed upstairs. And the couch was a present from Nicola. So three of her kids were with her, as she watched democracy nearly topple. And there's a photo of John Paul and his gang on the mantelpiece, so he was with her as well. They were all there. But especially Jack.

She finds Nicola's number in Favourites. It deliberately isn't on the top of the list. In case the others ever saw it there. The top is where the number should be, but not because Nicola is her favourite child. Because that's the number she's phoned most often – that's the number that's saved her. The grandkids are at the top, in order of age – youngest first. She's betting that whoever designed that part of the phone, or whoever it was that named it Favourites, didn't have children or he only had the one. She's betting it was a man.

—Hiya.

It's Nicola. She must have had the phone in her hand when Paula called.

—Hang on till I turn this thing down, hon, says Paula. —Now.

—How did it go? Nicola asks.

—Grand.

—Grand?

—Great – yeah.

Paula's the teenager – she's giving away the minimum.

—Did it hurt? Nicola asks her.

—No.

Nicola hasn't been vaccinated yet. For Paula, getting there ahead of her feels like an achievement. She feels a shiver run through her that might be something like happiness.

—And how're you feeling now?

—Grand.

—Tired?

—No.

She is, but she's not going to admit it. It isn't important. But she knows she's being a bit mean.

—It was a great day, really, she says.

—How was it –? Jesus –.

—Hang on now, says Paula. —I know it wasn't Tayto Park or Disneyland. But it was – it was a lovely day. Mary was with me. And Mandy.

Nicola tolerates Mary but she can't stand Mandy. Mandy's the same age as Nicola – she might even be a year or two younger. Paula can understand the hostility, her mother being pally with a woman her own age. She didn't have to mention Mandy, but she did anyway. Deliberately. She hears Nicola saying nothing, swallowing back the words.

—Mary got the call today as well, Paula says. —And Mandy gave us a lift. We made a day of it. Mandy wanted to go to McDonald's without her kids.

Still nothing from Nicola. Paula's feeling a bit cruel. Not enough, though, to stop her.

—So that's what we done, she says. —For the laugh. Just the drive-through, you know. We couldn't go in. But we brought the stuff on to Dollymount. And Mary had a flask of coffee and a few cakes.

She feels her forehead as she speaks.

—I think I might even be a little bit sunburnt, she says. —Anyway, we stayed there for the whole afternoon. The girls had a glass of wine as well.

—Jesus – you had a picnic?

—Yeah, says Paula. —I hadn't thought of it like that but that's what it was.

She laughs.

—Mad, she says. —How are you, hon?

She feels sated. She learnt that one from Joe. Sated. It's a simple sound and it surprised her that she didn't know the word when she heard it – she thought – the first time. She smiles now as she remembers when he said it, and where and why. But she won't be telling Nicola. Nicola's the best in the world but just now, just for the rest of the day, she can get lost and leave Paula alone. She thinks that and, immediately, the thought stops – it goes away.

—D'you know what it felt like, Nicola? she says. —The vaccination. The experience of it, like.

—What?

—I felt elated, says Paula.

—How come?

Fair play to Nicola, she's trying. There's no edge – aggression or sarcasm – in the question.

—I was just –. It felt like I'd got my exam results and I'd done really well.

She laughs. Nicola knows – there's no need to explain. Paula's never done an exam in her life. Not in school, and not since.

—And as well, she says. —I was doing me bit, you know. I won't be infecting anyone. Anyway, it was great.

—Good.

—And come here, says Paula.

She's liking Nicola, she's loving her. That 'good' – the way Nicola said it – it was soft. She'd understood. She'd spoken to Paula like an equal. Like she trusted her. There was even a little bit of envy in it.

—There were starlings, she says. —In Dollymount.

Paula can identify starlings, and she'd told Mary and Mandy what they were.

—They're not only fuckin' birds, Mary, she'd said, earlier. —They're starlings.

Joe had told her one day, a freezing cold day years ago, when they saw a whole flock, a murmuration – there's a word – a murmuration of them, changing shape in front of them, like a show. And later, they'd seen just one perched on the back of a chair outside a café and Joe had told her what it was. And she was elated today – again – when she saw them in Dollymount, on Bull Island, in among the parked cars and bikes, beside the Happy Out place. She loved being able to name them.

—They're gorgeous birds when you look at them, she tells Nicola. —The colours in their feathers – my God.

She feels a bit high. Nicola might think she's drunk. She can't tell her she isn't – she'd be proving she is.

—But there were loads of them, she says. —The starlings. Looking for food, crumbs and that. And Nicola – guess what?

—What?

—The noise they were making. They were imitating car locks.

—What?

—They're brilliant mimics, says Paula. —They copy the calls of other birds and – I swear to God – you know the noise a car makes when you point the key thing at it when you're locking it?

—Yeah.

—That's the noise they were making, says Paula. —The girls were amazed.

It had thrilled Paula, the expressions on their faces when they realised what they were hearing, what Paula was after telling them. She'd felt like a ringmaster, like she was organising it all with the birds.

—It's just been a lovely day, she says. —I'll be back to normal tomorrow, don't worry.

It's Nicola's turn to speak. But she says nothing.

—And how are you, hon? Paula asks again.

—Well –.

—Nicola –?

—Grand, says Nicola. —No – I'm grand. Just tired. I just wanted to know how you got on.

Nicola's gone. Paula drops the phone beside her. She'll phone her back tomorrow and have a proper chat, ask her properly how she is, be her mother and a pal. Not tonight, though. She wouldn't hear. Joe will be next – Joe will phone her. Joe and his 'sated'. She hasn't been fair to Joe. She thinks, sometimes. Sated Joe.

They were in bed. Joe's bed, in Howth. And he'd told her that the Japanese had a word for the mental state of a man immediately after orgasm.

26

—The state of a man? she'd said.

She was pulling the duvet back over herself but she didn't want it to look too urgent or obvious.

—Yes, he'd said.

—Like gasping and sweating, she said. —Is that the state you mean?

—I'm not gasping, said Joe.

—But you're sweating, she said. —You'd better be.

She put her hand on the meat of his back. It was slick, and still warm. She could feel his breaths on her palm, his polite gasps.

He laughed.

—Not that state, no, he said. —The mental state, I mean.

—What mental state?

—Good question.

—Are you not supposed to be brainless after a good ride?

—That's it, though, he said.

He sat up, a bit – he pushed himself up against the head-board. He didn't cover himself. He was a strange mix, Joe. He'd cringe when he heard the word 'fuck' but he dived right in when it came to sex. He'd have said anything about sex – like a scientist, nearly. And he stopped being self-conscious. He didn't care that he was seventy-two. He didn't care what she saw, or what he saw of himself.

—I read it, he said.

—Where?

—In the paper, he said. —It's a while ago now. The *Observer*, I think it might have been.

Joe read two papers on Sundays, cover to cover. He went out in any weather to get them. A war outside wouldn't have stopped him. Joe's habits weren't just habits. A couple of months in Joe's company had taught Paula that there was more to addiction than alcohol and betting.

—But the Japanese word, he said.

—What is it?

—I can't remember, he said.

27

—You don't speak Japanese, Joe, no?

—One of the few languages I haven't mastered, he said.

Even that, his answer – he'd never have responded like that if they'd been outside or in his kitchen. It would have taken him a while to cop on that she was slagging him. He was only this version of himself on the bed.

—But the word, he said. —Their one word, translated, means 'wise-man period' – if I'm remembering it right. The man is calm, wise, rational – those sort of – you know. Traits.

—Is that it?

—As much as I can remember, he said. —It intrigued me.

—They're gas people, the Japanese.

—You're not impressed, Paula?

—Women are the ones who have the periods and the pregnancies but the men get called wise after having a wank?

He laughed. Louder than he ever did elsewhere.

—And anyway, she said. —What's that shite doing in a newspaper?

He laughed again. It really did give her pleasure, making this fella laugh. He rarely resented it, that she was the funny one. He never came back at her for it.

He held her ankle and pretended he was going to pull her towards him.

—I can't speak for Japanese men, he said. —But speaking as an Irish citizen, I wouldn't be claiming to be wise or particularly rational after orgasm – easily attained in your company, by the way.

—Thanks very much.

—Credit where credit is due.

—You should be thanking the Viagra, not me.

—So should you, he said. —Truth be told. Will I tell you, though, what I do feel?

—Go on, so – what?

—Sated, he said.

She looked it up later, after he drove her home.

★

28

He'll phone her.

Why doesn't she phone him?

He'd texted her earlier, wishing her luck, telling her he was thinking of her. She wonders if that's true. She doesn't think about him much. She's not sure if that's true either. But when she thinks about putting her hand on his back, or tries to think about his hands on her – it's hard to do, it's been so long. Physical contact isn't really a memory. Or it's only a memory.

She nearly fell over – it was maybe a week ago – when she felt fingers on her neck, under her ear – under her right ear. There were no fingers – not real ones. She was alone, but this thing happened – the fingers landed on her neck, two of them, lightly but definitely, and moved down, brushed her skin, and she thought she felt the inside of a wrist press gently against her breast. And gone. She leaned in against the table – this was in the kitchen. She wanted to feel the pressure, the side of the table, against her thighs. To keep it going. The feeling. She groaned, moaned – she didn't know what – but the noise came from deep under her voice. The fingers were gone. They weren't Joe's – the last man who'd touched her. They weren't anyone's. The fingers were her own invention – her imagination. But they'd been real, pressing – tender. They'd had prints, and life. She'd been sure of that, even in the second that they'd been there. On her pulse.

They weren't Joe's. They might have been a woman's. That thought hadn't repulsed her. Far from. Still doesn't. But they'd come out of nowhere. No memory or fantasy. Fingers on her neck. Index finger and ring finger. And they weren't going around her neck; they weren't going to hold her, pull her or push her or choke her.

She squeezes her legs together now, on the couch. The window's there, to her left, a few steps away. She can see out through the net curtain. She'd see people outside, passing, if there are any. They could see her, or her outline, because of the light coming from the telly; she's not sure. But those fingers – they're not there but she can imagine they are, easily she can. Touching her neck.

She's a disgrace, the talk of the washhouse.

She laughs – she snorts.

She sees Joe's name on the screen these days and it takes her ages to wake up to the fact that it's him, and who he is and why his name is there at all. It's the Covid's doing. A year and a half, and they haven't touched each other. They've hardly seen each other. It was her decision – she wasn't going to move in with him. But his too – he hadn't objected or tried to persuade her. But that isn't fair; she knows it isn't. She hadn't been coy. He'd known it and he hadn't asked her again. She'd wanted her own space, that was what she'd said. I need my own space, Joe. She'd heard herself as she said it and felt nothing but relief when she got to the end. And she must have been convincing because he'd left it at that. She wishes now he hadn't. She wishes now that he'd skidded around the corner in his car and braked outside, one wheel up on the kerb – in the second week, say, of the first lockdown. That he'd hammered on the front door and told her to get out there and listen to him. She's grinning as she thinks this. She lets herself – she makes herself smile. Joe sweeping her off her feet. Joe kissing her feet. He's done that – she remembers it. She loved it. She thinks. But she feels nothing. Her runners are off, and her ankle socks. *They're not runners – they're trainers. Thanks, Nicola. Expensive trainers. Yes, hon.* Now that she thinks of it, it wasn't Nicola who gave her the trainers. It was Leanne. Again. She sits back a bit and lets go of a grunt while she's doing it – so she can release her feet from under her arse, so they can breathe and remember. But her feet remember nothing. They're only feet. She holds one. She rubs it.

—Dirty fuckin' things, said Mary. —They're as bad as the seagulls.

—They're starlings, said Paula.

30

—So what?

They were in Dollymount, on Bull Island. They'd been reluctant to get out of the car, to climb out of the atmosphere they'd created since they'd driven away from the Helix.

—It's too early in the year for that stuff out there, said Mary.

—The great outdoors, d'you mean? said Mandy.

—Yeah, said Mary. —The sky. Birds. Elephants.

—Meercats.

—Men on bikes.

—But it's lovely, said Paula.

—It's damp.

—How d'you know?

—It's always fuckin' damp. Look it, Paula. There – look it. The fuckin' sea.

They were getting out of the car. Paula had the brown McDonald's bag.

—I've a rug in the back, said Mandy. —I think I do.

She didn't.

—I definitely did, she said.

There was a plastic bag full of kids' clothes, burst, in the boot. She shoved it into a corner but there was no rug under it.

—Jayo must've taken it, said Mandy. —Why would he want it, though?

—There's no answer to that question, Mandy, love, said Mary.

—There's loads of answers to that question, Mandy, said Paula.

—You can keep them to yourselves.

—We can sit on our jackets.

—Brilliant idea – you're a fuckin' genius.

—Feck off, you.

They didn't go far. They could see the car from where they sat.

—Your lovely white trainers, Paula, said Mandy.

They were holding onto one another as they lowered themselves to the grass.

—They'll be wrecked.

31

—There's no muck, said Paula. —They're grand. Nicola gave them to me. For Christmas. And then there was the lockdown, so I've hardly worn them.

—They're gorgeous.

—Thanks – yeah.

—It's weird, this, said Mary. —I haven't been on the ground in years.

—It brings you back, I'd say, does it?

—I'm telling yeh.

—This stuff'll be cold, said Mandy.

It didn't matter. They sat, and ate the cold fries and burgers, laughed, and said nothing at all for long spells. It was mesmerising, being out in the air and so close to the ground and the sea. At home, she didn't like being on the floor, especially in the kitchen, even if she was just sitting with the grandkids, playing. It always made her a bit nervous, even dizzy. She'd been knocked to the floor so often – getting back up was always terrible, terrifying. Charlo's feet – apart, the way he stood – always there. She couldn't look up at him. She waited – expected to be hit again, knocked back down. Always. Lurking – the thought, the wobbliness. Even when she was only getting something from under the sink. Years after the last time he'd hit her.

But this was different. This was lovely.

—There are more dogs than people these days, said Mary.

—I'd like a dog, said Paula.

—Would you, though?

—I think so – yeah.

—You can have ours, Paula, said Mandy. —You're welcome to the fuckin' thing.

—Cindy? said Mary. —Cindy's lovely.

—If you don't mind standing in shit first thing in the morning, she's fuckin' adorable.

—Is she not trained?

—'Course she's trained, said Mandy. —She knows what she's doing. She knows fuckin' well. If he's up first, it's grand. Or the kids. She hears me on the stairs, but, she's dropping her

32

arse and taking a dump. If I could shove the shite back up her, I would – I swear to God.

Paula put her head back and looked at the sky as she laughed. She felt the cold of the grass on her neck. She felt the strain in her stomach muscles as she leaned back.

—No dog of Paula's would ever shite, said Mary. —That right, Paula?

Paula was sitting up again. She'd turned sideways, a bit, off her jacket, to do it. Whatever they were, the muscles in her stomach – they weren't up to the job of lifting her up.

—That's right, she said.

—Balls cut off, arse stitched up.

—My kind of guy.

—Most of the people here have two dogs, said Mary.

—That's a thing now, yeah – one isn't enough.

—What's that about?

—No idea.

—That fella Willo had the fight with –.

—Was Willo in a fight? said Mandy.

—He was, the eejit, said Mary. —The first night when the pubs opened before Christmas. Did I not tell you?

—I might have forgotten.

—It wasn't a real fight, really – more of a shove.

—Were you there, Mary?

—No, I wasn't, said Mary. —It would've been a real fight if I had been there. Willo was going to the toilet, mask on, you know, and this fella was coming out, no mask. And poor Willo told him to put his mask on and, of course, your man tells him to fuck off. So Willo goes on ahead in and does the needful – washes his hands and all – I have him well trained. But your man's waiting for him when he's coming out, the fuckin' dirtbird.

—What age is Willo?

—He's only sixty-four, said Mary.

—He's younger than you?

—Who says he is?

—Is he?

—Yeah, said Mary. —A year or two, just. Why?

—Well, said Mandy. —Fighting, like – at his age.

—Who says he was fighting?

—You did – in fairness.

—There was a fight, said Mary. —And Willo was there. Will I continue, Paula?

—Yes, please.

She knew the story. She'd heard three versions in the run-up to Christmas. Mary's version was different to the other two but that didn't matter – it wasn't the point. Paula could have listened to Mary all day.

—So your man's waiting outside the toilet.

—Who is he?

—I can't remember his name.

—Power, said Paula.

She couldn't resist.

—That's right, said Mary.

—Michael Power.

—That's right.

Michael Power was a friend of Paula's dead husband. Younger than Charlo. Kind of a protégé. An apprentice. A cunt. She was keeping it to herself.

—Anyway, said Mary. —He was outside, there. Blocking the way. And poor Willo couldn't get back to his pals at their table. There's no room for him to get around your man and he's a big unit, this fella.

He was. He was twice the size he'd been back when he'd knocked on Paula's door, a few days after Charlo was shot, offering his condolences and other services. That was nearly thirty years ago. Standing on the step, right at the door when she opened it. He was almost on top of her, with what he thought was his winning smile. Smiling even as he was telling her that he was sorry for her trouble. He leaned against the door jamb, looked past her down the hall. Charlo hadn't lived in the house – Paula had thrown him out long before he died.

34

Power's sleeve got caught in the door as she shut it, she did it that fast – she didn't give him the time to retreat. *For fuck sake – take it easy!* She remembered that time, the day the Guards called to tell her that Charlo was dead, and the days after. She'd have loved arms around her, hands open on her back. Not a man she knew – she'd wanted one of her madey-up men. Robert Kennedy, or Nicola's history teacher. She'd had a folder in her head full of eligible, non-existent men. Men who would pick her up without grunting or dropping or hurting her. Who didn't sweat, or only when they were on top of her, and then they'd sweat rum and black; she'd lick it off their shoulders and chests. But never Michael Power. Nothing about that man had ever gone into Paula's folder.

She still had the folder.

—And the dirty bastard starts coughing straight at Willo, said Mary.

—Ah, Jesus.

—Making himself cough, you know. And poor Willo, like – he's backing away. He has a few of the underlying conditions, Willo does. So he's supposed to be careful. But, like, he has nowhere to go except back into the toilet. The men's toilet in that place – the door, like. It's in a corner – tight, you know. And then there's the extra Covid screens around as well. So he's trapped and he doesn't know what to do. But he kind of takes a breath and he's ready to barge past your man. This fella – d'yis know him? He's fat as a fuckin' fool but it's hard fat – are you with me? He'd crush you.

One of the versions Paula heard, Willo got lodged between Power and the cigarette machine.

—But luckily now – luckily, said Mary. —Someone was trying to get past – what's his name again?

—Power.

—Somebody else was trying to get past Power to get into the toilet, so he had to shift a bit and Willo slipped through the gap. But Power grabbed his belt.

—For fuck sake, said Mandy.

—This wasn't any of Willo's doing, said Mary. —He was only coming back from the toilet, Mandy – be reasonable. Like – in fairness. He wasn't picking a fight.

—Yeah, okay – I'm hearing you.

—Willo's sprinting days are long gone but he must've been going at some speed all the same, cos he dragged the Power fella after him and they both toppled over.

Paula's version – another version – they smashed a table and one of the Covid screens on their way to the floor and they lay facing each other, like lovers in an old film, and started scratching each other's faces.

—They were both on the carpet –

—It's a wood floor.

—Fuck off interrupting. They were both on the floor, okay, and Power drew his head back and loafed Willo.

—What?

—Butted him, Mandy, said Mary. —Head-butted him.

Paula believed this version. Charlo had always preferred his forehead to his fists. She remembered – she didn't need to remember – getting up off the kitchen floor, reeling, trying to push the blood back up into her nose and her head, as she realised what had happened. How it was she'd ended up on the floor, against the fridge. Why she couldn't see properly, why she was breathing through her mouth. He'd butted her, but she hadn't seen it coming. She never did.

—Oh, my fuckin' God, said Mandy.

Her mouth stayed open till she spoke again.

—Serious? she said, and she closed her mouth.

She was a bitch, Paula was, noticing that – Mandy closing her mouth. But it was funny.

Mary nodded, quickly. For a second Paula thought that she was showing Mandy what a head-butt looked like.

—Serious as cancer, said Mary.

She paused the story till she took a bite from her quarter-pounder.

—I seen Willo, said Mandy. —I think it was last weekend. Saturday I think it was.

—It was back before Christmas this happened, said Mary. —I told you. And, like. There was nothing really broken. He caught him – the Power prick – he caught poor Willo on the cheek.

She put fingers onto her own right cheek, under her eye.

—He missed his nose.

—Thank God.

—Yeah – God, said Mary. —And he didn't break the bone – here.

She tapped her fingers, two of them, on her cheekbone.

—So there was no real damage done, she said. —As far as that went. Although the swelling was shocking, and the bruise. Purple. It shook him.

—It must've.

—Yeah, said Mary. —Yeah. So, anyway – when you saw him. Mandy – when you saw Willo, yeah? He's got a bit of foundation on – over the bruise.

—Ah – God love him.

—Even though it's months now and he doesn't really need it, said Mary.

There was ketchup – a little spot of it only, not a dollop – on Mary's cheek, where she'd put her fingers. Paula leaned across and took it off with one of her own fingers. Mary didn't flinch or even look at her. It was like she'd been expecting Paula to do it. Paula wiped her fingertip on one of the paper napkins from the McDonald's bag. She took her little bottle of sanitiser from the pocket of her jacket.

—But poor Willo, said Mary. —At a point in his life when you'd have thought there wasn't the remotest chance that he'd ever be getting into a fight.

—He got into one.

—It's humiliating, so it is, said Mary. —And really – just fuckin' absurd. Mad. But it happened. You saw him there, Mandy – on Saturday, yeah?

—Yeah.

—That was the first time he was outside the door. Since.

—Ah, no.

—Yeah, said Mary. —It's – what? Nearly six months, it must be. It's doing my fuckin' head in – never mind his. I don't really mean that. It's been terrible for him.

Paula could feel the cold under her now. The damp – the weather. But it felt like it was layers below her. It felt comfortable. Her ankles were bare. Bare – another word she liked; it did things for her, it always had. Her ankles weren't cold. She looked at one of them. What age did it look? She hadn't a clue. It didn't look too bad.

—The poor man, she said.

She meant it.

Mary and Mandy hadn't known Charlo. He was nearly thirty years dead. They knew Paula was a widow. They knew her husband had been shot dead by the Guards. And they knew – probably – that he'd been looking for it. It was what they'd have been told minutes after moving into their houses. She'd have been notorious before they got to know her. The gangster's moll and all that. She didn't care – only now and again, she did. Charlo was the father of her children. He'd been in love with Paula. He'd kissed the ankle she'd just been examining. It was one of the bones he'd never broken – she didn't let herself get too sentimental. She'd loved him, she'd ached for him. This was after they'd started going with each other, and for a long time after – she'd stopped herself from moaning out loud as she imagined she felt him, and actually did feel him, behind her, his hands at her hips, not holding them, delaying, teasing her. She'd loved every inch of him and he'd loved every bit of her. Once. She still believed that – she never doubted it. He was gentle when he'd wanted to be. Hard and gentle. When her hand on the back of his leg could make him want to do what she was wanting him to do. When he kissed her ankle as he was going into her. When his tongue on her neck could make her disappear. She never forgot that, despite everything

38

else. They were made for each other. But he'd terrified her too. From the start – she knew that now. Terrified her. And it was never something she'd wanted, part of a game – it was never theirs, always his. Him. His ability to terrify – his enthusiasm. She could well imagine Willo's terror, faced by Michael Power. A man trained by Charlo. The prospect of meeting Power again. Only the prospect, the possibility. She knew – she thought she knew what Willo had been going through.

She thought of something.

—Dogs.

—What dogs?

—You said something about dogs, said Paula.

—Did I? said Mary. —I didn't – did I? What did I say about dogs?

—Dogs and Michael Power.

—I'm with you now, said Mary. —Hang on a sec.

Mary grabbed the SuperValu bag she'd brought with her from the car and put it on her lap. She looked in, and took out a clear plastic box with four huge cupcakes in it. She dropped it on the ground between them.

—Sugar, she said.

Her hand was in the bag and she lifted out two little bottles of wine. Splits they were called – the bottle size. Paula remembered.

Mary's hand was back in the bag. She took out a can of the Italian lemonade, Sanpellegrino.

—Is this any good to you, Paula?

—You're a star, said Paula. —That's perfect.

Mary was looking down at the cupcakes.

—One of these yokes is blue, she said.

—They're the nicest, said Mandy.

—Okay, said Mary.

She twisted the cap off her bottle.

—No glasses – ah, well.

She put the neck to her mouth and tilted the bottle slightly.

—Grand, she said, when she'd taken it back down. —It's aged well. He was caught with a houseful of dogs and pups.

—Power was, said Paula.

—Yep.

—They were stolen.

—Yep.

—The Guards caught him.

—Red-handed, said Mary. —Red-pawed. Imagine it, though. Getting into that kind of bother. At his age?

—Is he married?

—She's long gone.

—Dead? said Mandy.

—Coolock, said Paula. —She's with another chap – so I heard.

—Who doesn't rob pups.

—Or batter my husband, said Mary.

That was when a dog, a little thing let off its lead, ran at the starlings. That was when Paula showed off her knowledge. When she got to say 'murmuration'.

She won't phone Joe. She'll wait till he phones her.

She puts the phone back beside her on the couch, the screen facing down so she won't be looking all the time to see if it's lighting up with a text or a WhatsApp. She has most of the buzzy things – the alerts – turned off. She did that on her own one day, after the quick buzz of a text nearly sent her toppling down the stairs, when she went for the phone in her back pocket and her elbow whacked the wall and propelled her forward. Her foot missed the next two steps and she didn't think she'd have the strength – when she'd grabbed the banister – to stop herself from falling. Even then she'd been reluctant to let go of the phone, so she could grab the banister with both hands. She was shaking when she got to the kitchen, and she sat and went into the Settings and turned off nearly everything. She'd impressed herself much more than she'd frightened herself.

She has her photos arranged in albums. She has her Favourites in the order she wants them, grandkids first by age, then her four children. Jack, Leanne, John Paul, Nicola. Top to bottom. That's the order – has been for a good while. Jack's at the top because he's so far away. Because he's her baby. Her thirty-two-year-old baby. Because he's lived through the best of her. Because he doesn't remember his father. He's her achievement, something she got right.

Leanne is under Jack because she's great. She's on the mend. Horrible words – 'on the mend'. The graveyards are full of people who were on the mend. But Leanne is winning. And she has been for a nice while now. Paula will always worry about Leanne, and she'll always admire her. Leanne is, she thinks, the most damaged of her children. She used to think that it was John Paul, especially in the years she didn't see him, when he didn't come near her. But now she thinks it's Leanne. Leanne will always bring guilt into the room. Paula's guilt. But Paula can look at her guilt and, sometimes, she can tell it to get lost. She can live with it. Most of the time.

Nicola's at the bottom of the children, not the bottom of the list itself – that's where Joe is – because she's so reliable. Dependable. Readable. Paula can anticipate Nicola's expressions before Paula speaks. She can see them without seeing Nicola. They don't change as she ages. She's the best in the world. Literally – Paula thinks that. Those exact words, several times a day. She'd be dead if it hadn't been for Nicola. She loves her, she's in awe of her. But she resents her for it. Little Miss fuckin' Perfect. She's never seen Paula, her mother, as an adult. They've rarely just had a chat. It's always a test, a cross-examination. The only thing missing is the white coat. She even had one once, a coat that was white, and she looked glorious in it, the bitch. She's never lets the guard down. Until, maybe, recently. It's Paula who's been keeping the guard up. Maybe. Who knows? Who knows why? Who knows anything?

John Paul's where he is because she doesn't know him. She has his number, she knows where he lives, he lets her see her grandchildren as often as she wants. But she's a visitor, or he is.

She can't blame him.

41

She hasn't adjusted the list in months. Her delete finger has hovered over Joe a few times. She isn't sure why – it isn't fair. The Covid isn't Joe's fault. She doesn't miss him. But she wants him to phone her, all the same. Earlier, in Dollymount, when the starlings flew – the murmuration. She missed him then – she thought of him. She wouldn't have had the word if she hadn't got it from Joe. And then – quickly – she resented it, the fact that without him she was ignorant, and she remembered his face and his voice as he explained things to her, educated her. But even as she's thinking that, now, she's pushing it away, making it disperse like the dog did with the starlings, and she remembers watching a film with him.

—Will we give *The Birds* a go, Paula?

—Ah, yeah – brilliant.

—Hitchcock.

—If you say so, Joe.

—One of his best.

—I seen it before. I love the horrors.

—It's not horror, strictly speaking.

—It fuckin' is so. Strictly speaking.

She annoyed him right the way through it. He wanted to just watch it and she wanted to be in it. She grabbed his leg and he screamed – he was furious until he started to laugh. He put the film back to where they'd been before she'd grabbed him, where the boys and girls are being brought out of the school and the birds that are perched in the playground, their wings begin to flutter really loudly and they fly up, like an explosion. She couldn't see now why she'd grabbed his leg, why she'd thought that she needed his protection or wanted his attention. When it was over and she stood, straightening herself up from the ball she'd been in when she was watching the film, he turned to her properly and smiled.

—I have to say, Paula, you add to the experience.

She wanted to slap him.

—The birds are brilliant but the humans are a bit shite, she said.

—You're right, actually.

She wanted to hug him. Hug and slap him. The patronising prick.

—Hitchcock gave Tippi Hedren a terrible time, apparently.

—That I can believe, said Paula. —She's good.

She sees the light of her phone now – there, gone, there, gone, making the couch glow. She can see crumbs and grit in the fabric. She picks up the phone.

It's Joe.

She doesn't answer. She doesn't know why not – and that's reason enough. Not knowing. She puts the phone back down beside her.

She'll answer if he tries again.

She flips the phone over, so the screen is facing up. She doesn't want to see the crumbs again, and the dirt. It's not dirt – it's not neglect. It's not just crumbs. It's the house – it's falling apart. If she's looking.

She doesn't look. And she doesn't want others looking. She's grand.

The phone lights up.

It's Nicola.

—Hiya, love.

—I'm outside, says Nicola. —I forgot my keys.

—Outside – here?

—Will you let me in?

—Will you look at this one, said Mary, quietly.

Paula had been in dreamland, watching a boat stacked with green and yellow containers coming into the port, going past the Poolbeg Lighthouse, blocking it. She was counting the containers, but not really. Trying to make out any figures, any humans, on the deck. But not really. She was drifting. Thinking that she could never have just sat like this even six or seven years ago. She'd have been afraid of the damp getting at her bones, where the bones had been broken. She wouldn't have

43

been able to stay still for this long – she wouldn't have known how to want to. The pain on the wet days was there – it was still there – but maybe it was because she was older and the aches were expected at this age; she'd caught up with herself. She didn't know. The Charlo times – she could hold them back. She could make them keep their distance. There was the Charlo she had the crack with, the madey-up Charlo, and there was the real one. The real Charlo stayed away for longer. Living on her own helped. That occurred to her one day, when she realised that she was listening out for the door, waiting for Leanne to come home – months after Leanne had gone. She wouldn't be hearing the door open and close, she wouldn't be looking at Leanne. She didn't have to make sure that the worry, the disappointment or the fear, that none of those things were on her face when she looked at her. Or the contempt. The hatred. She could even think that – that she'd sometimes hated her daughter, all of her children – without needing to sink into the ground here.

Guilt. That was what Charlo had left her. The family jewellery. A necklace, pearls of jet-black guilt. Choking her. She put her hand to her neck now. There was nothing there.

She looked at Mandy, asleep. She grinned. She laughed.

—For fuck sake, she said. —How does she manage that?

Mandy was lying on her jacket and her head was tucked into the hood, as if she'd been wearing it when she lay back. But she hadn't been. Paula had watched her stretching back, a few minutes before. She'd worked her head, her whole face, in under the hood since then. Her feet and legs were apart, the toes pointed up, like a cartoon.

—The state of her, said Mary.

Paula was pleased – she had Mary to herself again.

—That's what having kids does to you, she said.

—I remember, said Mary. —Just about. I fell asleep once with me head in the fuckin' fridge. I did – swear to God. Me head on a fuckin' shelf.

—You did not.

44

—I swear to God – this side of me face was orange for weeks after, from the cheese I was lying on.

—Orange is your colour.

—Mature Cheddar, said Mary. —Poor Willo was kissing that side of me face for months – any fuckin' excuse. He thought it was the taste of mature woman.

Paula laughed.

—He got me a box of Calvita for Valentine's Day, said Mary.

Paula laughed on top of her laugh – it nearly hurt.

—And how would you know, an'anyway? said Mary.

—What?

—That orange is me colour. Or any other colour.

This was Mary telling Paula that she felt the same way. That she was happy having Paula to herself.

—I know orange, said Paula.

—How, though? said Mary. —How d'you know?

—I just do.

It was why they'd become big friends. Mary worked in the dry cleaner's up the road, Brand New Cleaners, and – this was about eight years ago, maybe nine – she told Paula that there was a job going there. Part-time only, but it was Paula's if she wanted it – Mary would put the word in for her. This was after Paula had told Mary that she didn't think she'd be able to keep up her old job, the office cleaning.

The cleaning had been killing Paula. Literally killing her, she thought, when she'd met Mary on her way home, just off the bus. She could hardly walk. The pain in her back was excruciating, fuckin' cruel. Nothing she did would keep it under control. It used to flare up, but always went – it was like the moon. But then – this time – it had flared, ripped right up through her, and stayed. Six days before. She'd cried earlier, and she'd cry again when she got home. She'd stopped taking the Panadol – it made no difference. She'd felt the pull of the off-licence for the first time in ages, the night before, coming home, and the only thing that had stopped her, kept her on the path to the house, was embarrassment. She saw through the window, one

45

of the neighbour's kids – Rita Kavanagh's youngest, Eric – was working behind the counter.

She'd come home on the 29A this time. It was a longer walk from the bus stop but she didn't have to go past the off-licence or the pub. She didn't get the DART home any more, even though the station was nearer than any bus stop. There was no one working at the station any more. It was all automatic – unmanned, someone had called it. She was sometimes the only person getting off, onto an empty platform – but there were kids there sometimes, teenagers she didn't know. One of them had pushed her – not hard, but it had scared her. The station was in off the road – there was a bit of a lane to get through. And it was dark. She was shaking when she got home.

She'd been passing the Centra, not sure if there was milk at home, positive that neither Leanne nor Jack would have got any if there wasn't – they were both still living at home when this happened – when Mary stepped out of the shop and saw her.

—Christ, Paula – are you okay, hon?

Paula nodded.

—I'm grand, Mary – thanks.

But she started to cry.

Mary knocked on her door a few days later and told her about the job in Brand New. Paula cried again. Laughed, apologised –

—I'm an eejit.

And kept crying. She knew she'd be bringing home less money and she knew she needed every cent she earned, and more. But the pain seemed to stop clinging so tightly to her ribs before she'd even told Mary that she'd take the job. Just hearing the offer was enough.

Anyway, that was when they discovered that Paula was colour-blind. A few days into the new job, Paula had turned on the garment carousel – she loved that part of the job – and waited till the customer's skirt came slowly around the corner, and she'd let it pass.

—That one, Paula – it's gone past you, look it. The blue –
no, the blue, Paula.

Mary leaned past Paula and turned off the carousel and
took the skirt off the rack. The customer paid and left, and
Mary burst out laughing.

—You're fuckin' colour-blind.

—I'm not – I am not. How can I be colour-blind? I'm nearly
sixty, sure.

Mary cracked up. She leaned back against the counter.

—That's the best ever, she said. —Come here.

She pointed at a shirt.

—What colour's that one?

—Pink. Fuckin' pink, Mary – lay off.

—One down, said Mary. —You know your pinks, an'anyway.
This one here – quick.

—Blue.

—Sorry?

—Green.

Paula couldn't see the difference between some of the darker
shades of green and blue.

—Will I be sacked?

—What? said Mary. —Who'll sack you?

—Dermot.

Dermot was the owner. Paula had met him for about two
minutes the day she'd started. He'd seemed alright.

—Never mind Dermot, said Mary. —He'll never know.
And anyway, Dermot's grand. You'd need to have a white stick
before Dermot would sack you. It's fuckin' gas, but, isn't it?
What colour was your school uniform?

—I don't remember.

—You never knew.

—No – really. I can't remember.

Dermot might have been grand, but Paula was still scared
that she was going to lose the job she'd only started. She
couldn't begin to imagine going back to the cleaning, even
just walking to the bus stop, without wanting to curl up and

die – if her back would even let her curl up. But Mary and the other girls who worked in Brand New helped, and made sure Paula's colour-blindness remained their little secret. And their joke. They kept an eye out when Paula was at the carousel. On Paula's birthday they all sang that old one that Vicky Leandros used to sing.

—BLUE – BLUE – MY LOVE IS GREEN –

—You're fuckin' hilarious.

They had a cake for her as well.

—What colour's the icing, Paula?

—Fuck off, the lot of yis.

Herself and Mary became best friends. Like in school. Sometimes that was exactly how Paula felt. She'd go to work and realise that it wasn't Mary's shift and she'd want to go straight back home. She'd wondered if Mary had replaced Carmel, Paula's sister; Carmel was dead eight years. But Paula didn't think so – Mary was different. Paula and Carmel got on well, but Carmel had always been Paula's big sister. There'd been so much bad history, nearly all of it Paula's – they could never have been equals. Carmel had saved Paula too often. She'd pulled off Paula's shit-and-vomit-covered clothes and held her under the shower. Paula had never done that for Carmel. She'd never lent Carmel money for food. She'd never stood between Carmel and her husband as he came lungeing at her down the hall. There was none of that imbalance with Mary. Mary had found the job for Paula but two days later they were standing together, looking out the window.

—This is great, said Mary. —It's brilliant, isn't it, Paula?

—Yeah, said Paula.

—Look it, said Mary.

She pointed at the words, the shop name, printed on the window in front of them, just over their heads.

—We're Brand New, she said. —We can't ask for much more at our age, sure we can't?

Paula sometimes wished that she'd met Mary sooner in her life. But she knew – Mary wouldn't have been her friend now.

She'd have given up on Paula decades ago – forty years ago. More. She'd have crossed the road to avoid her. It was better this way. Much better.

She was feeling a bit stiff now from the sitting on the ground. But she didn't want to stand. It would look like an announcement. Time to go. And she didn't want to go. Ever.

—D'you know what we never thought of, Paula? said Mary.

—What?

—Our bladders.

—I brought mine with me, said Paula.

—You're fuckin' gas, said Mary. —Are you not bursting?

—I wasn't guzzling the vino.

—Fuck off now, said Mary. —It was only one of them kiddie bottles.

—It still put your woman to sleep – look it.

Mandy was still out for the count.

—Our designated driver, said Mary. —For fuck sake. We'll have to walk.

—It's not that far.

—It fuckin' is, said Mary. —Where am I going to go to the toilet? It's running down me legs here.

Paula looked around and pointed at the black circular thing down from them, past Happy Out, nearer the wooden bridge.

—Isn't that a public toilet? she said. —That thing over there.

—You mean the yoke with about a hundred people queuing outside it?

—Yeah.

—It really will be running down me legs if I have to go to the back of that queue.

—There's not that many, said Paula. —It looks like more cos they're all keeping the social distance.

—Well, your man at the back – look it.

Mary was starting to stand. She'd grabbed Paula's shoulder. She pressed down on it as she lifted herself.

—Putting on his mask – see him? With the red cap.

—Yeah, said Paula.

49

—Well, he's definitely going in for a crap and I'm not going in there straight after him – no fuckin' way am I. You can tell by the way he's standing – look it. His arse cheeks are hanging on for dear life.

She was hurting Paula. Her fingers were digging in as she levered herself up. For a second all of Mary's weight was right on top of Paula. But she let go, and swayed. She groaned as she straightened.

—It's fuckin' windy up here, she said.

She pointed across at the dunes and the few trees and the sea beyond them.

—I'm heading over there, she said. —There's bound to be a bush.

Paula laughed. Although she didn't want Mary to go.

—Don't forget your mask, she said.

Mary was already moving.

—I'll be wiping me fanny with it, she called back.

Paula saw a woman looking at Mary, then at Paula. She saw Paula looking back at her and hesitated, then looked away quickly. Paula kept looking in her direction, in case the woman looked again. She'd stare the bitch out of it. *Good girl, Paula – go over and slap her. Ah, fuck off, Charlo. Go on – she deserves it. Passing judgement on your pal.* She would. If she thought the woman – she was half Paula's age – deserved it. If she thought she was making little of Mary. If she saw her whispering to her friends there with her. If the four of them were laughing behind their hands. Or if they turned to look at Mary as she walked along behind the line of bike racks and stepped up onto the high grass. She'd go over there and belt her. It was in her. Not potential. Fact. She'd go over there and kick the snooty cow straight in the face.

It was nuts – she knew that. She'd no intention of doing anything. The woman wasn't a bitch. Probably. Not a particular bitch. She'd been amused at what Mary had said, the same way Paula had. It was funny how rage and happiness could be so close. If the woman looked over now, Paula would smile back over at her, and feel the exact same way she had a few seconds ago.

She's still holding the phone. It's still on. She can hear Nicola breathing – a couple of feet away – outside. She doesn't know if she should talk to her again. If she should talk as she stands up. As she goes out to the hall and the front door.

She needs both hands to get up off the couch. She's stiff after her day. That makes the decision for her. She presses the red button but – still – she's slow to throw the phone back on the couch. Slow to catch up. Slow to let go of Nicola.

She hates the door – she hates the fuckin' thing. She stood in front of it so many times, trying to push herself to open it and go. With blood on her face. One of her eyes battered shut. Not able to see the lock properly. Things swimming. She could never do it. Even though she'd been in and out all day, to the shops, to work. When it came to opening the door and going for good, she couldn't. Return trips only. She had Jack and Leanne with her once, schoolbags full of clothes. They stood in front of the door – it felt like hours. Until Leanne said she needed to go to the toilet. That was the end of it, the excuse she'd been waiting for.

She hates the pebbled glass, the fact that she can't see what's coming at her. It's years since she's had to worry. Since opening it had made her want to vomit. But it still kills her. The reminder – every time, especially after dark – it still grabs at her as she tries to leave. The handle seems to dance around as she goes to hold it.

This now – this. This terrifies her. Nicola outside. She'd prefer to pretend she's not here, she's not in. It's too late, though. The hall light is on. She'd turned it on earlier. Nicola will be looking at Paula's shape becoming sharper as she gets closer to the door. She'll already have seen that.

Don't be horrible, she thinks. It's Nicola. There's something happening – there has to be. She never does this, just turns up without texting ahead – especially since the lockdowns started. She needs you – she's depending on you.

But fuck – she resents it. And she immediately feels better, for thinking that. For allowing it, and then smothering it.

She opens the door.

Nicola's wearing a mask. It's a shock. Even though she's seen masks on Nicola dozens of times in the past year. But it looks wrong. Like she's trying to disguise herself.

—Alright, hon?

It's not Nicola. It's like parts of Nicola are missing – they've been rubbed out. It's not just that it's dark and Nicola's standing at the edge of the light. She's diminished – that's it. She's shrunk.

Paula steps out of the house. She holds the door, so it won't close on her. Her keys are inside.

Closer to her now, Nicola's more herself. But still, even with the mask, she looks frightened.

—Come in, hon, she says.

She opens the door wide and steps back into the hall.

—Come in.

She's not sure if this has ever happened before. Nicola has had her own key since she was twelve or thirteen. She's never lost the key, or forgotten it.

Paula says it again.

—Come in.

Nicola moves as Paula speaks. Paula gives her room, lets her pass. Shuts the door. Nicola stands in the hall. A few steps in. Paula brushes against her as she turns around. It's almost aggressive. Like Nicola is crowding Paula. Not letting her move.

Like Charlo.

Her father.

But her face – God – her face. It's her little girl. Paula puts her hand to the side of Nicola's face. Her skin is damp. Nicola pushes Paula's hand away – not too harshly. She lifts the elastic of the mask – yellow and grey diagonal stripes – she lifts it from behind her ear, and takes the mask away. She lets it fall.

Paula puts an arm around Nicola. Nicola lets her – trusts her. She wants her mother.

That's Paula. That's me, she thinks.

—Okay? Nicola?

—Yeah.

—Come in, hon – come on. Come in here and sit.

She leads Nicola the couple of steps from the doorway to the couch. It's like Nicola can't do it on her own. Paula makes her sit. Nicola isn't wearing her coat or a jacket. Just a hoodie that probably cost a fortune – like she walked straight out of the house.

—How did you get here, hon?

—Drove.

—Okay – grand.

Paula wonders where the car key is. There are no pockets in the hoodie.

—D'you want a cup of Rosie Lee?

It's their old joke, calling the chamomile and the peppermint and sage tea Rosie Lee.

Nicola shakes her head slightly.

—No – thanks.

Paula sits down beside her. She holds Nicola's hand in both of hers. Nicola's long fingers – she'd been a long baby.

—So, says Paula.

There's nothing else she can say. Nothing else she can think of. She takes her left hand off Nicola's. She puts it on Nicola's shoulder, her back, the back of Nicola's head – her hair. She puts it back on Nicola's shoulder. She waits.

Mandy woke when Mary sat down.

—Anyone see you? said Paula.

—Not that I noticed, said Mary. —Me mind was on other things.

She checked her empty wine bottle, held it up to the light.

—Meditation and concentration are the way to a life of serenity and dry knickers.

Mandy's head was still deep in her hood but they heard and saw her laughing.

—I live by those words, said Mary.

Paula watched Mandy pull the hood away from her face. Without sitting up, Mandy stretched out to the brown McDonald's bag and put her hand in. It came back out with a load of paper napkins.

—My turn, she said.

—Not here, Mandy, said Mary. —For fuck sake. Get up and go the extra mile.

Mandy groaned as she lifted herself.

—We'll go home when I get back, girls – okay?

—Grand.

—Mary, where did you go?

—Over there – d'you see that sideways bush thing, the tree, whatever it is. Over at the fence there. In behind there. It's grand. A bit smelly, just.

They watched Mandy head off, clutching the bunch of napkins.

—Jesus, don't make it obvious or anything, said Mary. —She's letting the side down, Paula.

—No class, said Paula.

—Not at all, said Mary. —She'll probably start whistling as well.

They said nothing for a while. The day was over. It was still bright but the heat had rolled away. Paula watched people zipping up jackets and tops as she felt the cold around her collar and at her ankles. In her hands, her knuckles. In the broken places.

—Thanks for this, Mary, she said.

—What?

—The day, said Paula.

—It has been one of the good ones, hasn't it? said Mary.

—It's been brilliant, said Paula.

—I'm sick of me husband, Paula, said Mary.

She was looking over the water, at the South Wall and the Poolbeg chimneys.

—Are you?

—I am. Kind of. Yeah.

She hadn't moved.

—But sure –.

Paula heard something. She looked – Mary's hands were up at her face.

—Ah, Mary –.

—No, I'm grand, said Mary. —Jesus, I hate crying.

She quickly wiped one cheek with a fist and brought her hands down.

—Alright –?

—I'm grand, said Mary. —Right as rain. Just –. D'you know what it is, Paula?

—What?

Paula was looking at Mary's face, trying to see what she'd missed.

—I envy you, said Mary.

—Sorry – wha'?

—It's true, said Mary. —I fuckin' envy you.

—Jesus – that's a first.

—No, I do, said Mary. —The way you're living.

Nothing rushed up through Paula, telling her friend to shut the fuck up – she hadn't a clue how Paula lived. She could wait, and listen – she'd be able to do that. She'd seen the state of Mary a minute ago. She looked, to see if Mandy was on her way back across the high grass. There was no sign of her.

—I was twenty when I got married, said Mary. —Fuckin' nuts. When you think about it. You know – now. Nuts. Twenty?

—Yeah, said Paula.

—He was nineteen. We were children, sure.

—Yeah.

—I wish he was dead, said Mary. —I don't – but I do.

—Would it not be easier if he just left?

—No – fuck that. I want him dead. Not literally.

—I know.

—It's more fun if he's dead, said Mary.

—Okay.

—I could wear me widow's weeds, then get on with me life.

Paula could see Mandy now, head down, making her way back. She looked up, to reassure herself that she was going in the right direction – Paula could see that from where she was. She lifted her arm and waved, saw Mandy seeing her and waving back.

—He's looking at me like I'm his mother, said Mary. —And I don't blame him, like, after what happened – don't get me wrong. But –.

—It's gone on a bit long?

—No, no – not that. Yeah – but no. I don't mind that. Although – I can't imagine that your fella would've locked himself away after he'd been slapped, Paula.

Charlo would have been doing the slapping. *Fuckin' sure I would've.* But Paula said nothing. She wanted to – she was angry, for just a moment. She didn't want her life and Charlo's part in it hauled out like this. She didn't want to listen to Mary's assumptions without responding, putting her right – telling her just to fuck off. But she swallowed back her words.

Mandy was nearly at them now.

—I realised, said Mary. —I recognised. He's been looking at me like that all along.

—Oh –.

—I think he has. I'm not being cruel – I don't think I am. But he won't get out of the fuckin' house. So I have to – d'you know what I mean?

Paula didn't need to answer. Mary wasn't looking at her. Her face was aimed at Mandy, waiting to smile at her. Mandy wasn't going to sit down. She was standing beside them. She wanted to go. She was looking back down the road, to the wooden bridge, the way back to her life.

—The party's over, Mandy, is it? said Mary.

—Sorry, said Mandy.

—No, no, you're grand. It's time to go.

They stood. They managed it without groaning or hanging

off each other. Then they started to clean up. Now they groaned as they were bending. They laughed. Their faces were close, Paula's and Mary's. Mary smiled quickly – uncertainly – then winked at Paula. Paula – just for a second – wanted to lean in and kiss her. Really kiss her.

—So, she says.

She's noticed – even now, with Nicola like this beside her – she's noticed how often she says that. So. Even when she's alone.

So is her word these days. Acceptance. Uncertainty. Anxiety. Fear. So. So. So. So. The last time she had sex, she saw the hearing aids on the table beside Joe's bed. So. It's become her soundtrack.

—So, she says now. —What's up?

She doesn't expect an answer. She'd love one, but she kind of accepts that there aren't any answers. Nothing is tidy, nothing is ever safe and done. Even Nicola – the safest thing in Paula's life. She's been waiting for this, expecting it.

—Can I stay here? says Nicola.

—'Course.

Paula doesn't hesitate.

For fuck sake, though.

—Why?

Nicola doesn't answer.

—Why, hon?

Nicola still says nothing.

Paula is looking for marks, before she knows she's doing it. Bruises on Nicola's wrists, broken skin on her knuckles. Fingermarks on her neck. She nearly gasps – she stops herself. When she realises that she's searching for violence on her daughter. When she realises that she's doing the right thing. When she pushes back the thought that the violence was properly meant for her. Paula. It's not even a thought. A reflex. An automatic thing. I deserve it. There is no violence, there are no marks – none that she can see.

—Can I stay? Nicola asks again.

—Yes, says Paula.

—Thanks.

—It's your home.

—It's not.

—It is, says Paula. —It used to be – it still is. It mightn't have been much of a home but –.

Nicola says nothing. She's staring at the floor – she seems to be. She's seeing something that isn't there. There's nothing there – except the carpet.

Paula asks again.

—Why do you want to stay, hon? You can stay as long as you like, by the way.

Nicola's still looking at the floor. She hasn't looked at Paula since she came into the room.

—I'll kill them, she says.

Paula isn't sure she heard Nicola – although she definitely did hear her. What she isn't sure about is *how* she heard what Nicola just said. I'll kill them. How Nicola wanted her to hear. What she'd meant.

Nicola has three children. Three girls.

I'll kill them. It can mean a lot of things. I love them. I'm proud of them. They drive me mad but they're fuckin' perfect. I'll kill anyone who tries to touch them, anyone who ever looks at them.

But Paula knows: Nicola means exactly what she's said. She'll kill them. Vanessa, Gillian and Lily. Nessa, Gill and Lily. She'll strangle them, smother them. She'll pull the life out of them. Paula heard Nicola, and she heard herself. She's wondering if Nicola is saying something she once heard Paula say. Paula doesn't know if she ever said it out loud. I'll kill you – I'll fuckin' kill you. I hate you! She doesn't remember – it doesn't matter. She meant it. She felt it. She believed it. She knew it.

Hearing it now – it's devastating. The guilt. The self-hatred. The lovely black hole. She'd hoped it had skipped a generation – or it had gone away altogether, because Paula had been good for so long.

But she's looking at it.

The thing.

The guilt. Whatever it is. The hate. It's not in her now. It's in her daughter. On her daughter. *In* her daughter. Her beautiful daughter, her perfect girl. The last person. The very last person Paula would have expected it to infect.

It's back. Paula can feel it – she can taste it. It would be so easy to sink into it. She wants to – that thought is already settling into her. She has company. It'll be lovely.

No.

No fuckin' way. That's not happening.

She's looking at her child. Maybe for the first time. It's Paula's turn.

Her chance.

Jesus, though – does this never stop?

24 February 2022

She felt a pull, muscles or tendons – she doesn't know what they're called – in the back of her legs, protesting, warning her to stop. When she stepped over the five-kilometre mark. The permitted 5K. She doesn't know if that's exact – she didn't check Google Maps to see exactly how far she'd come from home. But the backs of her legs were pulling at her for about five minutes and then it stopped and she was grand again, free to keep going. Like a young one rushing to meet her friends.

She's coming up to the corner of Talbot Street and she's hardly seen a soul. Town was always packed when she was a girl – and an adult. She remembers holding her mother's hand and, later, holding Charlo's hand. That just comes at her now – after they got married and they were in their flat at the top of Gardiner Street, her hand in Charlo's, and his thumb crossing and recrossing her wrist, softly, like a tongue.

She doesn't want Charlo in her head. She doesn't want to think of him – the thumb on her wrist, playing with her, promising love, sex, security, as they walked down Gardiner Street, into town. She often hoped they'd turn. He'd change their minds for them, about going to the pictures or for a drink, and he'd stop and they'd turn – they wouldn't say a word – and he'd bring them back up Gardiner Street, back to the flat and he'd drop her on their bed and the thumb would become his tongue until she was crying on his shoulder and he'd be in her and she'd explode slowly, she'd die, again and again.

She doesn't want this. She's not far from Gardiner Street but she's very far from wanting to remember Charlo as a lover.

She's an old woman. She doesn't mind thinking that. She's a vain ol' bitch. I'm an old woman, believe it or not. She's an old woman who's been thinking about her bastard of a husband kissing her shoulders, the back of her neck, thirty years after the Garda knocked on her door and told her he was dead – and she can still feel his lips if she wants to, and his hands. But she doesn't want to. If she could open her head and burn him out – all evidence of him – she'd do it. She'd have done it straight after Nicola came home and started talking – and screaming.

But she can't do it – it can't be done.

So.

Paula's walking into town. More accurately – more honestly – she's walking away from home.

She had to get away from Nicola.

—Jesus, Nicola – you're throwing away everything. Nicola?

—Grand.

—Ah, Nicola. Your lovely job, hon.

—Stop calling me hon – I fuckin' told you.

—Your job, though – just like that?

—Yep.

—The girls, Nicola – what about the girls? Nicola – for God's sake –!

It would never have occurred to Paula that she could have been the one to make the move, who'd stop halfway down Gardiner Street and make them turn back. She wonders what that would have been like. He wouldn't have liked it. Being told what to do. He'd have been cruel. Cruel sooner. But it's hard to know. Everything's hard to know.

She never got the chance to divorce him. She never had that satisfaction. There was no divorce when she got rid of him, when she hit him with the frying pan. It can still terrify her when she thinks of that, of what she did. He'd have killed her if she hadn't hit him hard enough. Or if she'd killed him – if she'd hit him too hard, or stabbed him. She'd have been out by now, out of jail. Long out. She can feel the pan in her hand, a good heavy pan it was, a present from his mother – she can feel her grip on the handle. It was his blood on the floor for a change. She'd bullied him out of the kitchen, down the hall, out the door, before he'd had the time to recover. When she saw him looking at Nicola.

There was still no divorce when he died. Would she have been a widow if she'd been divorced – a proper widow, an official one? She doesn't know. Widow or divorcee – she could have taken her pick. Divorcee. Every time. It's a great word, as sexy as fuck.

She doesn't know where this is coming from. She's a bit mad, she thinks, swinging from high to low, not that certain which is which. All over the place. She's not sure where she is.

She knows exactly where she is. But she hasn't a clue where she's going – that's the problem. She has no plan – no destination. She could phone Joe. She could cross the street, go into Connolly station, get on the DART – use her travel pass for the first time – and go out to Howth and see Joe.

No – she doesn't want that. Although she misses him. Not now, though. She misses no one. Except herself, maybe. Whatever that means.

She's walked out of her own house.

She'd been doing so well. Semi-retired – although she could never say that out loud, except maybe to Mary. Then the Covid comes along, and the lockdowns. And she managed – she was fine. She wasn't restless. She was thinking of gardening, half-thinking of getting a dog. She'd had her first vaccine.

Then Nicola was on the step. Nicola had done what Paula seems to be doing now. She'd walked out of her home – into Paula's. Nicola hadn't lived there since she was nineteen. And Paula can't think that it was ever cosy or warm when Nicola did live there. Paula can look back on those years and just about cope. She rarely wants to curl up – she doesn't feel like she's been thumped.

She bought a bottle of vodka for Nicola when she was sixteen, for Christmas. That's a memory that makes her want to curl up and die, even here, on the corner of Amiens Street and Talbot Street, outside the Spar. It's not a memory. It's a thing that's still happening, a thing that still eats Paula and always will.

Town could do with a good wash. Maybe because there are so few people. So few feet moving – there's nothing covering the path and it looks manky. It's like a filthy house, years of grime and grease. Her own house. But her house was never too bad. The fridge was often empty but it always looked emptier because it was clean. She was a cleaner, for fuck sake. The kitchen floor was always spotless because she had to mop up her own blood. That's an exaggeration – that's too dramatic. But it happened – she wiped her blood off the kitchen floor. She put the mop head in the sink and watched the water change colour, and she twisted the strands of the mop until most of the bloody water was squeezed out of it, and she went at the floor again while she told the kids – she told Nicola – to stay out till she was done. Her head throbbing, with the drink and the beating. And the shame. And rage.

But Nicola had rung her – out on the step – and she'd asked if she could come in.

The street is filthy. Filthy and empty. It's not the rubbish – it's not that kind of filth. There's virtually no rubbish on the street in front of her, no burst bags. The seagulls must be starving. It's under-the-skin filth. But she's here and – she doesn't know why – she's glad she's here. She's made it this far. It's some kind of achievement. A physical thing, at least. She still has some kind of strength.

She'll go on a bit further.

She met Maisie – that's the last time she was in town. Before the pandemic. Maisie's her granddaughter – one of her granddaughters. She's John Paul's girl. John Paul and Star's – their youngest. It was Maisie's birthday and Paula had treated her. That's nearly two years ago. It was the first time she'd been alone with one of John Paul's children, the first time John Paul and Star had trusted her.

That's not fair – she knows. She never asked. She waited for permission, for years. Passive aggression – that was what Joe told her it was. Hers, not theirs.

—I wasn't aggressive.

—I know.

—I'm never aggressive.

—I know.

—Joe – I'm never aggressive. Look at me.

—I am.

—Fuck off. That wasn't aggressive, by the way.

—I know.

—You're the one that's being passive aggressive.

—I know.

She's smiling now – she can feel it. Bloody Joe. They've been seeing each other for seventeen years. She couldn't believe that when she worked it out one day, when she was wondering why she bothered.

She can't believe she's got this far. And there's not a bother on her. She's sweating a bit. Glowing. But she's walked right out of her carefulness. It must be nine or ten kilometres she's done – probably more. She's not even thirsty. Although she'll get a bottle of water. She has a mask, and her cards – her debit card and her travel pass. She stormed out prepared. She must have known she'd be doing something like this. Unconsciously. Another of Joe's words. As if she didn't know the word herself, and what it meant. The fuckin' know-all. She has them – the mask and the cards – in her shirt pockets. She emptied her bag onto the couch one night and realised that she didn't need any of the stuff that she's been lugging around. There was a lighter she hadn't seen in years and a tube of hand cream that could just as easily stay at home. There was her lipstick. There was a wodge of masks, mostly blue, like a nest. One of them was black and had 'Glasgow Celtic' printed on it. She'd never worn it and she couldn't remember ever seeing it on anyone's face. Her reading glasses were in there, but she never wore them when she wasn't in the house, except at work, and she always left a spare pair there. There was a foil of Panadol with two left in it, and three empty foil packs. There was a charger for a phone she'd thrown out years ago. She'd emptied the bag after she noticed the groove on her right shoulder, where the bag went whenever she hoisted it. It wasn't just a red mark – it was a trench, years old. She'd been using the bag less and less, because she'd been going nowhere, except to the Centra every three or four days, and she'd noticed the ache – the jolt – when she'd taken it off her shoulder. It was one of the aches she'd twisted her body to accommodate – for years. She held the bag up in front of her face, a Tommy Hilfiger tote bag that Nicola had handed to her maybe ten years before, and she felt no affection for it. No hostility either – she wouldn't be throwing it out.

Today she's in her new uniform – jeans and a plaid shirt. This one, her favourite, is green and black, with two pockets. Nicola told her the pockets were sexy – the breast pockets – and that thought had kind of delighted Paula, although she'd said nothing. The mask is in one of the pockets and card and travel pass are in the other. The mask pocket is open, the cards pocket is buttoned. She has the front-door key in one of the jeans pockets and the phone is in the other.

It was Nicola who converted Paula to the plaid shirts – this was before she'd moved in and stayed, before the lockdowns. She'd given Paula this one, from FatFace. Then she told her weeks later, after she'd seen that Paula was wearing nothing else, that she'd bought it for Tony but it had been too tight across his stomach.

—Is it a man's shirt?
—Does it matter?
—No.

It didn't. Not at all. She was inside a man, somehow. It made a change. Another joke of her own that she hadn't been able to tell anyone, except Mary.

—Jesus Christ, Paula Spencer – your head should be fuckin' fumigated.

But little Maisie – she was a tiny thing, and she was right up beside Paula before Paula had a chance to see her coming. At the Spire on O'Connell Street. At the far end of the street she's standing on now.

—Hiya.

—Jesus, love –!

She'd laughed – they'd laughed. They'd hugged.

Paula smiles now as she looks up Talbot Street. She wants to keep going – the Spire has become her goal.

They'd gone to McDonald's that day and Maisie had explained the machine to her, how to order the stuff without going to the counter to do it.

—Can we not just go up and ask?

—This is how you're supposed to do it, like.

—I want to order my food from a human.

—You sound like my dad – he's always going on like that, like.

Paula had stopped seeing – for a second. Panic and happiness had it out inside her chest – they tumbled right through her. Her eyes filled with tears that stayed where they were, didn't roll out. And there, in front of the stupid machine, she loved John Paul. For the first time since he was a child – that was how she felt. And she stopped being frightened of him. Frightened of her own child.

A street with no people. That's what she's looking at. And not just any street. It's Talbot Street. It should be jammered. It's always been a wild street, always a bit mad.

A bus turns off Amiens Street and slowly passes her. She goes with it, as if she's using it for cover – she's hiding from snipers on the roofs across the street. It's been quiet all the way. Up Howth Road, along through Fairview, and the North Strand. It's not that there was no one – it's not like it was during the first lockdown when she could walk down the middle of the street. There were people, but she'd still felt like she was crossing boundaries, sneaking past border patrols. Pushing herself to be braver. Brave enough to walk away from home. She'd expected things to get busier as she got nearer to town. She thought she'd have to start being careful, weaving among the pedestrians, maybe even putting on her mask. But, she thinks now, it's got quieter and emptier the nearer to town she's got. It's like the film that Will Smith is in, him and the dog in the empty city.

She sees now, though, there are people – Roma – at the corner of Gardiner Street. Both corners. The women in their clothes – the long velvet skirts and the shawls, and their buggies parked up against the walls. She thinks of that old Cher song – 'Gypsies, Tramps and Thieves'. She loved that song when it was in the charts, years ago, when she was a teenager. She likes the name – Roma – but they all look like they've come out of somewhere two hundred years old. They scare her a bit. She doesn't know – it's the clothes, the old-style Gypsy clothes. Do they want to dress like that? Because the men don't – they dress like all the other modern-day fuckers from any part of the world. She doesn't see any of the men – it's just women and the kids. She'll smile if one of the women looks at her. They have their ways, she supposes. Their lives make sense to them. Just maybe not on Talbot Street. Or maybe there's a street like Talbot Street in whatever city in Romania they've come from. Bucharest – she's nearly certain that's the capital.

She loves that, when information pops up like that. Stuff she's not particularly interested in and wasn't aware she knew. She'd noticed it when she started going out with Joe. He'd be talking about something – explaining something – and she'd realise that she already knew. And she knew stuff, herself, that he hadn't a clue about. It was just that he did more of the talking. And less of the listening. She remembers the names of the different kinds of seagulls – herring gulls, black-headed gulls, Iceland gulls. She knows the names but she wouldn't be able to point them out, tell the differences – because, really, she couldn't give a shite about their names. It's not exactly vital information, just because Joe can tell the differences between them. There's one ahead of her now – a seagull – just landed in the middle of the street, and she knows what kind it is. A big fucker.

She knows she's smiling. She can smile as long as she keeps going forward. There's nothing ahead she has to worry about.

What would Charlo think of all this – all the foreigners, the Roma? He was dead long before they started to arrive. But she knows – he'd have been horrible. She can see him, going out of his way to push through them. He'd have stared straight at their crotches.

They'd gone upstairs in McDonald's – Maisie and herself. Maisie held the tray and lowered it onto the table like a pilot making a perfect landing. She took her own stuff off and shoved the tray gently across to Paula.

—Nanny, she said, after she'd finished her first nugget.

Paula couldn't believe she'd ordered chicken nuggets for herself. Stupid-looking things – and tasteless – thank God for the ketchup. Still, though, she was more than happy being here with this girl.

—Nanny, said Maisie again. —I don't want to call you Nanny any more.

Paula looked at Maisie's face. Maisie was afraid that she was hurting Paula's feelings. For a second – less than a second – she was. Paula felt something being pulled away from her. But she pulled back, and there was nothing to pull at – nothing was being taken from her.

—I *am* your Nanny, hon, she said. —And I'll tell you, Maisie, I'm very glad I am.

Maisie smiled.

—Me too.

They laughed. Paula watched Maisie dip another nugget into her ketchup.

—Are the nuggets to your liking? she asked.

—They're delightful, said Maisie.

They were laughing again.

—It's childish, said Maisie.

—Calling me Nanny?

—Yeah.

—So is eating nuggets, hon, said Paula.

She bit into one, just to make sure Maisie knew that she wasn't being too serious.

—Adults eat nuggets, said Maisie.

—Okay, said Paula. —You're right. So – what do you want to call me instead? It can't be Paula, though, hon. That'd be weird.

—No, Maisie agreed. —Granny.

—You want to call me Granny?

Maisie nodded.

—Grand, said Paula. —What's the difference?

—It's like Mama and Mam, said Maisie.

—Granny's like Mam, is it?

—Yeah.

—Grand.

—I can call you Granny?

—If you must, said Paula. —What do you call your other granny?

—Nanny Southside, said Maisie.

She was grinning.

—Excuse me? said Paula.

—That's what my dad calls yis, like. You're Nanny North-side and she's Nanny Southside.

Paula hadn't met Nanny Southside but she knew that she came from Fatima Mansions. She knew that, like her daughter, Star – original name, Carol – Nanny Southside was a recovering heroin addict and that she'd spent time in the female version of Mountjoy. And John Paul, Paula's son – another recovering heroin addict – called her Nanny Southside. And, again, she felt a rush of love for her son. A surge. One of the words she'd been hearing every day on the radio. That was what she was feeling. John Paul had a sense of humour. He made his children laugh. Paula hadn't known that. She'd never imagined it.

—Do you call her that to her face?

—Not really, like, said Maisie. —I call her Granny Fran.

—You can call me Granny Paula, so, said Paula.

—Just Granny, said Maisie.

—You get to choose, do you, madam?

—Yeah, said Maisie. —I do.

Paula's past Gardiner Street now, and past the Roma women. Everything's shut and most of the places look like they've been shut for years, like they're waiting to be knocked down. She can't believe that she isn't wrecked, herself. This isn't how she was a few years ago, when the walk from the bus stop after work could destroy her. But she can feel it in her feet and legs – she can keep going. Not forever – but she's not a bit tired.

She'll be grand as long as she keeps going forward.

Because she's running away. Walking away. She's two different people. She's the woman walking forward and she's the woman behind her, the woman who walked out of the house three hours ago. Because she couldn't stick it any more.

She'd come close to hitting her. Jesus – so close. The impossible bitch – the absolute impossible fuckin' bitch. Teenager in a menopausal body. The fuckin' wagon – acting younger than her kids.

—The girls – Nicola?

—They're fine.

—How can they be?

—They're fine I said.

—How –?

—Shut up. Just – just fuckin' shut up.

Her hand was on its way to Nicola's face. But Nicola had turned and she didn't see Paula stop herself – sit down at the kitchen table, shake. She could hear Nicola stomping up the stairs, back to her cave. She stood. She went to the front door.

She'll have to turn back. She knows that. But not yet. Maybe when she gets to O'Connell Street. She doesn't know yet – she hasn't decided. She can't.

She wonders if Maisie popped into her head because she feels so guilty about her other grandkids, Nicola's girls. About letting their mother stay with her, away from them. She keeps in touch – she texts them. Especially Lily. Poor Lily. She texts them but she hasn't seen them. In nearly a year.

So.

Most people think the street is named after Matt Talbot but Paula knows it isn't. It was already Talbot Street when Matt Talbot walked down it with his chains hidden under his clothes. It was named after the Earl of Talbot in eighteen-something-something and before that it was called Cope Street, which would be a much better name – a more honest and human name for this particular street. Especially with Paula on it. Coping. Not coping.

Her mother had a thing about Matt Talbot. She was always telling Paula little things about him when Paula was a child. She remembers a lot of it. He died on Granby Lane, behind Parnell Square, and his body was taken to Jervis Street Hospital. Paula found that out when she, herself, was in Jervis Street getting her tonsils out. There was a chain around his waist when they cut his clothes off, and other chains and cords around his legs and arms. But no barbed wire – that was just a vicious rumour, her mother told Paula. And the chain wasn't tight, she told her. Paula's smiling again. Thinking of her mother trying to make Matt Talbot seem reasonable. The chains were a symbol of his devotion to Mary, the Mother of God. He was the Blessed Virgin's slave – that was what the chains meant. Her mother telling her this while Paula sucked an ice-pop, to make her throat feel nicer.

There are people here, crossing ahead of her, at the corner of Marlborough Street. It's the junkies, the addicts, with that jerky walk they have – in a hurry, bouncing off one another. They're always around here but they stand out now because there's no one else. The Roma stand out for the same reason.

Does Paula, though – does she stand out? Does she look mad, the way she felt three hours ago? Is she the mad oul' one who nearly hit her possibly suicidal daughter?

North Earl Street's busy enough. It's as if anyone who's ventured into town has made their way to North Earl Street, a butt of a street between Talbot Street and O'Connell Street – real streets. North Earl Street is a short-arsed, aggressive little street, hardly started before it's over. Boyers used to be here – a good shop it was, like Arnotts, a place you could wander around. And the Kylemore Café, up at the corner. She sat in there with her mother and she sat in there with her own kids. Gone now, both of them. And Clerys, on the other side. There's a Sports Direct where Boyers was. It's open, but she'd never go in there. It's like a health-food shop or a strip club – the type of place she'd never go into. There's the statue of the writer, James Joyce – and more of the Roma, women and men, sitting and standing around him, at the base – the plinth. Joe's read that book by James Joyce, *Ulysses* – so he's said. More than once. But it's a dead loss, this street. And a bit rough. A bit more than she's ready for. It's gone from too few people to too many.

O'Connell Street. She's on it now. Her destination – she thinks. If she stops she'll seize up. That's the problem. There can't be a destination. But O'Connell Street feels like a border, or the river in Texas – the Rio Grande. Henry Street is over on the other side but – Jesus, she sees them now – there are tents all the way down the street. It's like two different cities, two different times of the day, divided by O'Connell Street. It's a line of tents, near enough to a straight line – organised. Like a refugee camp. Cheap tents, like the ones kids bring to festivals and don't bother bringing home.

What is the fuckin' world coming to?

There's safety in numbers, she supposes. The men and women who've decided to camp there – to live there – must feel safer than they would beside one of the canals or in the Phoenix Park. A woman alone at night in a little tent that's thinner than her shirt – she can't imagine it. She *can* imagine it. She's not going down there. It doesn't scare her – it's bright and there are people coming and going, between the lines of tents, normal-looking people from where she's standing. Normal? Paula has never felt normal – or not since she was in school. Normal now – here – means not being homeless or a drug addict. So she's normal. Although she's an addict – an alcoholic – and she's just walked out of her home. But she won't be going down Henry Street. She's not going to look into the unzipped front of a tent and see someone looking out at her. Someone she knows, someone she knew, someone who looks like someone. Herself.

She has to make her mind up for the first time since she walked out of the house. But that's not true. She's been making her mind up all along the way – keep going, keep going, keep going. She has to decide if she's stopped.

—Jesus – this is unbearable.

—Yeah.

—It's fuckin' unbearable.

—Yeah, yeah.

—I can't stand it. Nicola –?

—Grand.

No one should have to have middle-aged children. No one should have to look at them. They should be taken away when they get to Maisie's age, or – max – eighteen. Job done, good or bad. Leave your ma alone. Her life is her own now – the rest of her poxy life is hers.

She knows – she'll be going back.

She knows – she wants to.

She'll cross the street. She's come this far, so she'll make it formal. She'll cross, she'll go past the GPO, under the pillars – the columns. She'll go down to the river, go over the bridge, so she can know that she's crossed the Liffey to the Southside. Then she'll go back across the river by the new bridge, the Rosie Hackett. She can decide then if she's walking home or getting the DART or a bus – launching her travel pass. But she can feel herself stiffening, just standing here. Her legs are feeling fat and rigid, and she's beginning to feel the weight of her feet. It'll take a push to get her going again. But she has her plan. She just has to start – restart – put one foot in front of the other.

O'Connell Street's a mess. Jesus Christ, it's desperate. It's the widest street in Europe. She thinks that's true – or maybe it's just the bridge, O'Connell Bridge, that's the widest bridge in Europe. Jesus, though, she's full of interesting facts. Even the ones she isn't sure of. And she likes it – knowing things. She knows a lot.

She knows fuck all.

The put-down is automatic. It used to be Charlo's voice. Now it's her own. That's an improvement, she supposes. She owns her own self-loathing. She's a clever bitch, sometimes. Clever and vain.

She wants her home back. She wants her nice life back. She wishes Nicola would fuck off and leave her alone. The Charlo damage, the real Charlo pain – it isn't physical. It never was, once the bones were mended and the bruises faded back behind her skin. The real damage – she can't face her children, not even in her imagination. They're like a jury and she's always guilty – she knows she's guilty. Nothing will ever make her know or feel any different. He battered the mother out of her.

She hates her children.

She doesn't.

She hates herself. It's true. She thought she'd dealt with it, consigned it to the past. She could look in the mirror and smile at herself. That's nonsense, though, bullshit – the sentimentality of it disgusts her.

She's going mad. She's losing it. All these old phrases are making sense. She's off her rocker. She's out of it. Away with the fairies. Out of control. Out of her mind. Fuckin' bananas. Sick in the head. Mad as a hatter. She's been stuck inside the house too long.

74

What's a hatter? Someone who makes hats – she isn't sure. Why would a hatter be mad? Suddenly, she knows. The hatters used mercury for curing the felt they used for making the hats. They breathed in the vapour and went mad. Like your man in *Alice in Wonderland*. She's trying to remember the last time she wore a hat. Nicola's wedding – back to Nicola. A hat paid for by Nicola. Like a lot of other things.

She's exhausted – that's what she actually is.

She's afraid.

She'll go home. She'll go back down to Connolly. She'll get the DART. But she'll tap the Spire first. Like a swimmer tapping the end of the pool before she turns and swims back to the other end. She'll tap the Spire – the stupid big needle – and turn. She's made her point. She knows it now – she's reached her destination.

She steps out – she sees something. Something dead, on its back. Lying back, head back. It's a seagull. For a second she thinks – oh Christ – she thinks it's a baby. The way it's lying back, put lying there, its shape – like a swaddled baby. Its neck – she expects the head, the baby's head. Oh Jesus – how could that happen, a baby on the street, left there? But only for a glimpse, before she sees what she's really looking at. It's a seagull and Paula feels desperately sad. After the shock, she just feels sad. The poor thing. The way it's lying there, like it just gave up and died, put its head back on the pillow that isn't there. Lay back and died like a human.

She has to get away from here. Before she picks the thing up and puts it to her breast – it's only a fuckin' seagull. A maggoty dead bird.

A bike swipes her.

She didn't see it. She didn't look.

She must have looked – but it wasn't there.

She didn't see it.

She doesn't see it.

It doesn't hit her full on. It doesn't hit her at all – not really. The cyclist is on the ground, not Paula. She feels like she's been hit – the breath's knocked out of her. The shock – fuckin' Jesus. Not knowing what's happened – the stupidity, things tumbling all around her and she doesn't know what's happened. It's done, and she's still catching up. It definitely happened – the young lad is on the street, on his side. Curled up like he's trying to sleep. One of those yokes – one of those delivery bags – on his back.

She looks up the street to see if there's anything coming, a bus or a car, if he's going to be run over, if she should do some-thing, step out to stop them. There's nothing, though – he's the only thing on the road. She looks behind her – the seagull's still there, still dead on the edge of the path. She's kind of surprised – it would have made sense if it had disappeared.

Her stomach's burst open. She's looking down at herself. This is awful, fuckin' awful. She's torn, ripped, right across her front. There's no blood on her hands – she's gathering up the cloth, trying to pull her shirt back together. She's catching up, beginning to understand. It's buttons – that's all. The handle-bar of the bike pulled the buttons off her shirt. That's what's after happening. But it's terrible. She's exposed, falling apart, not what she was a minute ago.

The lad on the ground is moving.

No time has passed – a second or two. It feels like an eter-nity but it can't be. She remembers time being warped and squashed. She remembers it, even now – where she is now, with what's happening. Time has always played tricks. After Charlo had beaten her. Or when she knew he was going to, but she could still hope that he wouldn't. Time flew and stopped, and crawled, jumped backwards and forwards, and made her topple.

She hasn't been gawking at the poor kid on the ground. He's lying there because he's only after landing. Her shirt, though – her favourite shirt. It's ruined – it isn't just the buttons. It's been pulled off her, almost – it's ripped. The handlebar must have dug into her skin, her flesh – fuck it, her fat – because it's sore, it's stinging, and there's a deeper pain there too. She checks again – she looks at her front, she looks at her hands, one at a time, because she's holding the shirt together, trying to. There's no blood on her T-shirt. She's not bleeding – she hasn't been opened.

She checks again for traffic, and looks along the cycle path. She steps out to the young lad. He's one of those Deliveroo fellas, with the box on his back. Like a shell. He's a snail on the road.

He's moving.

She stops – she thinks about stepping back onto the path. What will he do if he blames her? He's foreign. He must be – they all are. A box full of pizzas on his back. It's not leaking – it isn't after bursting. There's no sauce or cheese on the street.

Her phone – where's her phone? She pats her pockets. It's there, it's still there – it's grand. Should she be phoning for an ambulance? Your man is moving, though, he's getting up. Should she be phoning the Guards? He was pulled off his bike by the buttons of her shirt. He was going too fast. He must have been – she didn't see him. He was there out of nowhere. She never saw him on the bike, just on the street. He'll say she wasn't looking. He'll say she stepped out in front of him. He'll say she was gawking back at a seagull.

She didn't see him – he wasn't there. She's sure she checked.

Where's the bike? It's disappeared. It's been stolen already. Jesus.

He's standing up. Crouched. Controlling the pain. She's been there, she's done that – she knows exactly what he's doing. She's feeling sorry for him.

—Are you alright, son?

Son?

When did she become the old woman who calls grown men son? Years ago – cop on. The poor lad is bleeding. A dark-skinned young fella – South American, she'd say. Brazil – that's where they come from. She just called a Brazilian man son. One of Pelé's grandkids. Where's his bike? He's thinking the same thing – she can tell.

She sees one of her buttons. He might be bleeding his guts out but she wants to bend down and pick up the button off her shirt.

She resists. It's going nowhere.

She holds his elbow.

His jacket is ripped – she sees. At the shoulder. It's the same colour as the box. That lovely blue. She knows it's blue. It's the dark blues that are tricky for her.

—Are you okay? she asks him.

She follows his eyes.

The bike is behind her. On the path. In away from the street. The wheels look the way they should – they don't look buckled or anything. How did it get there? Did it fly over her head while she was catching up with what was happening? Was she nearly decapitated by a Deliveroo bike? The back wheel is about a yard away from the dead seagull. The front wheel is still spinning slowly. The back wheel is on the ground, the front one is being held up off the path by one of the handlebars.

He's after saying something. She thinks he's just said he's okay.

She lets go of his elbow. She starts rubbing the muck off his jacket, and off his jeans. But she stops before she's started. Rubbing at the young lad's legs. Jesus, Paula. She'll be telling Mary all about this.

There are people here now. The gawkers. The rubberneckers – Nicola called them once when they were driving past a car crash.

She picks up the button, and the other one she sees now, beside it. She doesn't know how many are missing – more than two. She won't be checking. She's sore – very sore. Right below her boobs, right across.

The Deliveroo young lad has sat down beside his bike. He's holding one of the handlebars, afraid it'll be robbed. The poor kid – for this to happen. So far from home. Mind you, she's heard they're all drug mules – is that the word – mules? – cycling around the city, delivering heroin and what-have-you as well the pizzas and chow meins. She's heard they're living twenty in a room, paying mad rent for the share of a bunk bed. She's heard they raped a girl, some poor homeless young one – a whole gang of Deliveroo riders. She heard that one from someone who was collecting a suit and a dress in work, a woman who was going to her cousin's daughter's wedding in Longford, she told them, and she mentioned the rape when she saw a Deliveroo lad outside going by on his bike. She remembers herself and Mary sharing a look – will you listen to this one?

This poor lad here – he's a boy who's fallen off his bike and wants his mammy but she's thousands of miles from here, from him. He's not a boy. He's a grown man. She wishes the rubberneckers would fuck off. They're in the way, complicating things. There are five of them. Four – one of them has seen enough. And they're okay, the four that have stayed – two men, two women. They're wanting to help, to check that he's okay – they're not trying to make him get up.

She can't see any more buttons. She can't really check on the extent of the damage to the shirt. All she can do is try to keep it shut, keep herself decent.

It could be worse – it could have been worse. Jesus – that thought. It used to slither up to her – it could have been worse, Paula. As she lay on the floor, when she wasn't sure if she was living or dead. She'd hear it in Charlo's voice, in her mother's voice, her father's. But, worst of all, her own.

She remembers – it's daft – her jacket has a zip. She's been carrying it since she took it off in Fairview. She puts it on and zips it up.

Simple as that.

Leanne will do a job on the shirt for her. Leanne will make it look like the repairs are deliberate, a fashion thing – a statement. It's an amazing thing about Leanne, how she can be so precise and creative. An amazing thing to watch, the steadiness, the concentration – once it's thread or wool and not her life that she's concentrating on.

She asks him again.

—Are you okay?

He nods – he's okay.

He looks up at her. His face asks the question – is she okay? It's her turn to nod.

—I'm grand.

The rubberneckers have drifted off. There's no blood – there isn't going to be a fight. The street's empty again, like it was before the bike swiped Paula.

He's standing up – he's getting ready to stand. She puts her hand to his elbow, although she knows it's no real help. He's standing now, but huddled over, like he's hiding something under his jacket. And maybe he is. He groans as he bends to pick up the bike. He nearly topples – he's probably forgotten that he has the box on his back. She sees his hands now, his palms – they're dirty, they're grazed. She bends to help him with the bike. He lets her – he lets go of it. She can't remember the last time she held a bike in her hands, or cycled one. She'd love to do it now. Hop on this one and pedal off home. It's heavy, though – she thinks it's a mountain bike.

The young lad is standing but he's being careful with himself. Maybe he really is hurt. She's betting he's fine but she wishes she knew first aid. She's had so many different bones broken, so much of her has been mended or part-mended, she should be able to tell what's wrong with this lad just by glancing at him. She should be helpful, useful. But she's useless. She knows this – it's a relief.

No.

She's not having it. She's not going to be bullied back into victimhood. Especially not by herself.

—Come on, she says.

She's been looking across at the statue of James Joyce.

—Come on, she says again.

She pushes the bike a little bit, so she's right in front of him and he'll have to hear her. She's seeing his face – she thinks it might be the first time she's looked at it. He's a handsome lad, although the shock has made him look a bit thick.

—Over here, she says.

She knows that if she takes the bike with her he'll follow. She takes a few more steps and waits for him. He's right behind her. He's a bit straighter, she thinks. She's wondering about herself. Has she damaged anything? She doesn't think so – she's not sure. That stinging across the top of her belly – it's not too bad, it's hardly there. It's old pain, poked. But she'll be fine – she *is* fine.

The problem now – there are Roma sitting around James Joyce. On the plinth and on the ground. There's no room for Deliveroo. But there is. They're getting up. They've seen the young lad. Maybe they saw him flying off the bike. They're all up, the women, the kids, the man who's there with them.

—You're very good, she says. —Thanks.

A young woman smiles at her. A lovely-looking girl. Black-haired, smiling shyly. In her gorgeous years.

They have the whole plinth to themselves, Paula and Deliveroo. The Roma are hovering. But they're keeping their distance. She half-expects one of the kids to make a grab at the bike. There's one little lad who looks like a right imp – he reminds Paula of her John Paul. The same scampy look. One of the women has the back of his jacket in her grip. Paula can almost feel it in hers. She has been that woman. And she wishes she was again. She was gorgeous in her day, dangerous in her day. Desired. Here she is, pretending she wishes she was one of the Roma. She's an eejit, pathetic. A Roma girl with a boyfriend from Brazil, and a dead seagull for a child. Mad as a fuckin' hatter.

She's not sure about touching things. She's been very good about sanitising and washing her hands. She doesn't want to touch the plinth – it's bronze, like the statue. It's not the Roma, the fact that they've been sitting here. Coughing, maybe spitting – she doesn't know – but it's not that. Irish people cough and spit, Irish people sweat and breathe. Being alive is dangerous. But she had the bike in her hands, the young lad's sweat – it's already mixed with hers. She's gone way past not touching surfaces. She won't put her hands near her eyes or her mouth. God, but – what's she doing?

She leans the bike against James Joyce. She rests the saddle against one of his legs. She lets go of the bike and it stays there. Deliveroo is still huddled up. He's like a kid with a tummy ache trying to get a day off school.

—Sit here, she says.

He seems to understand. He sits and it doesn't seem to take too much out of him. He thanks her – he says thank you. The Roma women have moved away – they're heading down to Talbot Street.

She bends her legs, she puts her hands on his knees – she has to or she'll fall.

—Sorry.

She'd been going to get down on her hunkers in front of him, to get a good look at him, to see how he is. But she can't do it. Her legs are gone. If she bends any more she won't be getting back up. She'll keel over and he'll have to rescue her, or he'll just grab his bike and go. But she feels it – luckily she feels the stiffness before she bends too far. She can change her mind, and she does. She's walked too far – it's all caught up with her. She sits beside him – she has to.

—The bike's okay, she says. —I think.

She watches the side of his face as he tries to translate what she's said. His profile – he's very young. The boy is still there in his skin, even though he has a beard.

He looks over his shoulder at the bike that's leaning on the writer's leg behind him.

He nods.

She looks across to see the seagull but Deliveroo is in the way. She leans back, but hits James Joyce. She leans forward, looks past Deliveroo's chest. The seagull's there, its head on the path, its torso – does a bird have a torso? – on the road. He was avoiding the seagull and he hit Paula instead. That was what must have happened.

—Was it the seagull? she asks him.

He doesn't seem to know she's speaking to him.

—Were you on your way there or back?

She pats the box.

—Were you delivering stuff or coming back? she says.

He shakes his head and leans out a bit, and pulls his shoulders from under the straps, like it's an old-fashioned schoolbag and she's just asked him if he has homework. She doesn't know why she keeps seeing him as a kid. It's a man's sweat she's smelling. He puts the box on the ground. He taps it with his foot and it scoots away, close to weightless.

—You were coming back.

He nods.

She's going to say sorry but stops herself. She'd be admitting something that might not have happened. He'd be wanting her number, he'd be smelling the compo. It's why he's here, after all – to make money. And she's betting there's not that much in delivering pizzas. Would he even get tips? She doesn't know.

—Where're you from? she asks him.

She was right – he's from Brazil.

—Where?

He tells her – São Paulo.

—I've heard of there, she says. —Is it nice?

There's a zip on the sleeve of his jacket. He opens it and pulls out his phone. That's cool, she thinks. And it's fine, she thinks as she looks at it. The screen's not cracked or anything.

No one's phoned her since she left the house. She realises that now. She takes out her own phone and looks at the screen. She's missed nothing – no missed calls or texts. She's been at herself recently to stay away from the phone. To stop checking it every couple of minutes. To stop needing the relief and the disappointment. She doesn't need another addiction. So she's pleased, in a way. It's the first time she's looked at the phone in hours. And not one fucker has bothered to get in touch with her.

He turns the phone over in his hand. She sees the screen when he turns it again. There's a scroll of messages, a block of them down the screen. He needs it a lot more than she needs hers. For his work, for keeping in touch with home. All sorts of stuff – his life is in that phone. Photos of his nieces and nephews, his girlfriend. His mother, of course – his father's dead.

Where the fuck did that come from?

Mad as a hatter.

—You don't wear a helmet, no?

She makes a helmet of her hands, puts them over her head, to show him what she means.

He shakes his head.

—You should, she says. —You could've landed on your head.

She's sliding the fault back over to him – that's what she's doing. He should have been wearing a helmet.

He tells her he'll get one.

—Promise?

He nods.

He's looking at Paula and he's seeing his mother, even his grandmother. It's nice – she likes it. And it means he won't sue her.

He's fine – no real damage done. He should be back on his bike, delivering burgers and cocaine. Does he deliver drugs – is he one of those mules? He hasn't been rooting in his other pockets, checking on the little bags of powder or pills he might have hidden in there. He seems too calm to be doing anything too illegal. And he hasn't looked into the blue box at all. A strong wind would send it skidding across the street. Although the box is probably well padded, if it's for keeping food hot while he's cycling through the weather. And it's keeping its shape there – it can't be weightless.

She nods at the box.

—Pizzas – is it – you deliver?

He shakes his head, then nods.

—Not just pizzas?

He nods. Not just pizzas.

—How far?

He looks at her. He's getting a language lesson for nothing.

—How far do you go on your bike – delivering?

He shows her one finger.

—One kilometre?

She hears herself – the disbelief, the disappointment. She smiles.

—Is that all?

Two fingers he shows her – three, four, the whole hand. He says the numbers as he increases the fingers.

—Fair enough, she says. —That's better.

He smiles too. But he can't know that she's joking, that she's having him on. Unless his English is very good. He's only smiling because Paula reminds him of his mother or his granny.

She's after forgetting about her buttons. She's been too busy flirting with this fella. Has she been flirting? No, she fuckin' hasn't. Mammying him – that's what she's been doing. Maybe it's the same thing. Jesus – no way – she's not going there.

—Stay here, she says. —Stay put there a minute.

She doesn't know why she wants him to stay. If he goes, so will she – she'll have to. She'll have to make the move, go home.

She's enjoying herself. That's it.

She stands. She gets up as quick as she can. She's testing herself. She stands up straight – not a bother on her. She's brand new – no wooziness. Fuck, though – there's something not right. Something in her chest – she could whoop or cry out, both. She's scared and elated. It's not a bad combo. With tomato and mozzarella. She could climb into the blue box over there.

She's gas – she's fuckin' gas.

She wouldn't be standing like this, up straight and as young as she can be, if she had a fractured rib, even if George Clooney was strolling up to her. Who are the famous Brazilian men, besides Pelé? She can't think of any. There are footballers' names at the back of her mind. Who are the singers or the politicians?

—Bolsonaro, she says. —D'you like Bolsonaro?

He looks up at her. He shakes his head and does the thumbs-down thing.

—Just as well, says Paula. —Stay there.

It's amazing, really. Bolsonaro is the president of Brazil and a pal of Trump's. She knows this, she has this information, without help from anyone. Bolsonaro, right wing, climate denier. Like Trump. Like Orbán. Like Putin. Like Charlo would have been, she's sure. The things she knows, the things she thinks – she's delighted.

—Come here, she says. —Who's the president of Ireland?

She watches him work it out, what she's just asked him. He shakes his head – he doesn't know.

—You should be ashamed of yourself, she says. —Living here and not knowing Michael D. Higgins.

The name means nothing.

—Micky D – no?

She's smiling as she's talking, and she's moving away towards where the bike hit her. But she still feels a bit creepy as she listens to herself. She *is* flirting with him. Someone told her – Mary. Mary told her about women their age going to Morocco or Tunisia and paying young lads to keep them company and all that that covered. She was shocked when Mary told her, but then she wondered why. There was nothing particularly shocking about it.

—Would you do something like that? she'd asked Mary.

—No, I wouldn't – Jesus, no.

—Same here – yeah, no.

—I have Willo, sure – why would I go to Morocco? And come here – you could do that anywhere.

—Yeah.

—If you put your mind to it. Let's face it, hon. There's young fellas out there that'd get up on anything.

They were laughing, and keeping an eye on the door in case anyone came in and caught them. Mary turned on the carousel so Anozie down the back – the African fella ironing the curtains – wouldn't hear them. He was a serious Christian.

—There's no need to be flying off to fuckin' Morocco, said Mary.

—I'm not flying anywhere.

—A hole and a credit card – that's all you need, Paula, I'm telling yeh.

—I don't have a credit card.

She sees another button. It's right beside the seagull. Can she go over and pick it up and ignore the poor thing? What could she do? It's probably heavy – does she put it in the bin? It wouldn't fit. She'd have to push it and Christ knows what would happen then. She'd have to hold it, carry it. God knows how long it's been there – it could be full of maggots. The way it's lying there, she'd start crying. She'd pick it up like a baby. She'd bring it home, wrapped in what's left of her shirt. On the DART. Maggots crawling up over her shoulders. The button can stay there. It's so sad, though – the seagull. It reminds her of her seagulls at home, the seagulls she watches from Jack's – from Nicola's – bedroom window.

A thing just comes into her head, a memory. She was going to school. She was walking towards the bus stop. She could feel the wind on her legs – she was wearing her school uniform. She'd rolled the skirt up at the waist to make it shorter. The bus stop was just ahead, and the bin on the pole. The bin was green – everything was green back then, the buses, the bins, the postboxes. But it wasn't – the bin wasn't green. They'd painted it white. But it wasn't paint. It was maggots. The whole bin was covered in maggots, moving like one thing. The bin was completely covered, and part of the bus stop. She smelt it then – rotten fish. It was in the bin. She remembers – she wasn't disgusted, or particularly fascinated. Now she thinks – she never looked into the bin, to check what was dead. She'd just assumed it was fish. It could have been a seagull. Someone picked it up and dropped it in the bin. They weren't as fussy about hygiene back then. Someone could have put the sleeves of their jumper over their hands and picked up the dead bird, hit by a car or a lorry or just dropped out of the sky, and dumped it into the bin. There were no lids or anything. The bins were just buckets strapped to poles.

The fish was a seagull – Jesus, she's fuckin' mad. It's a good memory, though. Very vivid. It's one she could tell Joe. He'd verify it for her, the colour of the bin, the number of the bus – the whole fuckin' thing. She's a bitch and she likes being a bitch, in her head – she's hurting no one. She might phone Joe – she might answer his texts. She might.

She unzips her jacket and checks the shirt. The top two buttons survived because they weren't closed. And the bottom one is still there too, doing its job. There are four gone. There's the two she found already, in her pocket, and the one beside the seagull, but no sign of the last one. She looks for approaching bikes, then steps onto the street, the cycle path. She looks left, right, along the kerb but there's no sign of the last button.

Deliveroo is still sitting on the plinth. Maybe he's dazed, concussed. It would make sense – that was some tumble. There are no marks on his head but he must have been rattled. Maybe he isn't even Brazilian. Maybe she's the one who's concussed. She's feeling weird, she's feeling giddy. Mixed up. Tired yet wild. Unhinged – there's a fuckin' word. The hinges came off Paula years ago.

She could buy a new shirt. Penneys is just across the street, past the GPO. Maisie's favourite shop, she told Paula that time, and they'd gone in together and Maisie had told her about the girls in school who shoplifted in Penneys, how they took orders from other girls and sometimes even their mothers.

—Not you, but?

—No – I'd be too scared to, like.

Paula looks across the street, and down. There are so few people – it's hard to tell if Penneys is open. She can't make out if there's anyone going in or leaving. She doesn't have her glasses with her – she never brings them anywhere. Nicola offered to pay for lenses for her, or even laser surgery – before all of this happened – but Paula said no.

Bloody Nicola. The shirt, the phone in her pocket, so

much – her life – she owes to Nicola. She looks down at the shirt. It was like a skin, a layer of confidence – Nicola's. Even though it was bought for Tony and Nicola's confidence is under the floor with the mice. Nicola gave her more than a shirt when she took it out of the FatFace bag and handed it to Paula. Comfortable in her skin – that was how Paula felt before she'd even put it on. It was the timing, she thinks now – she's thought it before. She was ready for it. It's not that long ago – a year and a half, she's not sure – before the Covid. But Nicola, the woman who offered her the shirt, seems to be gone.

Replaced.

By the fairies.

It's dreadful.

She sits down again, beside Deliveroo. She doesn't know what else to do.

—Okay? she says.

He nods. He nods again. He's okay.

—Back to work, yeah?

Does he think she's telling him to go back to work? If he does, he's disobeying her. The pup. But really – this suits her fine. The plinth is a raft. James Joyce has the tiller – that's what his walking stick really is. She has nothing to worry about.

—D'you live with a lot of others? she asks Deliveroo.

He does – he nods. He says it. Yes.

—Lots, like – loads? Many, many?

She saw a thing on RTE – on *Prime Time*, she thinks it was – about young Brazilians, women and men, squashed into tiny, black-damp rooms with rows of bunks and all sorts of wires exposed, how they were being fleeced by the landlords and how a lot of them pretended to be language students just to get their visas, and how – she thinks she remembers this – some of the language schools didn't even exist.

He nods again – many.

—That's not great, is it?

He agrees. He shrugs.

—Are you able to sleep, even?

He shrugs again. He's speaking too. Single words just. It's a struggle. It's been the same with Nicola. Trying to get her to talk. Even a word. Or only a word. Monosyllabic. After weeks when Nicola didn't stop talking, when she didn't seem to sleep. Paula would have expected the monosyllables to be better than nothing, but they're not – they're worse. Especially when she remembers Nicola before. The plans, the orders, the arranging, knocking the world and Paula into shape. And her big laugh that Carmel, Paula's sister, told her was exactly like Paula's when Paula was a young one. The big, bullying laugh. Men stopped and looked. Women stopped and looked. Not so much at Nicola – although they did. At the air around her, looking for the laugh – it had to be visible.

Carmel would have been a help – she'd have been a great help now. She'd have listened to Paula, just listened. Denise, the other sister – the one that's still alive – is hopeless. She'd be jumping in, telling Paula about the other women she knows with daughters who are giving them worse grief than Paula is enduring. She refuses to eat a thing, Paula – nada. They've tried everything, literally everything. At least your Nicola is eating – is she?

She remembers trying to get Leanne to eat, when Leanne was a little one in the high chair. Holding the spoon to Leanne's mouth, holding it, holding it, pushing the spoon at the locked-tight lips, trying to be gentle, trying not to lose it. Hungover, dying, even drunk – trying to feed a child who wouldn't eat. Trying hard to care enough, to concentrate.

Getting words out of Nicola is like trying to get food into Leanne. Heartbreaking. Failure – abject fuckin' failure. She's lost – Paula is. How is she supposed to mother the woman who's been mothering her for thirty years? D'you want to talk about it? Nicola – hon? Listening to herself – Jesus. When you're ready, hon – I'm here. For fuck sake. Pathetic.

But it's grand here on the raft. She can chat and she doesn't have to care if Deliveroo doesn't answer. She's been talking to herself for months. She'd have thought, though, that the

90

Brazilians would be talkers. She knows they are. She's sitting beside the country's only silent Brazilian.

—D'you have any family here with you – no? Brothers or sisters?

No, he doesn't.

—That's a pity.

She doesn't think he understood her. How could he understand pity? How would you teach that – how would you learn it? Well – fuck it – she did. She's an expert on pity. Taking it, giving it, wishing people would shove their pity back up their arses. But she's still not sure what it means.

—What's your typical Brazilian food? she asks. —Go on – what's your favourite dinner?

She nods at the blue box.

—What would you like to find in that yoke?

He speaks – he doesn't hesitate.

—Full Irish breakfast, he says.

He isn't smiling – he hasn't turned to look at her. He's staring at the box. Like he's going to pull rashers and sausages, the full Irish, even the beans, out of it. He's not, though. His eyes – she sees now – his eyes are closed. He's asleep – he's fainted – he's after having a brain haemorrhage. Something rips through her – the poor kid is dead. First the fuckin' seagull, now this! But she knows – he isn't. She feels that in his weight against her. She hasn't jumped up or tried to scoot out of his way, along the plinth. It's not dead weight. He's just leaning against her. He trusts her. He's able to sleep because she's with him. She's looking out for him. She's looking after him.

That's just shite – she knows. The young lad's exhausted. He was able to keep going as long as he kept going. Coming off the bike – there's nothing left in him. What's she going to do now, though?

She gets her phone out – she does it without having to lean away from him. She wishes she had her glasses with her now. Trying to find the right yoke. She can feel her arm shake as she lifts the phone, so she can photograph the pair of them, herself

91

and Deliveroo. She can't really see the screen. And holding up the camera and trying to press the button with the same hand – how do they do it, all the young ones she sees taking their selfies all the time? They must go into training. She's hoping for the best here. She thinks she's taken the snap – it's hard to tell. She looks at the screen. She opens the photos. If this one didn't turn out properly, she won't be trying again. But it's okay, actually – it's not too bad. It's obviously her – she'd recognise herself. And the lump beside her is obviously a man and not obviously asleep. Obviously a young man. Somehow. It's the hair. It's the mad hair of a young man, deliberately mad. A decision – not an oul' lad's accident.

She's sending it to Mary. It'll give them both a laugh. GREETINGS FROM MOROCCO. Herself and Mary are friends in the same way that men are. They're mates, pals. They usually stand beside each other when they're chatting, the way she's seen men do. They're often working, so standing side by side at the counter comes natural. But even outside, they lean against Mary's wall or Paula's, or against Mary's car. If they met in a pub they'd be sitting side by side at the bar, staring ahead, into the bottles.

She'd had another bright idea. She'll take another selfie but this time she'll hold up her bank card as well. That'll slaughter Mary. But even as she thinks of it she starts to panic. If someone else saw it – the brutality of it, really. Even if it's just a joke between two friends. If someone else – Willo, say, or one of Mary's kids, or one of her own – Nicola – if they saw the photo on Mary's phone or hers. Even the one she's already taken. It's harmless – she's not exploiting anyone. She's been nice to the young lad. She's sitting here, aching and stiff, so he can stay asleep for a bit longer. She'll delete it – she'll have to. She heard of a girl – a woman, not a kid – who sent a selfie of her fanny. Is that a selfie or does it have to be just the face, or at least include the face? Anyway, she sent it to the wrong man. Or, if Paula's remembering it right, it wasn't a man she sent it to. It was Mary who told her this. She sent it to one of her daughters – it wasn't even the wrong man. And there's no such thing as the right daughter, especially with the message attached. She can't remember the message now but she remembers herself and Mary holding each other up. They made up messages of their own. DO YOU HAVE THIS IN GREY? She deletes the selfie, then lets herself laugh. Deliveroo's head is shaking away on her shoulder but he's out for the count. She'll tell Mary what she nearly did. It'll be just as funny.

She's never loved anyone the way she loves Mary. She's never had a friendship like this. Maybe it's because of their age. They don't have to be careful – they don't have to care. They're like two men who don't give a fuck. No – they're two women who don't give a fuck. It's definitely age. It's liberating. When Charlo was alive men didn't hug one another. They just nodded – one quick nod, like a half-hearted head-butt. But she's seen men since, big-bellied middle-aged men, hugging, really hugging – arms right around each other. Like bears in the zoo. Loving one another, although they'd never be able to say it. Women don't hug that way – they're always more careful. But Paula and Mary do. And kiss each other on the lips. Right on the smacker. And stand back and laugh.

A skinny lad is going past with a bag of cans and one in his hand. He sees the Deliveroo box and changes direction.

—There's nothing in it, says Paula.

The skinny lad keeps going but he taps the box with his foot as he's passing, to confirm that it's hollow. He walks on, straight onto O'Connell Street – the seagull doesn't interest him.

Listening to Nicola, being with her when she first arrived, Paula had felt drunk. More hungover – slow, trying to keep up. Forgetting – and remembering again, her head all over the place. Being with the woman – the girl – who used to be Nicola. That was the problem, the catastrophe. Paula didn't know who she was looking at or listening to. Some imposter. It only takes a slight adjustment for a beautiful face to turn ugly – she knows that. Bad news, sickness, the drink, an accident, even just tiredness – the face slides sideways, loosens, grows cross or stupid. But that wasn't it with Nicola. She'd been watching Nicola grow up, grow older – age. And it had thrilled her, when nothing else had even interested her. Just watching this woman walk into the kitchen, and thinking that she had grown up in this kitchen, and had seen so many terrible things happening in this kitchen. But here she was, like she'd slid off a magazine cover or she'd just been invented. Filling the fridge, chatting to her mother. Not chatting – instructing. Educating, reprimanding, cajoling, charming – the words for what Nicola did were fuckin' endless. Paula had marvelled at it, this thing in the kitchen – and sometimes hated it, the reminder. Never spoken but there, in every expression and gesture. I'm in command because I have to be. One slip – just the one – and I'd end up like you.

Ten months. It was supposed to be ten days – that had been the plan.

The raft Paula's on now, here beside Deliveroo – Nicola had always been the raft that Paula could cling to. The safe place, the best of herself. Something good came out of me. Jack too – her baby. She thinks about Jack now, sitting beside Deliveroo. It's funny to think that Jack is older than this lad – he must be ten years older. She's been proud of Jack too. She didn't deserve him – he should have been taken from her.

But Nicola – she needs to be thinking of Nicola. She never felt that she didn't deserve Nicola. Maybe because she wasn't a boy – she doesn't know. Maybe the love is different, and the guilt. Blue for a boy, pink for a girl. And Jack has been wise. Jack's gone. Nicola decided not to be wise. Paula had absorbed Nicola. She thinks now. She knows. She didn't lick it off a stone. She's her daughter's mother.

She'll have to go to the toilet. Where will she find a toilet? There's one across in Eason's, on the top floor. Mary told her about it. She'd been telling Paula about the book she was planning on writing.

—*Dublin's Hidden Toilets*. A little book, like – to fit in your pocket or your bag. With a little pouch in the back for a few sheets of the oul' Andrex.

Deliveroo is budging. He'll get an awful shock when he sees where he is and what he's decided to cuddle up to. But it's too late now – she can't scarper. Her left leg has gone dead – she's sure of it. She won't be able to stand. She'll keel over.

It's as if all of his weight rolls onto her – he's trying to shove her off the plinth, onto the chewing gum and the bird shit. He's not a big man but he's still toppling over on top of her. Then he's not – he's awake.

It's getting late – it's getting dark. But she can see his eyes. He hasn't a clue where he is – the street, the city, the country – and he hasn't a clue who he's looking at. His nightmare has come true. He's in Ireland, in the sagging arms of an ancient alcoholic.

—Sit up there – good lad.

He grunts – some sort of a cry comes out of him. It's not loud but it's awful. A baby, abandoned. But it stops before it starts. He's awake, he knows where he is, who he is. He looks behind him, for his bike.

—It's still there, she says.

He puts his hand on the frame, to make sure. His jacket, when he moves, sounds like metal parts rubbing against one another.

She's had enough of this.

She stands. She nearly topples. The blood rolls from one side of her head to the other. The tadpoles swim in front of her eyes. Then she's grand. The leg isn't dead – she can feel the blood rush down through it. She just wants to go.

—All set? she says.

Deliveroo looks a bit confused.

—Are you ready to get back to work? she says.

He understands. He nods – yes. He picks the bike up as if he's checking it's real, and puts it back down in front of him. He examines it from front to back. He holds onto the saddle. He needs his bike. He loves it.

She thinks of the rest of his day, ahead of him. His phone will be full of orders. She could hear it pinging away while he slept. He'll have to catch up – he'll be charging, head down, all of his weight on the pedals. All night, probably. He'll get home, and he'll have to wait till another lad gets out of the bed – the bunk bed, the top bunk – before he can lie down and sleep. And the aches of the accident – she suddenly remembers the accident – will catch up on him too. And he'll wish he was anywhere else except this damp kip of a room in this fuckin' dump of a city.

—You can come and live in my house if you want, she says.

That'll get rid of the bitch. That'll shove Nicola out, back to her own house and kids. No, though – she doesn't think that. She doesn't mean it. She doesn't want it.

She doesn't think he heard her. He's walking away, ready to get back up on his bike.

13 March 2022

She can hear the sea. The waves breaking. Bashing onto the stones, then dragging them into the sea. She's been drinking. She can feel it in her head. The throbbing. The pain is breaking through her. Pulling at her hair and what's under her scalp, then receding. Pulling again, and receding. It's dreadful. She can't open her eyes. She won't open them. She doesn't want to see where she is, what she's done. How far she's fallen.

Jesus.

Again.

She's afraid to move. Even an inch. To discover what she's done. She's damp, wet, lying on a beach, in her piss.

She's not cold, though – she knows that. She's not lying on the ground. She's covered.

Her head, though – the pain. The punishment.

She can't taste anything. The drink – the night before – isn't in her mouth.

The sea – it isn't the sea. It's her – Paula. Her breathing. She sounds like the tide. She knows the words – swash and backwash. She remembers them from school. More than fifty years ago. The in and out of the waves. That's the noise that's coming from her.

She's in bed. Her bed – in her own room. She hasn't opened her eyes but she knows. Despite the waves, despite the sea. She's in her bed. She wants to cry. Relief. Shame pushed back. She won't have to find her way home, stagger along the streets outside. She's home. She can feel it. The light, against her eyelids. It's the afternoon – the early afternoon. It's the light that comes through the curtains at the front of the house, on a sunny day in spring. She can't be anywhere else.

She's happy.

There's a skewer being pushed into her head, and out, and back in. It's being twisted, behind her eyes. The pain spreads out, and stays.

She's happy.

She stays still. Absolutely still. Her head is off the pillow. The pillow is behind her head. She can feel it, almost cuddling her. Holding her head in place, like hands. Telling her not to move.

She should be worried. And she is – she's definitely worried. She can hardly breathe – she's pulling in air through layers of wet cloth. She's not gasping, though – as long as she stays still.

She's hot. Wet hot.

She doesn't know how she got here. Nothing comes back. It's her own bed, so there's no big story. There can't be. It's not a nap, though – she didn't come upstairs for a snooze.

She still hasn't opened her eyes. Her breathing will become a problem if she moves. She knows that. If she moves – even just opens her eyes. She has to stay absolutely still. It's a test. A challenge. She can't hear a thing, except the swash and back-wash. She'll need water – she's thirsty – but she won't move.

Swash and backwash.

Deciduous and coniferous.

Pelagic and demersal.

Urban and rural.

Igneous and sedimentary. And metamorphic.

She doesn't remember liking geography. She doesn't remember learning the words. But there they are, in a queue. Keeping her company. She mustn't have been as thick as they told her she was, as thick as she'd always thought she was – knew she was. Thought she was.

Pelagic and demersal. She can't remember which is which – deepwater or shallow, oily or white-fleshed. She's a feeling demersal fish are deep and oily – good for the heart. The pelagics must be shallow and white, so – good for fuck all. She's amazed at herself – she's not panicking. She's doing exactly what she should be doing. If she moves she'll drown. She has no intention of moving. The way she's lying here, it's lovely. In her bed, in daylight. Protected by the pillow. She could stay like this forever. She could die this way. The thought doesn't scare her. Although she doesn't want to die. Her kids – their names, and their faces – fall on her. Gently. And the grandkids. All the faces. Especially the childhood faces – the babies, the toddlers, the first day of school. It's not a blizzard. It's nice. No tears or bruises, or terror.

Nicola.

Nicola is in the house.

Downstairs.

It's coming back. Paula's not alone. Nicola is downstairs. That face isn't a snowflake landing gently on Paula's cheek. The blotches, the anger – the dull eyes. Poor Nicola – stranded with her mother for nearly a year. Poor Paula, stranded with your woman downstairs.

Paula has the Covid – it's why she's here, why she's breathing like the Irish Sea. She tested positive. Yesterday. It must have been yesterday. After she came home from work. Came in to the smell of the dinner being cooked. She felt grand, felt absolutely fine. And then she didn't – like that, in the time it took her to get her jacket off. An ache like a huge hand coming down hard on her head, and she was shivering. She took the mask out of her jacket pocket. She was still out in the hall.

—Nicola!

—What?

—Don't come out here.

—What?

Paula saw the kitchen door opening.

—Don't come out, love!

—What's wrong?

99

Nicola was standing in the door, looking out at Paula. She saw the mask. She stayed where she was.

—Throw out one of the tests for us, said Paula.

She wasn't panicking, she wasn't frightened. But she felt fuckin' dreadful, and it was getting worse. She sat on the stairs.

Nicola was gone for a second, then back, at the kitchen door. She threw the antigen test to Paula. It landed near her feet but she had to stand, to get it. Her head swam, but she grabbed the box and sat back on the stair. She could hear the radio – the music – being lowered. Nicola had gone back into the kitchen. Paula's hands were shaking but she got the bits and pieces out of their wrappers. She shoved the swab up her nose, and turned it. Her eyes watered but she kept them closed and did the other nostril. She squeezed the drops from the tube, into the hole in the flat yoke – one, two, three, four. She stood up – slower this time – and turned on the hall light, so she could see better. She was dizzy again. She put her hand on the wall, for a second. By the time she sat back on the stairs she could see the two red bars.

—Yeah –, she called.

—Positive?

—Yeah, said Paula. —Shite.

—Go on up, said Nicola.

—I've no choice, said Paula. ——Do I?

—Well, I don't want it, said Nicola.

Paula laughed.

She remembers now.

She was kind of excited. She felt chosen.

—Come here, she said. —We'll have to pretend I have it again.

She was still sitting on the stairs, still looking at the red lines. Nicola was at the kitchen door. They weren't looking at one another.

Nicola laughed softly. Paula could hardly hear her – she seemed far off. The hand was starting to squeeze her head. The thing was taking over her.

100

—I'd forgotten about that, said Nicola.

—Yeah, said Paula. —Me too. But yeah – we've both had it before. Officially.

She'd told Tony and everyone else that herself and Nicola had the Covid, the day after Nicola had washed up on Paula's doorstep. A stroke of genius, she'd thought at the time. It had kept them all away for a while – them and all the questions.

She put the swab and the other bits into the plastic bag. What would she do with it now, though? Her hands had been all over it, and her breath. It was contaminated. And so was she – Jesus. She'd bring it with her. That was probably the safest thing to do.

She stood up carefully. She held on to the banister.

—I'll go on up, she said.

She turned on the stairs.

—Seeyeh, she said. —In what – ten days, is it?

She remembers – she was breathess by the time she got to her bedroom door. She remembers – Nicola had been playing music in the kitchen. For the first time that Paula could think of. That thought – Nicola listening to music – helped her out of her clothes and into the bed.

She still hasn't opened her eyes. She can't hear past her breath, her swash and her backwash. She's thirsty, but it doesn't matter. She doesn't know where her phone is. She doesn't care – she's sick of the fuckin' thing. She spends her days texting and waiting for texts. She's counted her steps from the house to work, from the house to the sea, from the fridge to the fuckin' telly. The phone is probably in her jacket pocket, downstairs. It can stay there.

Swash.

And backwash.

One thing she wishes – she'd like to be in Jack's room. Nicola's room. She'd like to hear the seagulls. Just to know they're out there. She never hears them here, at the front of the house – she doesn't know why not. She'd open her eyes if she was in Jack's room. She'd get up and open the curtains. She'd get back into the bed, put her glasses on, and watch the gulls gliding past the window. Coming and going, and coming back. Feeding their young, on the clubhouse roof. The gulls would know the difference between pelagic and demersal. There now – if she had the phone she'd be looking it up. And she'd forget it a few minutes later, and she'd have to check it again and she'd be feeling thick for having to do that. She's lying on her side. Her cheek is her thermometer. She's baking but there's no cold air on her cheek. Cold air replaces warm air. Convection. Cumulus. Nimbostratus. Clouds – the names of the different kinds of clouds. They're still in her head. She'd forgotten that clouds had names. Maybe that was what happened, what was happening – like the air. Your thoughts – the information and opinions and bits of gossip and shite that you accumulated, the things you thought were important – they heated up and rose, like air, convectional currents, through your brain, and the cold thoughts and ideas and images – all the things you'd for-gotten about, that had been up there for years, cooling – slid back down and replaced the warm thoughts. That was it, maybe – you never forgot. Your memories aren't memories. They're alive.

Her mother is flattening pastry on the kitchen table. Paula is watching her. I'll give you a go in a minute – don't worry. Paula is flattening pastry on her own kitchen table. She's using an empty milk bottle. Nicola is watching her. So is Leanne. So is John Paul. She's not drinking – she hasn't had a drink in months. She'll never drink again. She's humming. The kids watching – she loves it. I'll give yis a go in a minute – don't worry. She lets Leanne sprinkle the flour onto the table. She lets John Paul spread it around. Let's see, buster – are your hands clean? The radio is on in the kitchen – her mother's kitchen. The Bush wireless. Paula goes down to the shop to buy the battery for it. She has a ten-shilling note folded in her fist. Her mother has told her not to open her hand till she gets to the shop and she gives it to Mister Brady. And she doesn't. She makes it all the way there without meeting any of her friends, so she doesn't have to show them what she has. She watches Mister Brady unfolding the note. It's all here, he says, that's a relief. She needs both hands to carry the battery home. She can't open the back door. She puts the battery down on the step. She opens the door. She picks up the battery. Good girl. How was Mister Brady – did he say anything? He said it's all here. Why did he say that? She watches her mother putting the battery into the back of the wireless. I always pay him, says her mother. There was only ever that one time – when your daddy was on strike. Her mother puts the radio back on top of the fridge and turns it on. That's better. Paula knows the name of the man who's singing. It's Satchmo. There's a woman singing as well. Our love is here – to stay. Paula loves her mother. She loves being with her. I'll tell you what, though, Paula – never marry a shopkeeper.

She's awake. She's blank. She's been with her mother – she must have been asleep. Although she hasn't moved, she hasn't budged. Something woke her, jolted her.

A knock on the bedroom door. She hears it now, again. Nicola is out there – it must be Nicola. There's no one else in the house. It's barely a knock – Nicola doesn't want to wake her. She's just checking to see if Paula needs anything. Maybe checking that Paula is still alive. She'd come straight in if she was that worried. Nicola still isn't herself, but she isn't going to hesitate if she thinks Paula is dying. She's out there now – Paula can feel her. Her ear at the door. Trying to hear her mother's swash and backwash. She could just call out – Paula could. She could tell Nicola she's grand, or open her eyes and see if the glass beside the bed has water in it, tell Nicola that she'd love fresh water.

She does nothing. She doesn't open her eyes. She wants to get back to her mother. Her hands were covered in flour a minute ago. Her mother was inspecting her hands. Paula was inspecting John Paul's hands. She could feel Leanne's hair as she tightened her ponytail as Leanne pushed the star-shaped cutter into the pastry. That cutter is downstairs in the cutlery drawer, the only one left – the others are long gone. They were only ever used the once, she thinks. Nicola would be able to confirm that for her.

Paula's not giving up. She's not going to open her eyes. She's listening to herself. Nothing else.

She's standing beside the sea. She's on a beach and she's freezing. The sea is frozen solid. And the water – the ice – is black. The waves stand, frozen, ready to break onto the beach. There's no shine off the ice. There's a dead seagull at her feet – in front of her. It's windy – she sees the gull's feathers being ruffled. The eye she can see is open. Watching her. The wind makes no noise but her hair is blown across her face. It's not her hair – the hair she has now. It's the hair she had when she was a girl – it's long. The wind blows and the hair hides the seagull. There's someone beside her. She doesn't look – she can't. It's a man – she can feel it. The size of him – the shadow. She wants to step onto the ice, but she's scared. The man hasn't spoken – she's heard nothing, but his voice is in her head. It's safe – it's nice and thick, go on. She can't look. Go on – nothing will happen to you. She feels breath, air. She can move. There's a house on the sea. It should be a boat but it's a house – a wooden house. See? The house isn't sinking, is it? She knows who it is now – it's her father. Safe as houses. Her hair blows from her face – the seagull has gone. She steps onto the ice. Good girl – go on. She's in her bare feet. The ice isn't slippy – it isn't cold. She takes another step. A huge block of ice lifts up right in front of her, as the ice beneath her slides away and she sinks, she's being swallowed, and the block of ice continues to rise and it's going to topple, right on top of her – she can't move, she can't cry out.

She's crying.

Her own father. He made her do that. It was a dream – it

was only a dream. But it wasn't – it wasn't only anything. It was her father. The dreams she's been having, since the lockdowns started – they've been mad. Like films – the way she watched films when she was a child, in the Grand in Fairview or the Savoy. She believed everything in them, even the cartoons. She believed that men and women started singing when they were walking down the street. She believed that the birds and deer helped girls with the cleaning.

She's out of the dream but it's still all around the room, and close to her face. She'll have to move, get up, look out the window. Clear her head.

Her eyes are open.

She can see the curtains. She can see it's dark outside.

She sits up. Her arms shake as she does it. She's cold. The cold air is at her – it hurts. She's wet. She's been sweating. She sits on the side of the bed. It's dark but the curtains aren't that thick. She's thought about getting better, thicker ones – she's often thought about it. She decided she couldn't afford them. But really, she doesn't like it when it's too dark. She doesn't like waking up in blackness – or oblivion.

She sees the glass on the floor. She can't see if it's empty. It's near, beside her foot, but she can't reach it. She can't stretch enough – there's an ache in her shoulder, her hand is shaking. She slides off the bed, to the floor. It's colder here. Convection again – she should be up on the ceiling, crawling across it. Spiderwoman. The glass isn't empty. She drinks – she feels her arm shake as she brings the glass to her mouth. The water's warm. It's lovely, though – it's needed. She can feel it working inside her. She's out of the dream. The sea's a mile down the road and her father's been dead for years.

She puts the glass down beside her and it clinks against something – a plate. She must have eaten something – the plate is empty. She runs her tongue around her mouth. She can just about do it – her tongue feels like it's been punched. But there are no hints of what she might have eaten, nothing lodged between her teeth. She isn't hungry and she hasn't been hungry. But the plate is there – Exhibit A. She could turn on the light and search for clues – ketchup or salt, a crust under the bed.

She stands – uses the bed to help her. She sits back down, to catch her breath. Jesus. She's okay, she's fine. She's cold, though. She tries to wrap the duvet around herself. But the effort – she can feel the sweat, she can feel the cold attacking her. Her dressing gown is at the end of the bed. She stands again – slowly. She doesn't grab at the dressing gown – she'd topple over. She goes the few steps, so she doesn't have to stretch or bend. She puts it on, she ties it. She's out of her cocoon, she can hear things now and can't hear her swash and backwash – although she can feel it. Her chest is hurting her. She's not worried, though – she's not too worried. She'll go across to the toilet and get back to her burrow. She'll get back into the exact same position in the bed – she'll go back to where she was before the dream.

She'll see if she can say hello to Nicola while she's out there. She won't go downstairs – she won't even look down the stairs. But she'll make enough noise – Nicola will know she's up and alive and maybe she'll come to the bottom of the stairs and they can have a quick chat. Then Paula can disappear again. Maybe Nicola's asleep, though. It's dark outside. It could be three in the morning. It could be any time – she hasn't a clue. She hears it now, though – a voice. Out, somewhere – down the road. Another voice answering, a car door slamming.

There's a mask in her dressing-gown pocket. She puts it on. God, though – Jesus – she's smothering herself. She could text Nicola, let her know she's awake. No, she can't do that – she doesn't have her phone. And she doesn't want her phone. She doesn't want to see herself pecking at it. Peck, peck. Fuckin' peck. She's sick of the phone – the phone has made her sick.

She can see the shape of the door – the light is on outside on the landing. She opens the door – and, Jesus, the light. She's a vampire or a zombie, whatever the things are that hate the light. Vampires. Jack's door – Nicola's door – is open and the light is off. Paula steps across to the bathroom. The toilet seat is freezing – it cuts into her. She's too awake, too aware. There's nothing wrong with her. She looks at herself in the mirror as she washes her hands – and there's plenty wrong with her. Jesus – her hair. Where's it gone – is it always this thin? She gets away from the mirror. She's raving a bit – she's definitely sick. She needs to get back to the bed. Calm down, calm down. She's not to be fighting it. She can't hear the swash but she can feel it – the lack of it. The headache is crawling around from the back of her head, pulling at her hair.

She hears the front door being closed as she comes out of the bathroom. She braves it – she looks down. There's no one in the hall.

—Nic –.

She coughs.

—Nicola?

She can tell – the house is empty, except for herself. Nicola's just after leaving. Paula's alone. She needs to drink water but she's afraid to go near the stairs. She can feel herself falling, not able to hold onto the banister, no muscles in her arms, no bones in her fingers. Has Nicola decided to go home, now that Paula's the one that needs looking after? The self-centred bitch. The Big fuckin' Me.

That's not fair.

She looks into Nicola's room. It looks like a hotel room – the bed is made, there's nothing on the floor that shouldn't be there. But her case is standing in the corner, her dressing gown is hanging off the wardrobe door.

She'll be back.

Where is she, though? What's going on?

Paula gets back into her bed. She keeps her dressing gown on. She should go down and get water but she can't – she really can't. There's the water from the bathroom tap but it always has a weird taste, and a bit of a smell off it – she wouldn't be able for it. She lies back, she covers herself. She wants the water

107

brought to her. That's what she wants. She's still cold. She tries to find the shape, the exact way she'd been lying earlier. She uses her head to push the pillow back, so it feels like a cap. She straightens one leg, bends the other. She rests her hands on her tummy. The magic's gone, though. She's thinking – she's fretting. She shouldn't have shut the bedroom door. She's too by herself – she'll die alone.

She gets up again, carefully, and pulls one of the curtains back, a little bit. She can do it sitting on the side of the bed. She gets back down, under the duvet. The dressing gown is bunched underneath her. It's like lying on a cable. She hoists herself, lifts her bum so she can flatten it under her. She's being stupid, all this fussing. She has to get back to the way she was. Back to the swash and backwash. She's warming up. Where's Nicola, though? She hates being alone. She's been alone for years. She concentrates on the window. She can't see much – can't see anything. If she was sitting up it would be different. She'd see the roofs across the road, and the upstairs windows. Whose windows would she see? Mary O'Connor's, Avril Smith's. She saw Billy Smith at their bedroom window once, looking back across at Paula, in his vest. He might have said the same thing – she was looking back across at him. In his Marlon Brando vest – his wife beater. She remembers – it was night-time. And she remembers now too – Avril is in the hospice in Raheny. She's younger than Paula. She doesn't know who's in the house after Avril and Billy's. Poor Avril, though – she'll never see Avril again. She can't remember the last time she saw Avril. It can't be that long ago. Before the first of the lockdowns. It's not that long ago. It just feels like years – a different life.

Swash, backwash. It's not the same. She's not hearing the tide coming and going, pushing and pulling the sand and the stones.

Where's bloody Nicola?

The shaking's gone. That's something, anyway. She knows

about the breathing, how the Covid attacks the lungs. She knows about the headaches. She remembers someone on the radio or at work saying that the headaches don't last long with this new Omicron version. If that's the one she has. Did Nicola let Mary know that Paula wouldn't be going to work? Maybe she should go down and find her phone – and bring up a jug of water. She doesn't have a proper jug. A pot of water – a bucket. Text Mary, text Tony, text Lily. Text Joe. Maisie. Text, text, text. Peck, peck, peck. She doesn't want it. The people she knows and doesn't know, across the road and up and down the road. They're divided into the ones she knew before she stopped drinking and the ones after she stopped – they're the ones she doesn't know. Maybe it's age, though, not alcohol. The Smiths and the O'Connors have been living here nearly as long as Paula has. And Rita Kavanagh – three doors down, nearer the shops. And Lisa Higgins, a bit further down – she's been in that house since she was a child. They'd all remember Charlo. They'd remember seeing Paula in all sorts of states.

Billy and his vest – that was just after she'd thrown Charlo out. Maybe even later, after Charlo had died. She has to be fair to Billy. She doesn't know him well – she's never been in Billy and Avril's kitchen – but he never gave her the eye or assured her that she only had to ask if she ever needed anything done. Like some of the other dirtbirds. Some of Charlo's old pals. Michael Power. Brave after Charlo was dead and buried. Billy might have been looking across at pigeons on Paula's roof, not Paula. But she remembers thinking it was her. She remembers being amused and quickly disgusted. And she remembers looking out a few days later to see if Billy was looking back at her. And feeling relief – and disappointment. He's sitting with Avril now, in the hospice. Probably. Holding her hand. Looking after her. Wetting her lips with a sponge. Playing music for her. The music they both like. She remembers meeting Avril outside once, and Avril was dressed to go out. They were both going to see Aslan, in Vicar Street, her and Billy. That's who they'll be listening to now. Aslan. Christy Dignam. How can I protect you – in this crazy world? Poor Avril. Poor Billy.

She's still looking at the window. But it's different. It's bright. How did that happen? She wasn't asleep. She didn't wake up. It's been happening for days – she knows. There are no gaps between sleep and being awake. She doesn't know she's closing her eyes – she doesn't know she's after opening them. The room is full of things that should be in her head, thoughts and pictures that normally fade before she has her feet on the floor. On the window glass there – she can see her grand-daughter, Lily. Lily's fifteen – she's Nicola's youngest. She's looking in – no, looking out. Her back to Paula. It isn't Lily – it's only the curtain. Poor Lily. Gorgeous child. She's looking at her mother walking down the street.

The swash and the backwash are gone – completely. Paula waits – waits for them to come back. She wants them back. Lily isn't at the window, or in the glass. She just heard a press downstairs being shut. Nicola's in the house.

—Where were you? Paula asked her – probably yesterday – she isn't sure.

Nicola was outside on the landing. She'd just asked Paula if she wanted anything.

—What? said Nicola.

—Last night, said Paula. —Where were you?

—I wasn't anywhere.

—I thought I heard you going out.

The more she talked – Paula – the less sick she was. She was giving herself away.

—The shops, said Nicola. —I only went to the shops.

Paula remembered her mother asking the same question and Paula giving her the same answer, and Carmel, her sister, asking her a few minutes later – on the stairs – in what shop did they throw grass on your back. Fuck off, you, Carmel. Paula had gone into the bathroom and taken her jumper off and there was no grass on her back. She'd have told Nicola about Carmel and the grass – she might even have remembered the name of the fella she'd been snogging – if Nicola had been in the room with her, sitting on the bed. But she knew – she didn't have the energy to say that much. Literally, the energy – to speak loudly enough for Nicola to hear her.

She'd be able to tell Nicola now, she thinks. Something has definitely happened – there's been a shift. The tide's gone out, or the bed has moved inland, away from the sea. She'll sit up, and see how that goes. She arranges the pillows, gives them a wallop to make them fat. What's she doing now, though? She's been staring at the pillows. Was she back asleep for a few seconds, even though she's sitting up? It's fuckin' mad. She hadn't expected this sliding – this skidding – between her head and the outside world. She's awake, though. She's bringing the duvet up to her shoulders. She's looking out the bit of window – it's brighter than the last time she noticed. She thinks. She's aware of herself breathing. She knows – she feels – she has to be careful. She's being allowed to breathe, but that right could be pulled away from her. That's how it feels – that's what she thinks. She's not drifting.

Her stomach has growled.

Nicola's in the kitchen. Paula heard the press being shut – she's sure she did, a minute ago. She thinks she can hear the radio. That's right, she remembers now – she was delighted when she realised that Nicola had been listening to the radio, to music. When Paula came in from work – just before she knew the Covid had her. She'd heard the radio. How long ago was that? How many days? Three wouldn't surprise her. Seven – a week – would. So would one – it can't be only a day. But really, she doesn't know. She can't measure the time.

She can hear Nicola. She's coming up the stairs. It's a woman coming up the stairs, a middle-aged woman. She's not bounding. She's taking her time, measuring it. Paula's stomach growls again.

Nicola taps the door.

Paula doesn't pretend.

—Hiyeh, love.

—You're awake.

—So it seems.

—D'you want anything?

Paula remembers what she wanted to know.

—How long am I here, Nicola?

—Four days, says Nicola. —I think. Yeah – four.

—Jesus.

—Do you?

—What?

—Want something to eat.

—I'd love an egg.

—Boiled, scrambled?

—Surprise me.

—Poached it is, so, says Nicola.

That sounds like Nicola. Like Leanne, and Jack too – she thinks – and John Paul.

—Coffee or tea?

—This is lovely, says Paula. —It's like a hotel.

—Not from out here, it isn't, says Nicola.

—I think I could manage coffee.

—Okay, says Nicola. —I've left fresh water for you. And a couple of paracetamol.

—Nicola?

—What?

—Were you in the room?

—Your room?

—Yeah.

—No, says Nicola.

—At all?

—No, says Nicola. —I can't go in there. Not till you test negative. I'll bring a test up with your eggs.

—Don't bother, says Paula. —It'll only be positive – we'd be wasting it. I just thought –. I don't know what I thought, to be honest with you.

—Okay. Back in a bit.

She hears Nicola going back down the stairs, faster than she'd come up. What just happened there? Why had she asked Nicola if she'd been in the room? It hadn't been on Paula's mind. There was nothing on her mind. Nothing on her mind, or in her mind. She just felt she'd been close to Nicola – Nicola had been very close to her. Sitting on the bed while Paula slept. She'd been thinking of that, Nicola sitting on the bed, Paula telling her something – she can't remember what.

Nicola is after leaving the water outside, and the paracetamol. Paula will go and get them, before she forgets and Nicola finds them still there when she comes back up. Why does she care what Nicola sees or thinks? It's always been like this. The mother behaving like the daughter, the daughter acting like the mother. No, but – things have changed. It hasn't been like that these months. Derek Prenderville. That's the name – her head's beginning to work again. Derek Prenderville was the fella she'd been with when she told her mother she'd been at the shops. She went with him for a week. The water, the water – don't forget the bloody water. She pulls back the duvet. She feels something – a weight, something heavier than the duvet – resisting. It's Nicola's iPad. She's no memory of having it here with her. But then she does. She remembers Nicola telling her how to get Sky Go on it, through the bedroom door. She remembers pretending to follow Nicola's instructions. She remembers waking up – thinking she'd woken up – and hearing Nicola asking her if she needed the code.

The water. Her dressing gown is on the bed, at her feet. She pulls it to her and finds her mask in one of the pockets. She puts it on. She sits on the side of the bed. She stands. Not too bad. No swimming, no dizziness. She opens the curtain a bit more. She doesn't look out. If she does that, she'll forget she's on a mission to the landing. She bends down – no bother – and picks up the empty glass. She'll leave it outside when she's collecting the full one. She's made it to the door. She's impressed. Bed to door, without wandering off in her head. She can feel the exertion in her chest, though, the effort. She's not out of the woods – she can't be fooling herself.

She opens the door. It's not a glass of water that's waiting for her. It's the measuring jug, full. And two paracetamol, in their foil. She'll need the glass she's holding. She'll need both hands for the things on the floor. She goes back into the room and puts the glass on the windowsill. She looks out the window, but stops herself. That way lies madness. More madness. Different madness. She's like a dog chasing leaves on a windy day. She goes back to the door. Nicola's rationing the drugs. She doesn't trust Paula. That goes back – and back and back. She's not rationing the water, though – the jug is heavy. More proof that Paula's not herself. She can't lift it with one hand – she knows it'll tilt and water will spill onto the floor. She goes back in and puts the paracetamol beside the glass. She goes to the door and picks up the jug with both hands. The jug is new. Paula didn't have a measuring jug – she'd gone without one for years. But she'd bought it when she was shopping in town with Nicola – they were in Arnotts' basement. Paula had paid for it, even though it was Nicola who'd said they needed it. Paula had paid with her card and Nicola hadn't objected, hadn't tried to stop her, or taken it and stood in front of Paula at the till. She brings the jug over to the windowsill. An elegant thing it is, really – a lovely green handle on it. She'd told Nicola about her colour-blindness, so she'd asked her to confirm that it was green. It's one of those obvious greens. Obvious to Paula, anyway. It even has a designer, a name on the handle. Joseph Joseph. She could have got a cheaper one or she could have refused to buy it at all. But she'd bought it – she'd been delighted buying it. And now it's on her windowsill, for all the neighbours to see. She's getting notions, that one. She'd have been drinking gin out of that thing not so long ago. Maybe she still is.

She's sitting back on the bed when she sees that the door is still open. She's up again. Her stomach growls – it nearly barks. There's no sign of Nicola. She listens while she's at the door. She can't hear anything – a wooden spoon tapping the inside of a pot or the spatula scratching across the pan. She shuts the door. She takes off the mask – it's beginning to make her sweat. She gets back into bed, just in time to hear Nicola on the stairs. Maybe she'll chance it – she'll ask Nicola just to bring it in, leave it at the end of the bed. But she gets up again. She's not going to be hopeless. She hears Nicola outside. She hears her tapping the door.

—Your breakfast's here.

She hardly ever calls Paula Ma or Mammy. She hardly ever calls her anything.

—Ah, thanks, hon, says Paula. —I'm starving.

—You got your water.

—I did, yeah, says Paula. —Thanks. It was Derek Prender-ville, by the way.

—What was?

—The fella I was telling you about, says Paula. —When Carmel said I had grass on my back.

—I've no idea what you're talking about.

—Ah, you do, says Paula. —No, hang on – you don't. Sorry.

—Who's Derek Prenderville?

—You don't want to know, love.

—I do, says Nicola. —And did you just say you had grass on your back?

—No, I didn't.

—I think you did.

—I'll give you the gory details when I'm better.

—I'll be waiting.

—I know you will, says Paula. —Now – step away from the door, ma'am.

She puts the bloody mask on again and she opens the bedroom door. Nicola is standing on the stairs, a few steps down.

—There's no way that's two metres, says Paula.

She's smiling. Nicola will see the creases at her eyes.

—Near enough, says Nicola.

Paula looks down. Her old friend, the tray with the beanbag

bottom, is at her feet, slightly sideways, like a ship in a storm. She sees the scrambled eggs on two slices of toast. She can smell them too.

—There's nothing wrong with me sense of smell, anyway, she tells Nicola. —That's good, isn't it?

She bends down, aching a bit – a bit fluey.

—This is brilliant, Nicola, she says. —You're a star.

—Mine's downstairs, says Nicola.

—Off you go, says Paula.

She's standing up again, reluctant to move till she knows she won't wobble.

—Talk later, she says. —Thanks again. This is massive.

She brings the tray to the bed, then goes back and shuts the door. She can hear herself wheezing, and feel it, as she gets into the bed. She's definitely not out of the woods. She leans out and pulls the tray towards her. She might be wheezy and woozy but she's ravenous. She lifts a forkful of the egg to her mouth, then puts it back down on the plate. She takes off the mask and drops it onto the floor. She picks up the fork again.

The window's open. Not wide – just enough to feel the air and to hear a bit more from outside.

—What month is it again? she asks Nicola.

Nicola is sitting on the other side of the bedroom door.

—March, says Nicola.

Paula thinks she can hear Nicola sighing, impatient at her mother's dimness. She's probably asked the question twice already – she hasn't a clue.

—It's like summer, she says.

—It's Saint Patrick's Day, says Nicola.

—Is it? says Paula.

—Yeah, says Nicola. —You could've watched the parade on the iPad.

—I can think of better things to be watching, to be honest with you.

Talking is like physical exercise. She can feel herself running out of breath before she finishes what she wants to say.

—Are you meeting the girls or anything? she asks.

—No, says Nicola. —There's nothing planned.

—Do you want to?

There's nothing for a while – Paula can't hear a thing, not even from out on the street.

—Yeah, Nicola says then. —But not particularly.

It's so hard hearing Nicola talk like that. It hurts – it's almost physical. But Paula recognises the truth in it. She was that way, herself – she hasn't forgotten. There were times when the last thing she wanted was the company of her children. Their needs and demands, their hands grabbing at her. Their disapproval, their hatred. Their love. But having to listen to Nicola – it sounds dreadful. Nicola is all the things that Paula isn't – wasn't. Intelligent, independent, organised. Paula has often thought that Nicola was put on Earth to taunt her. It's rough, hearing Nicola being human. Being cruel and cold. Paula resists the urge to jump in. Ah, you do – 'course you do. The weather and all – you could have a picnic. It's just as well she can't focus on anything. The Covid's a bit of a break for her.

—No plans, so?

—No.

—Grand.

—I talked to Tony.

—Did you?

—Yeah.

—And?

—Nothing, really. Just talked.

—How is he?

—Seems okay.

Paula knows how Tony is. She spoke to him, herself, the morning the Covid whacked her – a few days ago, only.

—How are *you*, love? she asks. —More to the point.

—I'm okay, says Nicola.

117

—Is it lonely out there?

—A bit.

Paula isn't sure she heard that right. She can't ask Nicola to repeat what she said. Is Nicola getting restless? Is she missing the girls and her old life – her proper life?

Paula's been playing the long game. That thought – in those words – only announced itself recently when she'd been talking to Joe on the phone, after she'd finished the call.

—What are you going to do? he'd asked.

She hadn't hesitated.

—Nothing.

—You're going to let it keep going the way it is?

—Yeah.

She's playing the long game. She'll tell him that the next time he calls – if he calls. Or when she calls him. If she does. She doesn't know if she will – he's a pain in the arse. But she knows – the long game explains what she's been doing, and why what she's doing, near enough to nothing, has been right. Since she walked out of the house, herself, and walked into town – how long ago is that? She doesn't know where it comes from – the long game. Probably football – but she doesn't know and she doesn't really care. It fits – it's what Paula's doing. She's waiting. She's letting Nicola deal with her demons, face up to her own decisions.

It hasn't been easy – it's been fuckin' excruciating – but she might have just heard Nicola admitting that she's lonely. That she's sitting on a kitchen chair outside the door for her own benefit, not her mother's. That Paula is keeping her company and not the other way round.

Paula says nothing now, to Nicola. The light seems different – she isn't sure. She might have been drifting. She doesn't know when she's been drifting, or when she's back. And that's the word – drifting. It isn't sleep – it doesn't feel like sleep. Sleep is different. She's doing that too – sleeping. She's tired but it's not a struggle. It doesn't matter what time it is, or what she's supposed to be doing.

There's a fly buzzing around, somewhere. Inside the room.

—You there, Nicola?

—Yeah.

—Are you not cold?

—No.

—I might do a test later, says Paula. —See how red the red line is.

—Okay.

—I won't be negative, though, I don't think. But isn't the red supposed to get lighter when you're on the mend?

—I don't know, says Nicola. —But it makes sense.

—Yeah, says Paula. —I think someone told me. Someone who had it.

—Who had it?

—Well – Mandy, says Paula. —You remember Mandy.

—Yeah.

Paula feels herself smiling – she knows that Nicola can't stand Mandy.

—She had it, says Paula. —The whole house had it.

—Was she bad?

—She said she was, says Paula. —Yeah, she was. Her fella was nearly hospitalised.

—How can you be nearly hospitalised?

That sounds like Nicola now, her imperial majesty. The goddess out on the landing. The queen of black and white.

—It was touch and go, says Paula. —But I know what you mean. She likes her drama, Mandy does.

—Can't have been nice, though, says Nicola. —All of them at the same time.

—No, says Paula. —Awful. Imagine being that sick with a houseful of kids that are all sick as well – Jesus.

—Maybe that's why her husband was trying to escape.

Paula laughs. She feels like she's been running.

—Is going into a Covid ward escape?

—Well, that depends, says Nicola.

—Into what's it called – the ICU?

119

—Still depends.

—I don't know –.

Nicola says nothing more. Paula closes her eyes. It's a decision – she knows she's doing it.

She's cold. It's dark out there. It's dark in the room.

—Nicola –?

No answer.

She says it louder.

—Nicola –?

Nothing.

That's a relief. She'd hate to find out that Nicola had been out there all the time that Paula's been asleep. It was day when she closed her eyes – she remembers that.

She sits on the side of the bed. She stands. She's not too shaky. She shuts the window. She pulls the curtain over but leaves a chink. She doesn't look out. She doesn't know why not. She puts on her dressing gown. Tightens it. That's nice – she can feel it doing its job, getting her warm. She stands at the door. But she hesitates. She doesn't want to open it and see Nicola keeling over, onto Paula's feet, because she's been sleeping there, leaning against the door. She doesn't want to see Nicola sitting on the landing floor, looking up at her. There are lots of things she doesn't want to see. They've been frightening her for months. Nicola on the bathroom tiles, Nicola in the bath, Nicola hanging from the attic hatch, Nicola at the bottom of the stairs. Nicola passed out. Nicola covered in blood or vomit. Nicola dead.

She opens the door.

The landing is empty. Except for two paracetamol, on the chair that Nicola brought up from the kitchen. Paula listens. The telly isn't on, or the radio. She can't smell food. She can't hear anything. She goes across to the bathroom. It's the only exercise she's getting these days.

She looks in the mirror as she's washing her hands. She

120

looks pale – she looks washed-white. She brushes her teeth. The toothpaste – the mint, or whatever it is – makes her hungry. The taste is mad, way stronger than it should be.

She comes back out. She stands on the landing. The light is off in the hall and in the kitchen. It doesn't frighten her now, the prospect of going down the stairs – the drop. She must be on the mend. She doesn't have to tell anyone – she can stay sick for another while. She can't hear anything. She looks at Jack's bedroom door. It's shut. Nicola must be in there, asleep. Paula hadn't noticed it when she'd come out of her own room.

She bends to pick up the paracetamol. She stands up straight. She's grand. The way she feels, it should be midday. She looks out the window. She pulls back the curtain so she can see more. Not a sinner out there, a couple of hall and porch lights on – that's all. And – hang on – a fox. Walking down the middle of the road, not a bother on her. What a brilliant thing to see. Paula's delighted – she is. Thrilled. The fox moves off the road and goes under the streetlight outside Smiths'. The colour – it's so beautiful, it's golden – there's no mistaking that colour. It's gone into Smiths' front garden. Paula waits, but it doesn't come back out. She can't see it, although she can see most of the garden – Smiths don't have a hedge. Maybe Paula drifted off while she was standing here. She misses the fox. She'd love to see her again – it was definitely a girl. She lets the curtain drop.

—D'you want your phone?

Does she?

—No, she says. —I don't think so. Thanks.

—Okay.

Not having the phone – it's a bit like not having a drink. But that's not true. She hasn't missed the phone. She hasn't been wondering how everyone else is getting on without her. She's been off in her own world. She hasn't missed the phone. And that was never the case with the drink. Ever. She doesn't miss the drink – it's been years since she's had one – but she has to tell herself she doesn't miss it, or need it or want it, every day, throughout the day. Including when she wakes. Especially when she wakes. Especially now, when she's still a bit mad, raving a bit – when everything else seems a bit mad too. She's confident – she'll always be able to keep it at a distance.

She might have one, though, when she knows she's definitely dying. Just the one. For the road. A final toast. Seeyis now – keep in touch. But it would never be just a taste, a dignified sip. She'd be drinking for oblivion again, and she won't be doing that.

She likes the word, though.

Is Nicola still out there?

—You there, Nicola?

—Yeah.

—Google oblivion for us, will you.

—What?

—Oblivion.

—The perfume?

—Is there perfume?

—I don't know. Sounds like it.

She hears Nicola laugh. A short burst, like she's telling herself to laugh.

—The word, says Paula.

—Just the meaning of the word?

—Yeah – that's all.

—I could just get your phone, you know. You've my iPad there with you.

—Jesus, Nicola, are you not even curious about why I want to look it up?

—I am. But.

—It worries you.

—Well –. Yeah.

—No need, hon, says Paula. —I only want to know what it means – exactly. That's all. I'll tell you why then. Are you looking it up there?

It doesn't take long.

—The state of being unaware or unconscious of what is happening around one.

—One?

—You – it means.

—I know, yeah – it just sounds weird. Is that it, though?

Nicola reads it again.

—The state of being unaware or unconscious of what is happening around one. And then it gives an example. Of it being used.

—Something to do with drinking, I bet.

—They drank themselves into oblivion.

—I should've put money on it.

—There's another example, says Nicola. —He was another minor poet who was consigned to oblivion.

—The drink one is better, says Paula. —The minor poet can fuck off with himself.

—He can drink himself into oblivion.

—He can, says Paula. —Are there any women poets, though?

—There'd be loads of them.

—Name one.

—No.

—Does it say where it comes from?

—Oblivion?

—Yeah.

—Latin, says Nicola. —Oblivio. Forgetfulness.

—What?

—Forgetfulness.

—What?

—You're very funny.

—Name a woman that's a poet but you're not to look it up.

—Can it be a singer?

—If she writes her own words.

—Kate Bush.

—I like her.

—Taylor Swift.

—Don't really know her stuff.

—The girls are mad into her.

—I know, says Paula. —Absolutely. All three. And Maisie as well – she loves Taylor Swift. That's some tribute, though, isn't it? All the girls love her.

—Beyoncé.

—Ah, yeah, says Paula. —Our lady of the ceiling. That's brilliant. Beyoncé's our poet, so. Shakespeare can –?

—Fuck off.

—Yeah, says Paula. —I'm enjoying this, Nicola.

—So am I.

—That thing about oblivion, says Paula. —The definition, like.

—Forgetfulness.

—That's not it, says Paula. —That's not what I think it means. It's not enough. It's not just about forgetting or even being unconscious. It's death. Am I being a bit dark?

—No.

—When I was drinking, says Paula. —Waking up was the horrible part, not the oblivion. I was just thinking about it there.

—Why?

—Just. Missing my phone or not missing my phone. I was comparing it to alcohol. In my head, like. Addiction to the phone and addiction to the drinking. But there's no comparison. I don't think. And just so you know. I don't want oblivion. I don't want to go there, ever. Okay?

—Okay.

—What about you, Nicola? Do you?

Paula waits. She lets herself wait.

—No. No, I don't.

She can hear the voices below her. Not below – not in the house. They're outside. Under the window. She's been lying on top of the bed, hearing them – a hum, really. She'd been reading a book. Marian Keyes. She doesn't remember putting the book down beside her. She checks – her glasses are on her head. She doesn't think she's been sleeping long. Nothing's changed outside, except the voices. The hum that's become Nicola and a man.

She could go to the window. But she won't. She'd hate to be seen. Nicola looking up and catching her – or the man. Anyway, she's no distance from the window – it's open. She can hear enough – she can fill in the gaps. Nicola's at the door. He's the two metres back, on the path. His voice is clearer. He's definitely out in the open, and Nicola's half-inside, under the porch.

It's Tony – she knows the voice.

That's good. They're talking. Talking it through. She doesn't know how much Nicola has told him, about what she saw in his brother's back garden that day, or what she'd heard his brother say – or what she'd thought and what has happened since. She doesn't know if they've been face to face since Nicola came here. She's guessing they've met up some of the times that Nicola's been out of the house. Paula gave up asking. Where were you? How're the girls? Have you been near the house since? The answers weren't worth the anxiety. Out. They're grand, I think. No. She was forcing Nicola into being a teenager.

But the real point – the reason Paula had stopped asking – she was letting Nicola get on with it. It was hard sharing the house with a middle-aged woman, especially when the woman was your daughter and she'd walked away from her family and motherhood. But that was Paula's problem – she'd decided, coming home from town that day, the Deliveroo day. And she'd felt the hard lump in her gut begin to soften when she'd stopped expecting Nicola to go home.

They're talking out there now, Nicola and Tony. That's good – it has to be. But Paula isn't holding her breath. She needs all the breath she's getting. It's all Nicola's business. Although Paula is listening to any words she can catch.

She wishes she had her phone now. She could text Mary, keep her up to date. Have a bit of crack. She hasn't thought about Mary. Or anything or anyone else, really.

The curtain – a breeze makes the curtain flutter. It's as if the curtain moves and lets the words in.

It's Tony.

—She's falling asleep crying.

He's talking about Lily, their youngest – Paula's sure he is. She can't hear what Nicola is saying.

Then it's Tony again.

—Did you even hear what I said?

Paula listens, and she's not feeling too sorry for Tony. He's trying to make Nicola feel guilty. As if Nicola needs any encouragement. He said something to Paula – this was when Nicola had first arrived here and stayed, a few days after she'd come into the house. What are we going to do with her, Paula? And she'd answered him. She'll see sense – don't worry. Something like that – she isn't sure exactly what she said.

—She has her Junior Cert coming up, says Tony now. —Or had you forgotten? I sent you her mock results.

Nicola says something.

—Did you even look at them?

Nicola has shut the front door. Paula feels it more than she hears it, like the whole house has moved, then settled. Nicola didn't slam the door – it's just what the house always does.

—Open the fuckin' door –!

Paula waits. For the thump on the door. The broken glass. The splintered wood.

—Nicola –!

He doesn't hit the door.

—Fuckin' –. Fuckin' mad fuckin' bitch.

He's not shouting now. If he was, she thinks she'd go to the window and tell him to fuck off out of her garden. She wishes now that the window was closed, so she'd be able to hear Nicola downstairs. Walking back down to the kitchen. Turning up the radio, pulling open the cutlery drawer. Paula could get up and go down – put on her mask, stay on the stairs. Check that she's okay. Ask her why she's after upsetting poor Tony.

That's the inbuilt thing, the almost natural thing. What did

126

you say to Tony? Fuck the inbuilt thing – it isn't inbuilt or natural. It was put in there. The poor man. People saw her after she'd been battered numb and they'd sympathised with Charlo. And she had too – she'd been the one to blame. She'd believed that. She'd got what was coming to her. What are we going to do with her, Paula? She'd nearly fallen for it. She *had* fallen for it. She'll be grand – don't worry. Give her time.

Even now.

Even now, she's feeling sorry for him, out there. Being driven demented. Coping – trying to cope on his own.

And actually, there's nothing wrong with feeling sorry for him. She waits.

Tony and Nicola have been together since Nicola was fifteen or sixteen. And he hasn't suddenly become a bad man. He's not going to batter the door down. He's not going to start throwing rocks at the windows. He's just being what he's always been. A man. What are we going to do with her, Paula? The man is the man and the woman is the problem. It's like the drink – she's been having to fight it every day, the urge to give the expected answer. She'll see sense – don't worry. Since realising that it wasn't the answer that she'd wanted to give, that she'd just clicked on, like the central heating. She'll be grand – don't worry. Give her time.

If Nicola comes up now and tells Paula she's going back to Tony and the girls, she'll be delighted. She'll be over the fuckin' moon. But Nicola isn't going to come up and tell Paula that, and that's grand too. It'll have to be. It's a mess. It's heartbreaking.

She waits.

She can't help thinking of Lily. Poor Lily. Hadn't a clue what was going on, why her mother had suddenly walked off and left her. Gone, like a death.

Nicola will talk to her. Maybe she already has.

Paula doesn't know if Tony is still down there. He hasn't said anything else – she hasn't heard him. It doesn't matter. He can say what he wants. She wishes she had her phone. She could text Lily, just say Hello – or call her for a chat.

She wishes she had her phone.

She wishes she had a drink.

She wishes she could make Tony happy.

She stands. She shuts the window. The garden's empty. Tony isn't out on the street. He's gone. Unless he's right up against the front door. She wouldn't be able to see him from where she's standing – he could be sitting on the step. Charlo sat on that step. Talking to her through the letter box. Telling her he was going to kill her. Telling her he loved her.

She goes to the door. She waits – she checks her breathing. It's not as bad as it was – not nearly as dramatic. She goes out to the landing. She puts on her mask. She'll do a test – she'll get Nicola to bring her up a test. She stands at the top of the stairs. She hasn't gone down in a long time – it feels like a long time. Her legs ache a bit – like when she walked all the way into town. That feels like a different life. A different body.

She's on the stairs. She shouldn't be out here – she's being very bold. That's what she thinks – she feels. She's two-thirds of the way down.

—Nicola?

—Yeah.

She's delighted. Nicola heard her the first time. And suddenly, she's panicking – she's given too much away. She's been pretending to be sick. The proof is in her voice – not a bother on her. She's a shirker, a malingerer. A cod. She's enjoying herself and she shouldn't be.

—Everything alright?

Nicola's at the kitchen door.

—Yeah, she says.

—All good?

—Yeah –. Yeah.

Paula puts both hands on the banister and turns so she can look properly at Nicola.

—I heard you there with Tony, she says.

—Yeah, says Nicola. —He was here.

—Was he in the house?

—No, says Nicola. —It's a leper colony, remember.

—You're alright?

—Yeah.

—Good, says Paula. —Good. I just thought – I'd ask, you know. Make sure.

—Grand, says Nicola.

—I'm feeling more meself, by the way.

—Good.

—I'll do one of the tests, if there's one going spare.

—I'll bring it up to you.

—Grand, says Paula. —I just came down to see how you were. I'll go back up.

—Yeah, says Nicola. —Go on ahead.

She's a bit lost – Paula is. She reminds herself to go back up to her room. She doesn't want to go – that's it. She wants to stay with Nicola.

Nicola's still there, waiting for her to disappear.

—D'you want tea? says Nicola.

—Coffee.

—Is it not a bit late for coffee? says Nicola. —You mightn't be able to sleep.

—Don't worry about that, hon, says Paula. —I could fall asleep on me way up the stairs. It's unbelievable.

—Okay, says Nicola.

—Come here, though, says Paula.

She's after remembering something – something she'd meant to tell Nicola earlier, or yesterday.

—I was listening to the radio on your iPad, she says.

Nicola had explained to her how to get RTE on the iPad. Paula had been able to follow her, to concentrate long enough – Nicola was giving her the instructions through the door. She'd heard Nicola clapping after Paula got the radio going – Ronan Collins was wishing someone a happy sixty-fifth birthday. She'd laughed – they'd both laughed.

—There'll be no stopping you now, said Nicola.

—Where's the volume on this yoke?

—Buttons on the top – left side.

—Where?

—Maybe the bottom.

—Is this them? Hang on –.

The volume went down.

—Oh shite – what've I done?

And then she brought it back up.

—Great, she said. —Thanks, hon.

She was pleased, although she wasn't particularly interested in listening to the radio. She shut it down – the app – and opened it again, just to prove to herself that she could. She'd felt like a pilot. Or a record producer.

—Anyway, she tells Nicola now.

She looks – dips her head – to make sure that Nicola is still there.

—I was only half-listening, she says. —But there was this ad on, for bathroom tiles – or just general bathroom stuff, you know.

She's breathless – not breathless, exactly, but she has to wait before she can go on.

—Anyway, she says. —The ad's on and I thought I heard the girl in the ad say erectile bathrooms. Tiles and that – I thought it was erectile bathrooms.

Nicola laughs, and Paula watches her laughing. It's not just polite, it's not just to get her mother back up the stairs. Paula laughs too – she's not far from crying.

—All those erectile dysfunction ads, she says. —I suppose it was only a matter of time before they snuck into all the other ads.

—Leaked in.

—Ah now, says Paula. —Keep it clean.

She's tempted to tell Nicola about Joe's Viagra, to prove her credentials. But she won't. Not now. Not yet.

—I'll go back up, she says.

—I'll bring up your tea.

—Thanks, hon. But I wanted coffee.

—Okay.

—And me test.

—Yeah.

—Did Tony leave biscuits?

—Yeah.

They both start laughing again.

It's not Tony's voice this time.

It's John Paul.

Jesus Christ – it's John Paul. She's positive. What does he want? God – that's terrible, that thought, the first thing she thinks of – what does he want? It's dreadful. She smothers it – she absolutely smothers it. It wasn't really a thought – she doesn't feel it.

She's wide awake, she's trying to hear what they're saying. She reminds herself – she has to – they're brother and sister, John Paul and Nicola. It's hard to remember that, sometimes. They can't stand one another. They hate each other.

She listens.

—The broccoli's dense in vitamin C, yeah.

That's John Paul. He's talking about broccoli.

—She'll love it.

That's Nicola, and there's none of the efficiency that's usually in her voice when she doesn't like who she's talking to. Paula has heard that voice often enough. She's been shredded by it.

—She loves her soup, says Nicola.

Paula can tell, somehow – Nicola smiled when she said that. She's smiling at John Paul. They're even laughing quietly. She can't hear that but she knows they are. They're bringing each other back to when they were kids, sitting downstairs in the kitchen, while their mother – brand new, absolutely a new woman – lowered the pot of soup onto the table. Soup was always the announcement, a fresh start. Now – out there – they're able to laugh about it, share it.

131

John Paul's rumble – he's talking again.

—Anyway, tell her I was asking for her.

Something about the way he's speaking – he's been inside the house. He's been in the kitchen, chatting with Nicola. They've been down there chatting while Paula's been drifting.

—I will, yeah, says Nicola. —She'll be delighted you were here.

They were down there chatting *because* she's been drifting. Because she's up here. Because she has the Covid and she's out of the way. They don't have to fight over her. Because they love her. Despite everything. They love her. They love each other too. The proof of it is in her ears. John Paul has brought her soup. Is he thanking her for all the soup she gave him in the past, all the false starts and broken promises? She doesn't think so. He's her son. He's brought her broccoli soup that he made, himself. He wants her to be proud. He wants her to be grateful. He wants her to stay alive.

They're still down there, both of them.

—Seeyeh, Nicola.

—Bye.

He wants Nicola to be proud of him too. Paula heard that too, when he was telling her about the vitamin C. He wanted Nicola to approve.

She hears him on the path. His van will be parked outside. She could chance a look, even wave if he looks up and sees her – what harm? But she'll stay where she is. This happened – what she heard, what she now knows – because she is where she is.

She hears him start the van. She hears it move off. Then she hears the click below her, the front door being closed, the slight shake of the house. Nicola had stayed at the door till John Paul had gone up the road.

Will she bring the soup up to her? Or will she pour it down the sink? It's a cruel thought, and out of date. She can't even bother hating herself for thinking it. She picks up the book. She loves Marian Keyes. This one – *The Break* – is Nicola's. She hasn't a clue where she stopped reading. She's not even certain she started. Her eyes won't stay on the page. She puts it back down, nice and near, beside her.

—Did you know he could cook like that?

—Yeah.

—How come?

—He told me.

They laugh lightly. Two sisters sharing a joke. Two mothers sharing a child.

—Did you taste it, though?

—Yeah, says Nicola.

—It is, like – it's fuckin' delicious, says Paula.

—Why are you surprised?

—I'm not, says Paula. —Well, I am. But I'm not as well. There was a lot more than broccoli in it, though, wasn't there?

—Oh, yeah.

—Is there any left, is there?

—Loads.

—Good.

—Do you want some?

—No, says Paula. —Later.

She doesn't want to send Nicola rushing down for more of her little brother's soup.

—D'you want your phone? says Nicola.

—No.

—Mary was asking for you.

—Are you trying to tempt me? says Paula.

—Just telling you, says Nicola. —She was.

—I'll phone her tomorrow.

—Grand.

If she lies here and does nothing everything will mend. She's learning things she wouldn't have seen downstairs.

133

She's playing the long game. And she's beginning to think she's good at it. She thinks she hears Nicola standing up. She thinks she hears her going downstairs. She could call out now, check, ask her if she's there. But she won't. She just has to stay where she is.

12 January 2023

She's doing her sums. And it's harder than it used to be. In the old days, she knew how much she had in her pocket before she stepped into a shop. Even when she was drunk and staggering, she knew to the penny or the cent how much she had. And how much she didn't have. And how much she should have had. And how much she wouldn't have for the next day when she staggered back out.

Now, though, she has no cash. She's a bit uncertain and nervous. Very nervous. She's let herself think that she's the bee's fuckin' knees with her debit card – Cash-Free Paula – but now she wishes she had real money. She'd know where she was.

She does know where she is. She's in Lidl. She's after walking here. She left the house and came straight here, to do the shop. That's not right, though. The shop – like, the big shop, the weekly shop – she doesn't do that any more. And really – to be honest – to be harsh – by the time she'd become organised enough to do a big shop, to afford a big shop, it was a bit too late. There was just herself and Jack in the house – and sometimes Leanne.

She'll have to start doing a list again.

Fuckin' lists – she hates them. She thought she'd left them behind.

If she stands here long enough – she's in front of the cereals – a young one or a young lad in a Lidl fleece will come along and change the prices. She doesn't even know why she's at the cereals.

She's frightened. She's actually frightened. She can't take anything off the shelves. Her basket is empty. She literally isn't able to pick anything up. She sees herself having to put it back, having to go around the shop, putting back the things that she can't afford. She remembers doing that, and seeing it – back in the good old days. Women taking things out of the baskets and trolleys, kids hanging off them, crying, and the women themselves crying. And she'd done it too. She remembers, she couldn't look left or right, at people glancing at her as she tried to make it seem like she'd changed her mind, that she'd thought of something better and nicer, when – actually – she was trying not to get sick, trying not to groan or cry out. The imaginary blinkers, the dark screens that pressed into both sides of her face and made her blind and wet-eyed. Shame. She remembers putting a jar of bolognese sauce back onto a shelf but she couldn't see what she was doing – she couldn't judge the distance – she was going to drop it, smash it into the other jars, bring people running with mops and handcuffs.

She'll have to get out. Go out. Calm down. Come back in. Go home, come back later. Tomorrow. Think a bit. Think it through. Stop catastrophising. Find a cash machine and check exactly how much she has in her account – she's able to do that. Come back in and do her shop. It's only a fuckin' supermarket. She's entitled to be here. She can afford what she needs – she knows she can.

She'll put a few things in the basket – things she knows she needs – and go and pay for them. She knows she has money. Enough food for a few days, and washing powder. And a four-pack of toilet paper. Four rolls should see her through this war in Ukraine.

It's not the prices. Although it's frightening how quickly they're going up. Genuinely frightening. It's reasonable to be frightened. Her electricity bill – Jesus. She'd had no idea that the switch in the hall turned on the floodlights in Croke Park. Her house is suddenly a mansion. She's afraid to turn on the lights.

She's alone. That's what has her this way. She has no safety net.

She's been alone for years.

No. She hasn't. She's never been alone. She's been like a child alone in the dark, in her bedroom, but she knows that her mammy is downstairs.

Paula only knows that now – now, recently. She's never been on her own. She's always been looked after.

And that's stopped.

Her mammy isn't downstairs.

She's on her own. Go on ahead, love, put those cornflakes in your basket and see what happens. Humiliate yourself – go on. Your Nicola won't be coming to the rescue – with her Prada and her this and that. Left you all on your ownio, she has.

The electricity bill was a shock. But the real shock is the fact that Paula will be the one paying it. All the help from Nicola has stopped. All the handouts that have allowed Paula to think of herself as independent – they're gone. And they won't be coming back. She doesn't feel bitter – it's right and proper. But it's terrifying. Here – now – it's crippling.

But fuck this – she walks on. She won't walk out – there's no need for the drama. She'd be the only one watching. She doesn't put the cornflakes in her basket. She doesn't want them. If she changes her mind, she can come back. But if she's going to change her mind, she needs to be in charge of her mind.

Breathe in, breathe out. She's grand, she's grand. Swash, and backwash. The words are back, like birds that flew off for the winter. She hasn't thought of them in months – it must be since the Covid. They're flying around the supermarket, under the ceiling. Swash and backwash. Her own flock of words. She's never liked that word, 'cereal'. It's too like 'serial'. The two of them – cereal and serial – were traps, put there to make you stupid. 'There' and 'their'. She remembers being walloped for mixing them. Not really walloped, but made to feel like a dunce because she kept getting them wrong. Will it ever penetrate that skull of yours, Paula O'Leary? She can't remember the name of the teacher but she can hear her voice. If the teacher came around the corner of the aisle up here – an ancient oul' thing she'd be by now, probably with a carer – Paula would stop and say, Yeah, Miss, it will, and keep walking.

The walking is good, even in here. It's funny that, how moving always helps. Her basket is still empty. But that's her choice – it's not destitution. She's always had to be careful. There's no harm in being careful. She grabs a net of satsumas – she's up and running. She's developed a taste for them since Nicola invaded the house. She loves a satsuma first thing in the morning.

Nicola's in a house in Artane. She's sharing with two other women. She's renting a room off them. They're a couple – she doesn't know if they're married. One of them's a teacher. Nicola didn't bother telling her what the other one did, or Paula didn't catch it. Teacher is easy. The other one probably has one of those jobs that Paula will never understand.

—Are they nice?

—They seem alright, yeah.

—Is your room nice?

Nicola looked at her.

—It's fine.

—Is it bigger than your one here?

—Way bigger, said Nicola. —You have no idea how much bigger.

—Okay.

—A donkey refuge, it is – massive.

—Grand.

—There's a bus from the door to the bed.

—I only asked, said Paula.

That was a couple of weeks ago. Thirteen days ago.

—I'm sorry for being sarcastic, said Nicola.

—Dating back how long, hon?

Reality's a cunt. Paula's going to get a T-shirt done with that on the front, right across her chest. She'll get a few, hand them out. She'll give one to her old teacher, Miss Whatever, when she comes around the corner here, pushing her walker. Look it, Miss – I put the apostrophe in the right place and all.

She'll change it a bit.

The Reality's A Cunt.

The reality of getting what you wished for.

—Will you be bringing Beyoncé with you?

Nicola smiled.

—I don't think so, she said.

—You'll miss her, said Paula.

—I probably will.

Paula has been tempted to pull the Beyoncé poster off the ceiling. It feels a bit ludicrous up there, with only Paula in the house. But she worries that Jack would miss it – see it gone – when he comes home. But when will that be? If ever. She hasn't seen Jack in years – more than three years. Except on Zoom. And she hates Zoom. She absolutely hates it. She's never comfortable when it's on and she just feels so sad when it's over, seeing him but not really seeing him. It's better than nothing, Paula. She's heard that so often over the last few years. She's said it, herself. But she's not so sure. She drags herself around after a Zoom call with Jack. An ordinary phone call would be easier. It's not Jack she's gazing at on her phone, or on Nicola's iPad. It's a cartoon – a hologram.

That's another thing gone and not coming back – Nicola's iPad.

He's a little bollix. She doesn't mind thinking that. She doesn't mind saying it. She has said it. To Mary. To Joe. To Nicola. Even to John Paul. And Leanne has said it to her. He could come home for a week – less, even. It wouldn't kill him.

She'd love a soft bread roll with ham in it, and tomato. She often has a ham and tomato roll for her lunch, when she's working with Mary – the Centra beside them does nice rolls. She'll have her roll – damn the expense. She puts a four-pack of tomatoes into her basket. She'll go back past the bakery for the roll. She can get the ham on the way. She has it all worked out.

—Like, with Jack, she told Nicola, about a month ago. —I always thought he was the one I'd got right, you know. That I'd done a reasonably good job with him.

—You did.

—But I never see him.

—He's in America, said Nicola. —Be fair.

—To who?

—Both of you, said Nicola. —The rest of us are here. He's not. You can't expect him to call in for a chat.

She doesn't get upset when she talks about Jack – there's never a shake in her voice. She renewed her passport a few months back. She's been waiting for Jack to invite her – even drop a hint that she might like to visit him in Chicago.

—I'll come with you, said Mary.

—He hasn't asked me, Mare.

—Doesn't matter, said Mary. —Fuck'm – we'll just go. I'd love to see it – where is he again?

—Chicago.

—Brilliant, said Mary. —The Windy City. Perfect spot for a couple of oul' ones.

This was before Paula realised that she was poor, all over again. She hasn't looked at the price of a return flight to Chicago. A year ago – more – two years ago, Nicola would have had her phone out if Paula had mentioned Chicago, and she'd have been tapping away, looking at flights, telling Paula to go and get her passport number so she could confirm the booking for her. Paula would have objected but she'd have been thrilled. It would have happened because Nicola would have made it happen.

That's stopped. It had to. But she wonders if she'll ever really catch up with it – the fact that Nicola isn't her fairy godmother. She'll have to. She wants to.

He is a little bollix, though. Maybe it's something to be

proud of. He really is independent. He's flown away, flown the coop. He doesn't need her. He doesn't need to think about her. He's an adult. A real adult. She knows nothing about him. He used to like Beyoncé. She'd googled Beyoncé a few nights ago, as she lay on Jack's old bed – and Nicola's old bed – looking up at her on the ceiling. She'd wondered if that was why Jack was in Chicago, because that was where Beyoncé came from. But Beyoncé didn't come from Chicago – she was from Texas, somewhere. Stupid – thinking that Jack would have gone all that way, to that particular city, because he'd fancied the girl when he was a teenager. He teaches in a college there – she can't remember the name of it. She has it written down somewhere. It's a long name, with 'Northeastern' in it. Her son teaches in a college – a university, the real deal – in the United States of America. She has two sons. One is a recovering heroin addict, the other is a college professor. One son made her soup when she had the Covid and the other one didn't even phone her. He's a little bollix and she's proud of it.

Nicola's seeing the girls again. They go to the pictures, or just meet for coffee, go for walks. They all seem fine – even Lily. They probably are fine. Why wouldn't they be? But talking to the girls, just being with them, is tricky. Paula's afraid she'll say something wrong, betray Nicola – interfere. But it'll be fine – she'll get the hang of it, and so will they. Tony has stopped phoning her and texting her, and that's fine too. It's a relief. He'll get the hang of it – or he won't. Here, now – Paula really doesn't care.

She grabs two chicken fillets for three euro. That's her dinner. And her tomorrow's dinner. Her protein. Nicola is always on about the protein and the carbs. She never sees chicken and spuds – it's proteins and carbs. Paula won't miss any of that – she'll eat what she wants. She'll get spuds. She'll get spinach. She's not mad about spinach, though – it always feels like she's eating an experiment. She's still trying to impress Nicola – that's what she's doing. Thinking of Nicola's approval when she sees the spinach on Paula's plate.

She takes the bag of spinach out of the basket and flings it back on top of the other bags. She'll get a can of peas. She hasn't had a can of peas in years.

She's figuring out where the peas are – she's after getting lost again – when she sees it. A woman putting a bottle of body lotion onto the shelf. Paula just did that a minute ago, with the bag of spinach. This is different – this is awful. It's like watching the woman falling over. But at least she'd be able to run across – Paula would – and help the woman to get back up. They could laugh away the embarrassment. This is shame, though – Paula knows it. She sees it. A young woman she is. Walking away now. Paula goes across, closer to the shelf, so she can see the price of the lotion. Cien Body Milk – it's €1.79. She takes a bottle – she's not sure if it's the same one. She puts it in her basket.

She's never minded the door from this side – the outside. She was never afraid of coming home, of what would be waiting behind it. She pushes the door open now, and goes in.

The emptiness doesn't scare her. The hall's no emptier than it was before Nicola arrived and stayed. It's business as usual. It's getting dark outside. It'll be darker in the house. She wishes – she half-wishes – that Nicola had hung on for a few more months, till the days started to get a bit longer. But really – she doesn't mind being alone in the house. She's the queen of all she surveys. Queen of all the switches. She turns on the light in the hall. She goes down to the kitchen, opens the door wide so she can see properly. She puts the shopping on the table. She turns on the light. She goes back down to the front door and turns off the light. Then she's back into the kitchen. She's definitely getting more exercise, jogging from switch to switch.

She keeps her jacket on. The cold is on her face, her cheeks. It's colder in here than it was outside. The heat will come on soon, for an hour. She'll see how that goes for a while, see what it does to the bill. An hour in the mornings, an hour in the evenings. She might adjust it for the days she isn't working, when she'll be spending more time in the house. She'll manage. She always has.

She checks the time. It's a quarter to four. She'll put on the kettle. She doesn't use anything electrical – she turns nothing on – between five and seven. They're the big times. When everyone in the country uses the electricity. She saw that on the news. In from work, in from school, hungry, sweating, cold and giddy – cookers, kettles, showers, mixers, Gameboys, laptops, dishwashers, washing machines, sex toys. That's when there'll be a power cut. Paula has candles where she knows they are – she has a box of matches on the table. Her own idea, her own planning – nothing to do with Nicola. She'd nearly be wishing for a power cut. She could go along the street knocking on doors, offering candles.

She's grand. She breathes deep and agrees with herself – she's grand. The anxiety's gone, back wherever it hides. Lurks.

She's alone. She's not lonely. She heard a story – Mary told her – about a woman who had the Covid, back at the start when it was terrifying and they were still calling it the coronavirus. The woman wasn't able to get out of bed, she was totally wiped, afraid to breathe, afraid to move, for six days.

—She lay in her own filth, Paula, God love her – she couldn't even open her eyes.

But then she did open them and she saw her cat at the end of the bed, looking at her, staring at her – deciding which part of her to eat first.

—And that got her out of the scratcher.

Paula doesn't have a cat. She won't be getting a cat. She's had two vaccines and a booster. She's already had the Covid. She's not going to be eaten by a cat.

She's alone.

She's on her own. She can hear the little girls next door, bouncing around the place, and their mother giving out to them in Polish. There's no anger in her voice, no anger coming through the wall.

Paula takes the bottle of body lotion from the bag. She's

wondering why she bought it. Or why she didn't run after the woman and give it to her. That would have been dreadful, though – it would have made the poor woman feel worse. Less than two euro. It wouldn't have been an act of solidarity. It would just have added to the woman's humiliation, added shame to the shame. Paula can easily picture it, the woman running away from her. And there was something about the woman. Her coat, Paula thinks now – it was a good coat, a coat Paula would have liked. It was a coat that Nicola would have worn – that's it. The woman wasn't used to her poverty. The glimpse Paula had of her face – she was pale, she looked like she was going to be sick.

She'll use the lotion – Paula will use it. It can join the other bottles in the bathroom. It's like a game of chess up there, the bottles and tubs lined up along both sides of the bath. Most of them are Nicola's – were Nicola's.

It's defiance. That's what it is. Her two-quid bottle of skin milk. It's symbolic. It doesn't matter how much it actually cost – it's what it stands for. The bit of luxury, the bit of self-regard. The bit of fun. Keeping her skin soft. For who – for what? For herself – fuck off. If Joe was here he could tell her if she was right to call it a symbol. She'd hit him on the head with it. Do symbols hurt, Joe? Similes, metaphors – more of the words from school. Her head is full of them. Released by the Covid, she sometimes thinks.

She can't make her mind up about Joe. If she likes him – if she likes him enough. Even, if she loves him. She saw his face – they were sitting on a bench in Howth, opposite his apartment block. They'd gone for a walk, just along the pier, to the lighthouse and back. Last week this was. Paula had gone there on the DART – Joe had driven her home. But his face – his profile. He'd looked so sad. And she only remembered in the car on the way home – his wife had died, his ex-wife. Less than a year before. And his face, too, while she was looking at it, while they were sitting on the bench. It changed – his face lit up. She followed his eyes and saw a toddler, a roundy little lad, running through a gang of seagulls, over on the grass. And he pointed – but said nothing.

—What sort of gulls are they, Joe?

He smiled. He knew she was slagging him.

She definitely likes him. It's the Zoom version of him that she doesn't like – the text version, the phone version. He put his hand on her leg – when they were on the bench. She put her hand on his hand. But she's glad he isn't here now. And she'd never live in his place. They spent the afternoon there, in his bedroom, and she was happy when she left.

That's a thing she'll definitely do. She'll bring Joe to the house. She'll hold his hand and bring him upstairs and she'll stay in bed and listen to him leaving – going down the stairs, opening the door, closing it. She'll tell him not to say anything when he's going – she'll just want to listen to his steps.

Maybe she doesn't have to make her mind up about Joe – maybe that's the trick.

She'd love a new kettle. Just to be picking up something with a different handle, a different weight. The inside of this one is a bit of a horror film. You'd half-expect sharks – or the little ones that eat people when they fall into that river in South America. Piranhas. They used to be big – popular – when she was a kid. You don't hear much mention of them these days. He has teeth like a piranha. That's a simile. 'Like' and 'as' – they're the simile words.

She stands in the kitchen.

She doesn't know what to do.

She's devastated.

She breathes in – inhales. And she exhales. Is it true, though? That she's devastated. Well, she is. She absolutely is. It's not just a word. It's the sadness in her breath, and how hard it is to exhale. She's on her own. There's a cat out there somewhere, licking its lips.

She doesn't want tea. She's after wasting the power that went into boiling the kettle. Every light in the country will go out now, because of that. She'll be on the news – the woman who brought Ireland to a standstill. Putin's pal. Putin's ally. Putin's oul' slapper.

She doesn't know what to do. She doesn't know if she should sit, if she should take her coat off, if she can make herself at home in her own fuckin' home. She's standing here at the sink, waiting for permission – waiting for something to happen. For the opposite of a power cut. A surge. A jolt. A click. The switch is right in front of her. She's waiting for Nicola to lean forward and turn it on for her. That's not going to happen. Those days are gone.

Grand.

Nicola is her daughter. She inhales – and exhales. Nicola is her daughter. Her child. She's gone out on her own. And so has Paula. She's out on her own. She's an orphan. She's sixty-seven years old and she's finally an orphan. An orphan with a travel pass. Nicola isn't her mother.

They both know that.

It's devastating.

It's wonderful.

It's devastating.

—I can remember – I had Jack in my arms. I was sitting – Jesus, Nicola, I was sitting here, exactly here. And he was bleeding – there was blood all over him. I couldn't figure it out – I couldn't see where it was coming from.

—You.

—Yeah. Me.

—I'm not playing this game.

—What –? What game?

—You Think That's Bad.

—There is no game, Nicola.

—I'm not playing it.

—Sorry, Nicola, I don't know what you're on about. Honestly.

—You were going to tell me that you know exactly what I'm going through. You've already more or less told me that you had it worse – because I never bled on top of one of my children.

146

An experience I've been deprived of, thank Christ. But you're going to tell me that it'll be grand because you've been through far worse and you're still sitting in the same fuckin' chair that you sat in when you bled on your blue-eyed boy and – sure, look at you – you're grand.

—Jesus, Nicola. You really hate me, don't you?

—Yeah.

Fuck this – she's going to have her roll. There's no electricity involved, so she won't be putting the economy at risk.

She should be delighted. She *is* delighted. She has the house to herself again. And it's a long time since she thought that Nicola would be going back to her old life, back to Tony and the girls. She'd stopped hoping for that a year ago. Nicola had fallen apart – Paula had seen that happening – and she'd put herself back together, differently. Paula had seen that too. But she hadn't known it – not at first. The old Nicola would come back – she'd get over it. She'd go back to selling her gym equipment, back to running the world. She just needed rest. Someone to hear her. Rest and a shoulder to cry on. Paula would look after her. Paula would be her mother. She remembers thinking that, deciding it – like she was deciding to have her ham and tomato roll. She hadn't a clue.

She still hasn't a clue.

It's automatic – it's always automatic. The put-down, the dismissal. Will it ever penetrate that skull of yours, Paula O'Leary?

—We're living our best life, Paula.

—Jesus, said Paula. —Are we?

—I'm telling you, said Mary.

They were sitting in the back of the cleaner's, in the heat – the steam – and they were doing what Paula is doing now, eating ham and tomato rolls, although Mary had onion in hers as well.

—Not a care in the world, said Mary.

—Okay.

A man had come in half an hour before and he'd started giving out about a stain that was still on his lapel. He talked to them like they'd been waiting on their side of the counter just for him.

—I specifically pointed out the stain, he said.

—To me? said Mary.

—It might have been you – I'm not a hundred per cent sure. He looked at Paula.

—When was this? said Mary.

—Does it matter?

—Yeah, said Mary.

He looked at Paula again. He was waiting for her to take over, to see reason.

—I think it was Tuesday, he said.

He was still holding the jacket. Paula couldn't see the stain. She'd have needed her glasses for that. They were on top of her head and they were staying there. She knew – she hadn't been working on Tuesday. But it didn't matter. She hadn't seen this maggot before. That didn't matter either. She was interested in what was happening, in what was happening in herself. She didn't care – he could give out and threaten as much as he wanted.

—I was here meself on Tuesday, said Mary. —But I don't remember that jacket.

—My wife brought it in.

—On Tuesday?

—I think so, he said. —I have the receipt.

—Grand, said Mary. —Give us it here.

She took the jacket off him.

—And you were with your wife, were you?

—I was at work.

—Good man, said Mary. —But you said you pointed out the stain.

She pointed at the lapel. She prodded it.

148

—This stain here, yeah?

—I showed it to my wife, he said.

—Ah, said Mary. —Now I get you. And she specifically pointed it out to me, yeah? On your behalf, like.

—Yes, he said. —If it was you.

—You wouldn't have a photo of her there on you, would you? Just for verification.

Paula thought she'd piss herself. Mary had brought the lapel up to her face.

—Looks oily, she said. —An Indian, was it?

Paula was waiting for your man to explode. But his face – she wasn't even sure if he'd heard Mary.

—I'd definitely remember this one, said Mary. —If it was me that she showed it to. A woman showing another woman a stain – you don't forget things like that in this game.

Mary looked up from the lapel.

—And you rubbed it in, she said. —Did you?

—I used a napkin, he said.

—Ah well, said Mary. —Look it, we'll do our best.

—Thank you.

—We'll give it our best shot, said Mary. —Me and Paula here. But – just so you know – the horse might have bolted.

—I understand, he said.

—Going at it like that with the napkin, said Mary.

She shook her head.

—I know, he said.

—But leave it with us, said Mary.

The door wasn't quite shut when they let themselves laugh.

—Cunt, said Mary.

—Yeah.

—Fuckin' poxbottle.

Mary picked up the jacket.

—I'll tell you, Paula, she said. —We'll be leaving this stain exactly where it is and we'll be adding a few of our own.

Our best life. That was what Mary called it. Where they were now. She'd heard someone saying it on the telly.

—One of those You're Shite an' I'm Massive programmes, said Mary. —You know – on RTE. This poor bitch was after doing a mini-marathon and she looked like she'd shat herself, the poor girl, and the main girl – the presenter, like – she was screaming at her, 'You're living your best life, you're living your best life.' Her kids – the girl that done the mini-marathon – they were there, and they were supposed to be hugging her cos they were so proud of their mam and that. But they were holding back, you know. And you could tell – they were nervous about what they'd find when their hands met on the other side.

—Ah, stop it.

—And her fella – the fuckin' head on him. A big fuckin' Irish head – you know what I mean? Nowhere else. Half-pig, half-cocker spaniel. And she's living her best life? I was, like, No, you're not, hon. I am. And what's the secret? Go on, Paula – ask me.

—Ask you what?

—What's the secret.

—Go on – what's the secret, Mare?

—I don't give a shite, said Mary. —That's my reality show. I don't give a shite.

—I'd watch that one.

—You're in it, hon.

Paula's eating at the sink. As if she's in a hurry – she's grabbing a quick bite before she dashes back out. Or as if she's afraid that she'll bring it back up, that she'll need somewhere to vomit, quickly. It happened before, she remembers now. The morning after Nicola came home. Exactly that – Paula puked straight into the sink. She'd no time to do anything else.

She won't be vomiting now. She might never vomit again.

She pulls a chair from under the table, and sits. She could put on the radio – hang the expense. But she's happy enough with the silence. Just herself – the sound of her chewing, breathing.

What's going to happen?

Nothing.

Age. Getting older. Spoiling her grandkids, loving her kids. Not waiting for anything. Mary's right. Not giving a shite. Easier said than done, of course. Mary worries about plenty. Worrying about the right things, though. That's the trick. Maybe. Jesus, though. This – for the rest of her life.

She's a mother. Because the house is empty.

She doesn't feel it. She doesn't know what it's supposed to feel like. How could she, though? She thinks about her mother sometimes, what she might have felt when Paula and the rest had gone and left her alone. Paula hasn't a clue. She never asked her. She never thought about her mother at the time. She doesn't think her mother would have told her. Ah, sure – I'm grand. She mightn't have understood the question. Paula's not even sure there is a question. It's just what happens. And her mother would have understood that. Never marry a shop-keeper, Paula. She thinks they'd like each other, if her mother was still alive – they'd get on. She'd chat – she can nearly hear them chatting.

She's alone in the house with the dead. Even the texts have dried up. She's not getting any. Hardly any. No harm, though. She believes that – she thinks she believes it. She picks up her phone. She pecks one to Mary. I DNT GIVE A SHITE X. She looks at it, then she deletes it. She doesn't want another back from Mary, and having to send one back to her. It's a pain in the arse. She'll see Mary the day after tomorrow, at work. She'll tell her about the girl – the woman – in Lidl, and the lotion. She'll tell her she bought the lotion herself. She'll tell her she feels great – free – now that she won't be depending on Nicola. That it's great for her, and great for Nicola. Probably great for Nicola's children. Even Lily. She told Mary about Lily. About what Nicola saw. About what Nicola did – and didn't do.

—Jesus Christ, Paula – it's just as well we can't buy guns in this fuckin' country.

151

They can't buy guns but, still, Charlo had one when he died. He'd just murdered a woman with it. The kitchen – where she's sitting, the whole house – it's full of him. His voice.

And now there's Nicola's too.

—No one will ever do that to my children, Nicola had said.

Paula will never forget it – she'll never be able to. She'd looked at Nicola and she'd thought – she knew – she was going to hear something that she wouldn't survive hearing.

—Do what, Nicola?

She was hoping Nicola wouldn't answer. And then – stronger, stronger – she was hoping she would. She had to – Nicola had to talk.

But Nicola said nothing.

—What, Nicola? said Paula. —Did your father –?

Paula sat up.

—Do you remember the time – the morning I threw him out of the house?

—Yeah –.

—I saw him looking at you. Inappropriately – is that word okay with you?

—Yeah.

—The minute I saw him, said Paula. —And I saw you. I grabbed the pan and I hit him. Do you remember?

—Yeah.

—That's what happened.

—Yeah.

—Now, said Paula. —That's all I saw. It was enough – more than enough. The second I saw him. But, like I say, that's all I saw. That's what I remember seeing.

Nicola said nothing.

—Love –? Nicola?

—What?

—Was there more?

—More what?

—You know what I mean, Nicola – was there more?

Nicola looked away from Paula.

—Yeah.

She knew when she saw Nicola looking at her. She knew that she was going to have to rip herself apart. She could only help Nicola if Nicola saw her changing, shifting. Squirming. Suffering. She wanted to kill Nicola. And Nicola wanted to kill her. Both of them staring at their mothers. Blood in their eyes. Fuck you! Nicola screaming at her with a voice that Paula hadn't heard before. Fuck you, fuck you, fuck you, fuck you! Paula nodded. And nodded. And nodded. And looked straight back at the forty-six-year-old teenager. Her little girl, her big girl.

Jesus, Jesus, Jesus.

It feels like a minute ago. But Paula works it out – it's a year and a half ago, a little bit more. When Nicola came into the house and stayed.

She inhales and exhales. Swash, and backwash. She feels herself smiling – she's not sure why. She puts her finger – her nail – to her front teeth and dislodges the bit of ham that's stuck there.

She'll be grand. She'll be more than grand.

When Nicola was leaving, when she was at the door, Paula put her hand – her palm – to Nicola's cheek and left it there. And Nicola let her do it.

—Seeyeh.

—Yeah, said Nicola. —Bye.

—I love you, said Paula.

She felt Nicola's smile on her palm.

She looks at her hand now, her palm. She can still feel it, Nicola's smile. She'll always feel it.

Two

7 May 2021

—I'll kill them.

Paula wondered if Nicola had already killed them. The way she was sitting, the only thing missing was the blood on her hands, dripping onto the floor. Her face – the way she was staring at the rug – she looked like someone who'd already committed the murders. She wasn't really staring at the floor. She wasn't staring at anything. Anything that was in the room.

The room was filthy – Paula saw that now. It wasn't dirt, though – it was age. They'd be growing old together, her and the house. Nicola hardly ever came into this room. She always went straight for the kitchen.

The way Nicola was sitting, it was like she was on the toilet, hunched over. Paula had never seen her like this.

—Sit back, hon – why don't you sit back?

She held Nicola's elbow and pulled gently, and Nicola came with her. She lifted herself, and sat back. But she was up again immediately, up off the couch, standing, looking around. Not for anything on the floor or on the table. She needed to go somewhere. She was at a junction or a crossroads, unsure – startled.

She sat again, dropped again, beside Paula. Hunched, switched off. She was being played with. Possessed – not Nicola.

Paula was scared. She was feeling possessed, herself. One minute, she was sitting back in the warmth of a great day – the next, she was ready to phone for an ambulance or the Guards.

She tried again. She held Nicola's arm, just above the elbow.

—That's right – sit back, hon. Let yourself – you'll enjoy it.

She climbed onto the couch, on her knees, beside Nicola. There was a gap – a few inches – between the back of the couch and the wall, and she'd pushed a duvet in there, so she could have it handy whenever she wanted it. There was no cover on it, and it was stained, thin in some sections and bulging in the corners. But Nicola didn't object. She let herself be covered, be smothered, by a duvet that was caked in milk, jam, piss, vomit and every kind of alcohol known to woman. But no – that wasn't right. The last time – the final time – Paula had promised herself that she'd never drink again, she'd got rid of every old duvet and sheet and blanket and pillowcase – one at a time, pay day after pay day, for months – until she had nothing left that released old fumes every time she lay down and tried to let herself sleep. This duvet wasn't too bad. She was under it now too.

—D'you want to talk, Nicola?

—No.

But she did. She might not have wanted to talk but Paula heard – she thought she heard – a kind of click coming from Nicola's throat. It sounded almost like the latch on a gate, or a noise you'd make to show that you were changing your mind. And – whatever the noise was – Nicola started to talk.

—I can't sleep, I can't breathe properly, I can't close my eyes even – even though they're really sore, they're stinging me all the time, I can hardly see with them, like, I can't close them – and nothing works – I've tried all sorts of drops and stuff and they're all useless and a complete waste of money, I can't cry.

—D'you want to cry?

—Yeah – no. Yeah. But I can't.

—How come –?

—I never cry, she said.

Paula wanted to contradict her. She wanted to remember the times she'd seen and heard Nicola cry. On her wedding day, at the births of her children. After her miscarriage. At the communions, or her granny's funeral. She couldn't think of a time when Nicola had cried when she was a child, even when she was sitting on the floor beside Paula while Paula did. She must have, but Paula couldn't hear her. There was nothing – no time she could recall. She couldn't hear the baby cry, or the girl, or the woman. Crying for something she wanted, or over a boyfriend. Or the threat of her father – the terror. She must have cried when she was a baby – she must have cried when Paula gave birth to her. Paula must have heard her. But she couldn't remember. Not here.

She could remember Jack crying. She could see him, she could feel him in her arms as she comforted him – she could feel it working. Here we are again, she sang – happy as can be. Leanne cried. Leanne never stopped crying. Leanne was never full, never comfortable, never still. Leanne's rage always came with tears, the child's and the adult's. John Paul – she could see John Paul crying. In the hospital after his stomach had been pumped – was that the last time? It was impossible to imagine John Paul crying now. But who knew? She didn't.

The sheer terror, though, when Nicola saw Charlo staring at her, looking her up and down – did that dam the tears? Or her useless mother, who saw it happening and pretended she didn't. That wasn't true, though – that wasn't what had happened. Paula saw Charlo, saw him pinning Nicola with his eyes, staring at her like he stared at women – and he was gone, out of the house, covered in his own blood, less than a minute after she grabbed the frying pan and brought it down on his head. And he never got back in. Paula made sure of that. But before – before she finally saw? Nicola had told her that he'd never touched her, afterwards – after they knew he was gone for good. Jesus, what a conversation to be having with your child. Did he ever do anything – even playing? Did he ever touch you in a bad way? She'd said he hadn't, and that had been that.

—I'm sorry, said Paula now. —I'm so sorry.

—Shut up.

Nicola spoke so softly, Paula wasn't positive she'd heard her. But Nicola said it again, in the same way, same voice.

—Shut up.

Paula didn't know what to do or say. Defend herself, apologise again – she hadn't a clue. She wanted to escape, get out from under the duvet. Go sit by herself on the stairs. A safe place, where she could see what was coming. She could feel Nicola's heat – the menopausal bitch. And smell her. Her perfect child, her saviour, was turning into a mad, unwashed oul' one.

—Okay, said Paula.

She didn't move. Didn't budge. If she got up and left, she could never come back into the room – she could never face Nicola again. That was what she felt, that was what she knew. This thing had been coming at her for decades. She knew that now – even if she hadn't known anything about it five minutes before.

—Okay, she said again – she thought she was saying it again. Softly. Calmly. Nothing aggressive in the word, or provocative. Just acknowledgement – that she'd been told to shut up. Because she'd said she was sorry.

—Nicola –?

Nicola didn't speak or shift.

—Nicola – hon –?

—What?

—I'm glad you're here.

The silence – it was silence. She couldn't hear a thing from outside. She could hear the buzzing in her right ear, the tinnitus, louder than it had ever been. The dull buzz that never stopped. She didn't know when it had started – she didn't even know it had a name until years after she'd first been aware of it and aware too that it was the first thing – the only thing – she knew every morning when she woke. She didn't know if it was Charlo damage – she couldn't pin it to a beating. Or one of those things – age, bad luck, family history. It was Joe who'd given her the name for it, when he'd been describing his own. She hadn't told him then that she had it too and that hers, by the sound of it, was way worse than his.

It was all she could hear now – nothing else. It wasn't

pandemic silence. It was a black hole and it was going to swallow everything.

—I'm glad you're here, she said again. —I am.

She wanted to hug Nicola. But she wouldn't. She might hug her too hard, try to reverse the roles, force them back to where they'd been, Nicola the mother, Paula the helpless, hopeless child. Or Nicola might push her back, or hit out. And Paula would cry. She wasn't going to cry – she definitely wasn't going to cry. Not until Nicola cried.

It was fuckin' ridiculous, thinking like that. It was no help to Nicola, and no help to herself. Denise, her younger sister, had shaved her head when Carmel was having her chemotherapy. In solidarity, she'd said. And Paula had wanted to kill her – the sentimentality of that. D'you think Carmel wants to be bald, Denise?

She could hardly breathe. She was going to vomit. She was going to break.

—You're safe here, hon, she said. —Nicola –.

She waited for the attack. Because she deserved it – she had it coming to her. For saying something like that. Playing, she was – let's pretend I'm your mother. Maybe it would be for the best if Nicola let go and battered her. Maybe it would clear the air and they could start again. Start all over again. She could be the mother and Nicola could be the child, and maybe then she'd cry.

Jesus.

Paula couldn't remember the last time she'd cried. She cried all the time – she just couldn't remember if it was a day ago, or four days or a week. The last time she spoke to Jack – that was probably it, when the Zoom thing was over. And it wasn't sadness. It was pride, really – or even happiness. Just seeing him. He had a screen behind him, an artificial thing that wasn't really in the room. A mad thing, some sort of huge painting, with people made of triangles and bits of fur – Jack had told her all about it, who'd painted it. But she couldn't remember any of the details. She hadn't cared. The colours all around

Jack – the brightness, the garishness – had made his cheeks glow and shimmer a bit. He was a slender, handsome man with a little boy's fat cheeks. Surrealist – that was the style of the art. But the surreal thing on the screen had been Jack, not the art. She knew what 'surreal' meant. And Jack knew she did, and hadn't explained it to her. He knew his mother was intelligent and that was what had made her cry. But she didn't know if that was the last time.

Her phone buzzed, under the duvet somewhere. She didn't feel it, just heard it. A text. She wouldn't go searching for it. She was betting it was Tony, wondering where Nicola was.

—Are you hungry, love?

Nicola didn't answer.

—Same here, said Paula.

Nicola's phone had been quiet. Maybe she didn't have it with her. Come to think of it, Nicola didn't have her bag. Nicola without her bag was nearly the same as Nicola without her head. Where Nicola went her bag went with her – she always had the best of bags. But why wasn't anyone phoning her? Maybe they didn't know she was gone. The girls all had their own rooms – it was a four-bedroom house. They mightn't have noticed, the way kids noticed nothing. And they were well able to look after themselves – Paula had often seen that.

Kids noticed nothing.

What a lie that was. The proof was right beside her.

Jesus.

—Did you try Optrex, hon?

—Yeah.

—There's a spray –.

—Yeah.

—It's very good but I'll tell you – it's expensive.

This was the way to go. Get her chatting.

—Eighteen euro or something I paid for it, said Paula. —I couldn't believe it.

—I paid for it.

—Did you?

—Yeah.

—You shouldn't have – are you sure?

—Yeah. I was with you.

—You shouldn't have.

Paula was nearly hoping to hear the sarcasm, although Nicola was rarely nasty, or deliberately hurtful. She was matter-of-fact, Nicola was, and she'd told Paula that she was the one who'd paid for the Optrex Actimist. And it just happened to hurt.

Paula's phone was at it again, a call this time. Like a finger, poking at her. Do it. Do it. Do it. She thought she knew where it was, near her right foot – she could have grabbed it without too much fuss, without having to make Nicola shift.

—Feckin' phone, she said.

She was hoping Nicola would agree or respond, give Paula permission to find it. But Nicola said nothing and Paula let the phone ring out.

—Nicola, she said. —If you want to sleep –

—I can't –.

—If you want to, though. If you want to try. I'll stay with you.

—I can't sleep, said Nicola.

—I know.

The way they were on the couch – the way Paula was half-lying back – she couldn't see Nicola properly. The duvet was between them, like a hill or a sand dune. They weren't even touching. It was ridiculous – it wasn't even comfortable. It was agony – her back was killing her. She'd have to shift herself.

The phone went again. The doorbell would be next – that was her bet. Tony was eliminating all the other possibilities. He'd be on his way. He was probably phoning from the car. The thought was a bit frightening.

—Did you have a row with Tony, hon?

—No, I didn't.

—I was just asking. I'm not judging.

163

—It's nothing to do with Tony.

—I know.

She fought the temptation – he's worried about you, he just wants to know where you are. She didn't know if Tony did care where Nicola was. But even if he did – and he more than likely did – it didn't matter.

But the fingers were poking at her again – poor Tony, poor Tony.

Fuck Tony.

She sat up. She groaned – she couldn't help it. She felt the phone – when she moved her hand, the phone was there. She picked it up but she didn't look at the screen. She dropped it onto the floor.

She could see Nicola now and, God, she looked dreadful. Paula had turned on the main light when they'd come in from the hall. The bulb didn't have a shade – it had never had a shade. She'd always been going to get one. She usually turned on a small lamp she had on the other side of the couch, near the window. It was cosier. The room was too bright now and Nicola was too bright. Her skin was white, like she'd been in water for way too long, and blotched too, swollen-looking – and damp.

—D'you want to give it a try? Paula asked her.

—What?

—Sleep.

Nicola looked at her, and away.

—No, I don't.

Paula said nothing back.

Let the bitch sweat. Paula had. It was Little Miss Perfect's turn. She could drench the couch, so she could. She'd paid for it. But she hadn't – Paula remembered. Paula had bought this one – another day out, up to IKEA with Mary. It was the old one that Nicola had bought. And no – now that she thought about it, the complete history of Paula Spencer's couches – the old one had dated right back to when they'd moved into the house, her and Charlo – and Nicola. Paula had had sex on that couch. Nicola had had her mumps, her measles and her chicken-pox wrapped up on that couch.

She had to get up. She had to do something. Something useful, anything at all. She could feel her thoughts – she could feel herself – getting ugly.

She slipped out from under the duvet. She stood – she didn't groan. That was better – already it was better. She went to the lamp – something else she'd bought, herself – and turned it on. She went across to the door and turned off the overhead light.

—There now – that's nicer.

The bit of gloom was working wonders. Nicola had stopped looking like some sort of crazy lump. She looked hungover. Maybe she was. Or just sick. The couch looked less catastrophic now that Paula wasn't sitting in the middle of it. She'd go, and come back, and they could start again.

—I'll just go up and make your bed, she said. —Back in a bit. Okay?

—Okay.

Paula was reclaiming the house. It was days since she'd been in the hall – that was what it felt like. She stood there, a bit lost, unsure. She turned off the hall light but that made the place too dark. She turned it on again.

—Ignore that, she said.

She'd make Nicola's bed. Where was that, though – which bed was it? She was going up the stairs. Which bed was the best – which room? There was no bed here that Nicola would have thought of as hers. Paula was fairly sure of that. Even if she did want to sleep in her old room, it had been Leanne's room too – it had been Leanne's until recently. There wasn't a picture or a poster left that would have been Nicola's. There used to be a *Dirty Dancing* poster. Paula remembered that one. But it was long gone, like poor Patrick Swayze. And Leanne had left the room like she'd be coming back in a minute. It was still Leanne's room – and it was a kip. Paula had closed the door on it.

She'd give Nicola her own room. It was easily the nicest. Paula could sleep in Jack's. But she knew – before she got to the landing – she knew it wouldn't work. Nicola would never agree – she'd never let Paula make the sacrifice. And she'd seen Paula in all sorts of states in that room – she'd been on her hands and knees, with a bucket and rubber gloves, cleaning up after her mother's disasters. Jack's was the best bet. Jack's room was the safest.

She looked in – she never shut the door of this room. She turned on the light. It was grand. She just had to get all the stuff off the bed – she'd shift it across to Leanne's. A couple of bags of old clothes, and a box that the radiator in her own room had come in. She'd bring the radiator in as well, in case Nicola wanted the heat – although it wasn't cold.

God, though, she was a different woman – the day she'd gone through earlier had been lived by someone else. She was a lost old woman doing her best. She'd aged – caught up with herself – just coming up the stairs. What the fuck was happening?

She dropped one of the clothes bags so she could open Leanne's door. She didn't bother with the light. She threw the bag she'd been holding onto the bed, then saw that the other one, the one she'd dropped, had burst. Ancient knickers, socks, a pair of jeans, the denim so thin it had split, opened like a mouth, at one of the knees. She flung the clothes on the bed, went back into Jack's room and got the cardboard box. It was empty, except for the polystyrene wrapping that came with electrical stuff. She brought it into Leanne's room. She didn't want to throw it – she just lowered it to the floor. She shut Leanne's door and wondered – again – why she shut that one and not Jack's.

She knew exactly why.

There was a sheet and a duvet on the bed. They looked okay – the bed was made and all – but they'd been there since the last time Jack had been home, a year and a half before, the Christmas before the Covid kicked off. She'd put a clean sheet on the bed, and a duvet cover – only the best for madam. It was good. Doing this for Nicola. Simple things, easily done. No words, no landmines – no wrongness.

She heard the door, downstairs – the front door – being opened.

She was at the hot press, rooting for the best-looking sheet. She stepped back, so the hot press door wasn't in her way – and listened. She'd heard the front door opening, but she hadn't heard it shut.

—Nicola?

The house was empty again – Paula was nearly sure of it. Oh Christ, she'd let her down. Nicola had seen her face, heard her voice – felt her anger, her uselessness. What had brought Nicola to the door in the first place, self-preservation, had pushed her back out the door. She'd trusted Paula but knew now that she could never trust her.

The bitch – the fuckin' bitch – she'd set her up.

Stay calm, she told herself.

—Nicola – you there?

She could have gone to her bedroom window. Her room was at the front of the house. She'd have been able to see Nicola driving off, or taking her bag from the car – or getting into Tony's car.

Trust her – trust Nicola. Trust yourself. Nicola would be back, or she wouldn't be.

Jesus, though.

She pulled the sheet out from under three or four others. She shut the door of the hot press. It wobbled as she pushed. It wasn't a real door – the original door. That one had been smashed by Leanne – Paula would never forget it. Leanne had destroyed it with a hammer she'd had under her bed. It was only later – long after she'd stopped shaking – that Paula had wondered why Leanne had a hammer. A yellow-handled hammer – a professional hammer – that still had the price tag on it. Leanne had bought it – or stolen it – in McQuillan Tools on Capel Street, and brought it home and put it under the bed – ready. For what? Paula had never asked her. She'd found pills – she didn't know what they were. She found them in a ziplock bag hidden behind the towels and she flushed them down the toilet and wondered, as she flushed again because one of the pills was still sliding around the bottom of the bowl, she wondered what she was doing. Living in a film again. And then she watched Leanne – another woman living in her own film – smash the door. She worked at the door for half an hour, methodically, took it apart, punching holes, then prising the panels away off the frame. Paula watched, mesmerised. She wondered where the strength came from, and the skill. If she hadn't known Leanne, she'd have thought how great it was that girls were becoming carpenters. Then she realised it – she knew. She was the door – she was the one being taken apart. She went downstairs, out to the front step, and phoned Nicola.

She'd never spoken to Leanne about it. Tony had put up this door, temporarily. Ten years ago. It was grand. It worked – it opened and closed. It just felt like it would buckle or come off the hinges if she pulled at it too vigorously.

She'd never catch up – make her peace. There was too much. Too fuckin' much. There was no such thing as the past.

She pulled the old sheet off the bed, threw it out onto the landing. She flapped the fresh one, out and up – and down. She'd promised herself that she'd never iron a sheet again. She'd done it for years, ironed other people's sheets and duvet covers, their towels, even their underpants and socks. Such a waste of fuckin' time. This sheet here – it was one of those fitted ones with the elastic in the corners.

She heard something – distant. A bleep – a car noise. Outside. Nicola had locked her car. She was walking back to the house.

The last corner – she had to pull the bed out from the wall. She didn't want to. She didn't want to test her back. But she did it – she had to.

She shoved the bed back into place – she pushed with her knees.

She got the old cover off the duvet and got the fresh one

on. She buttoned it up. She went back for pillowcases – she'd forgotten them.

She heard it – the front door, the sound of the door being quietly shut from inside. Nicola was back, she was in.

Paula went into Jack's room and put the covers on the pillows. She thumped the sides of each pillow, gave them a good wallop to make them fat. She closed the curtains. She went across to her room and unplugged the radiator. She hurried it like a toddler, out, and into Jack's room. She plugged it in. She looked at Jack's old posters – the bands, the singers. Manchester United – Gary Neville, Wayne Rooney. She liked Wayne Rooney – and Coleen. But she wondered if she should take the pictures down, make it Nicola's room. It was about time it stopped being the Jack Spencer Museum. She'd open Leanne's door too, and keep it open – and let the ghosts out. The posters could wait. She'd had a nice thought. She went back across to her room and took the throw blanket from the end of the bed. It was a lovely thing, like an Indian blanket. She'd bought it in an outdoor market, off a table – from a Romanian lad – in Gorey. She'd gone there with Mary for the day – she couldn't remember the excuse, why they'd been in Gorey. But the blanket had cost a tenner. A wedding fair – that was why they were there. Someone belonging to Mary – a cousin's daughter, no one too close – had set up her own wedding-cake business and they'd gone down to Wexford to have a look and give her the support.

—Mind you, Paula, the cake in the middle – the one with the black marzipan girl and the white marzipan fella on the top?

—It was lovely.

—It was lopsided.

—It was not.

—The Leaning Tower of Pisa – I'm telling you.

They were in the foyer of the hotel where the wedding fair was on, and the cake-girl's mother had heard them. But that had just made them laugh more when they got outside and around the corner.

—The head on her – she should be making cakes for fuckin' funerals.

She hesitated at her bedroom door. She might want the throw, herself. She loved the weight of it, when she woke up in the night, after she went to the toilet. She'd be too hot waking up but cold coming back and pulling the throw from the end of the bed and lying back as it came with her – God, it was lovely. Luxury. She kept going – she was giving the throw to Nicola.

God, though. What a fuckin' day. The upheaval – she knew what that word meant. The shock. The guilt, the fear. She stood at the top of the stairs. She could let herself fall down them and Nicola would have to look after her. Life would get back to normal.

She went down the stairs. The grime on the walls – it wasn't too bad. Shoulders, hands, living. She was off the stairs, straight into the lounge – she didn't hold back. There was a Lidl bag on the floor, at the door. She looked down as she passed it. A bottle of wine and a net of satsumas. And another bottle on the coffee table.

Sweet fuckin' Jesus.

She could smell it.

There was something else in the Lidl bag. She realised what it was now that she'd seen the bottle on the table, and the glass. It was the cardboard packaging for a set of two wine glasses, ripped at the side – one glass missing. There was no corkscrew in the house but the bottle was a screw top. The top was on the floor, beside Paula's phone.

She sat down. The duvet was on the floor too. She shoved it under the table with her foot. She leaned down and picked up her phone. She checked the screen. There were texts from Tony, and a few WhatsApp things. She put the phone on the table.

She really could smell the wine, right under her nose – in her nose. In her mouth. She'd been with Mary and Mandy earlier while they drank their little bottles and it hadn't been a

170

problem. That had been outside, but it wasn't about inside or outside or the size of the bottle. It was history. Repeating itself. She wouldn't be able to watch Nicola knocking back a bottle of – she looked at the label – Barossa Valley. Not like this. She'd be sick. Or she'd join her. The other bottle was at the door, with a brand-new glass keeping it company.

—You bought new glasses and all, she said.

—Well, said Nicola. —You know me.

It was still Nicola sitting beside her – the real Nicola, not some imposter left by the alcohol fairies.

—I knew you didn't have any, said Nicola. —And I didn't fancy drinking out of a jam jar. Or the bottle.

—That's a relief.

She was joking – she hoped she sounded like she was joking. And it was a huge relief.

—I brought nothing else, said Nicola.

—That's fine.

—Nothing, said Nicola.

—Grand.

—I'm not going back.

—That's fine too, said Paula. —D'you want to watch something on the telly?

—No.

—Grand.

—I don't want to do anything.

—And that's grand too.

—I want to die.

—Don't say that, hon.

—It's true.

—D'you want to talk about it?

—No.

Paula knew the feeling – she'd wanted to be dead. But she kept that to herself. Me too, hon – been there. She swallowed the urge to run ahead of Nicola.

She watched Nicola drink. She held the glass in both hands. But they weren't shaking. She wasn't rushing or desperate. She was tasting what was in her mouth. She leaned out and put the glass on the table.

—Not die, she said. —I don't want to die, like – just stop.

—You want it to stop.

—Yeah.

Paula could have told her – it never stopped. It just retreated into some corner for a while. But it was there, lurking, sneering, patient. That news could wait, though. And Paula wouldn't be delivering it. She wouldn't need to.

Nicola was in Jack's bed, in Paula's pyjamas. Which Nicola had bought for her. Two weeks after Nicola had made one of her snap inspections and found Paula in a pair of ancient leggings and an old T-shirt of Leanne's with 'Fuck Your Thoughts and Prayers' printed across the front. Nicola had arrived with a Marks & Spencer bag full of pyjamas, for herself and the girls.

—And I got you some as well while I was at it, she'd told Paula.

She'd spent a couple of hundred quid so she wouldn't embarrass Paula or herself. She was wearing those pyjamas now – it didn't matter who'd paid for them.

Paula had turned Nicola's phone off.

She'd texted Tony.

SHES WITH ME

ILL COME OVER

NO BETTER STAY AWAY FOR NOW

WHATSUP?

You know yourself what's fuckin' up, she'd wanted to answer him.

SHES GRAND JUST NEEDS A REST

GIRLS ARE WONDERING

GIRLS ARE ALWAYS WONDERING – ITS WHAT GIRLS DO LOL

Tony hadn't texted since – it must have been an hour ago. And she didn't think he was likely to come to the house. There'd been messages from the girls too – on Nicola's phone – but

Paula had left them alone. Nicola could deal with them after she'd slept – if she slept. The girls would be grand. Vanessa was twenty-two and Gillian was twenty. Lily, the youngest, was fifteen, nearly sixteen. Paula wasn't too worried about the girls. Nicola was her worry. Right and proper. Nicola was going to get all of her attention.

Her phone buzzed, under her leg. She picked it up and brought her hand out from under the throw, so she could read the text. It was after twelve but Mary was still awake, keeping Paula company. SHE ASLEEP YET X Nicola's eyes were closed but Paula didn't think she was sleeping. If Paula moved – stood – the eyes would snap open. NOT SURE X Maybe it was what Paula needed to think – if she moved she'd wake Nicola. So she wouldn't move. That was the deal. The contract. She'd stay here till Nicola was snoring. She wished she'd given a bit of thought to the chair, though. It was the straight-backed chair that was under Jack's desk, one of the four chairs that came with the table downstairs in the kitchen. She was torturing herself – maybe deliberately. She should have brought up a different chair while Nicola was brushing her teeth – with Paula's toothbrush. But there wasn't a different chair – a suitable chair – in the house. There was the armchair that went with the couch but she'd never have been able to get that up the stairs, and the only other chairs were in the kitchen, same as this one.

The landing light was on and the door was slightly open. The floodlights at the all-weather pitch across the way were sometimes on and they lit the room like there was a Garda raid going on outside, but there'd been no football or training at night for months. The landing light was all she needed. She could see Nicola. She was lying on her back – she was too rigid. There was no way she was sleeping. Her face looked healthier, although that might have been the dark. But definitely – she looked calmer, more herself. In control. Beautiful. And she'd been more herself going up the stairs. Paula had stood in the hall and watched her. She'd thought at the start that she

173

was going to have to help her up and she'd wondered how she was going to manage. Nicola was no midget and Paula's back was a disaster area. But it was good – it was reassuring – watching Nicola go up the stairs. Like Nicola.

Paula would stay awake. She'd be there whenever Nicola opened her eyes. She'd be smiling.

The thought had settled in her – she'd always expected this to happen. She'd been waiting for it, even if she hadn't been aware, even if the actual thought had never occurred to her. She knew – she'd been waiting. Dreading.

She put her elbows on the bed, so she could have a closer look at Nicola. As her arms sank into the duvet, Nicola turned – Paula thought she was going to sit up, that she'd disturbed her. Paula was lifting her weight back off the bed. But Nicola was asleep. Her head didn't really rise up off the pillow. She was turning so she'd be lying on her side, facing Paula.

Paula leaned in further. Her back gave out to her but she kept going – it wasn't far, it was inches – till her lips were on Nicola's forehead.

She sat up again. Jesus, though – her back. It wasn't just a place in her spine – it was the whole fuckin' motorway. She was okay again in a couple of seconds, and Nicola's smell was still with her.

Sanctuary. That was what she was giving Nicola – sanctuary.

She loved words. Even now – here.

SHES FAST ASLEEP X

How did fast and asleep get put together? She used to hate it when one word could have different meanings – or different spellings. It felt wrong, deliberate – a code that she was never going to crack. But she had. Eventually.

Mary hadn't answered. She must have been asleep.

She'd text Joe, but not now. In the morning. She'd ask him how he was.

Sanctuary.

The word kept swinging back at her.

Like a feather in the air.

The bells, the bells.

Asylum.

A madhouse or a safe place – both. She loved that. This place had been one and now it was going to be the other.

Safe asylum.

She whispered it.

—Asylum. Asylum, asylum.

She sat up – Christ, though, keeping her daughter safe was breaking her fuckin' back.

She looked at Nicola.

She put her elbows on the bed again – fuck the pain.

—I love you, she whispered.

She meant it. No tricks, no extra meanings.

The room was wrong. Where was she?

She remembered – but she didn't.

She was in Jack's room but she wasn't supposed to be in bed – she wasn't supposed to be waking up. She'd been sitting beside Nicola. She'd been protecting Nicola. But she was in the bed, under the duvet.

She was alone.

It had happened – exactly what she hadn't wanted to happen. She was the one in bed and Nicola was the one downstairs. In charge. Looking after her mother. It was morning – Paula was facing the window. It wasn't as bright as it would have been if she'd been in her own room. Her room got the morning sun. This room lit up later, when the sun crossed over the roof.

What was she going to do? How was she going to reverse this – get it back to the way it had been last night? God, she was fuckin' useless.

But she remembered.

She remembered – and she felt Nicola shift behind her. Nicola was in the bed too.

Nicola had woken – last night. She'd seen Paula sitting on the chair. She'd pushed herself – shifted herself – back to the other side of the bed, against the wall. She'd lifted the duvet. She'd told Paula to get in.

—Here.

Just the one word. She'd turned the other way and Paula had slid into the bed. Because it was what Nicola had wanted.

And here she was.

She hadn't lost it – she was still in charge. She could still be Nicola's mother.

It was hard to guess the time. If she'd woken up in her own room she'd have known exactly. She'd only have had to look at the curtains and the day outside behind them. She'd have heard front doors opening, cars starting, heels on the path, kids shouting, the Polish baby next door.

She turned carefully. Nicola was curled up. Paula put her hand on her back and felt her heat – she was damp. She felt her breathing, heard a slight wheeze.

Did Nicola have the Covid – was that it? And it was only occurring to Paula now – God, she was an eejit. Especially after the day she'd had the day before, getting her first jab – it should have been the first thing she'd thought of. But no, that wasn't right. Nicola was more important than Paula's health – than life or death.

She checked that – was it true? Was she being sentimental because it was cosy under the duvet and her menopausal daughter was her hot-water bottle? It was true. She'd have died for Nicola. She'd have let her into the house, regardless. The vaccine hadn't made her safe, though – immune. It took a week for the stuff to kick in. Or was it two? She'd wear a mask from now on – now that Nicola had seen clearly that Paula hadn't hesitated. She'd seen Paula's face – now Paula could hide it.

She could hear the family next door now. The little girls' room must have been on the other side of the wall. She thought she heard one of them laughing. She heard what she guessed was the bathroom door, opening and closing, opening, closing.

She'd woken up but she hadn't fallen asleep – that was what it felt like. She wasn't tired. She'd slept – she must have slept well. She measured her sleep by the state of her eyes. When she was tired her eyes began to sting and water. When she wasn't, they were grand. Now – here – they were brand new. She had the eyes of a teenager.

She shouldn't have slept. But that was just stupid. She'd have been no good to Nicola if she'd stayed awake on the chair all night. It was a mother the girl needed, not a fuckin' martyr. Nicola had seen her there – and that was enough. She'd seen Paula on her all-night vigil – that was the point. She was here in the bed because Nicola had wanted her here.

Vigil.

Were all the right words religious?

She'd wanted to keep a vigil, to prove something – to herself. But this was much more practical. She'd be of more use rested.

But she didn't feel rested. She felt sick. She felt inadequate. She felt weak. She was lying here because it was handier. She was just shite.

She pushed that one away, that accusation, and it slithered away easily enough, off the bed.

Accusation – more religion.

She wasn't shite. What a boast that was. What a tattoo that would make, on her neck. She could imagine someone – Jack, Leanne, the priest – saying it at her funeral.

There was a queue of messages and WhatsApps waiting for her. There was one from Mary.

DID U SLEEP YRSELF? X

JUST AWAKE. N STILL ASLEEP X

There were two from Tony.

ALL OK?

STORY?

She thought about it. She'd have to send him something. He wasn't the enemy, as far as she knew.

SHES ASLEEP. EXHAUSTED NEEDS REST. ALL GOOD.

That would stop him from battering on the door, she thought. Battering wasn't fair, though. Tony wasn't a batterer. She'd always thought he was a bit soft. *A bit of a puff, if you ask me. Fuck off, Charlo.* She wasn't letting that bastard into her head.

Why was she stopping Tony from coming to the house? He was Nicola's husband, a man, the most likely suspect. Jesus, though, she wouldn't think like that. Not yet. Nicola had said that she'd wanted to kill them. So none of them were getting in. Simple as that. That was Paula's job. Bouncer. Nurse and bouncer. The eulogy was coming along nicely. She wasn't shite. She was a bouncer, nurse and mother.

She needed to get up and switch herself on. But she was lying up against Nicola – it was a single bed. She was an animal, protecting her young.

The phone shook in her hand – a text. She held it close to her eyes.

It was Mary.

GREAT. POOR THING. TALK LATER X

She was thinking about answering, about how she'd answer, or if she'd answer – she wasn't going to spend all the time answering texts – when the phone rang. She dropped it – it jumped out of her hand. It bounced off her cheek and landed somewhere beside her. She found it – she had it in her hand again. Nicola was moving. Paula looked at the screen. It was Tony – of course it was. She pressed red. He could wait.

—Hiyeh, love, she said.

Nicola didn't answer.

She was still sleeping.

The tray was one of those ones with a kind of beanbag for a base, so you could sit with it on your lap while you ate your dinner and caught up with your soaps. Jack had got it for her years ago – her birthday present. When he was still in school. She'd found it – she knew she still had it – lodged in the gap between the fridge and the washing machine. She needed the butt of the brush to pull it out. It was manky, covered in grime and cobwebs.

She was giddy. She had to stay calm.

She wasn't giddy – she was efficient. She was washing a tray. She'd be making toast. She was perfectly calm.

The wine bottles were out of the lounge. The wine glass was washed and upside down on the draining board. The net of satsumas was on the table behind her. She'd put one of them on the tray with the toast and the tea. A satsuma or any kind of orange – any fruit, really – would have been too much for Paula first thing in the morning. But Nicola had brought them with her – she'd chosen satsumas when she'd forgotten nearly everything else.

She turned off the tap. She got a knife and went around the edges of the tray with the tip, to make sure she'd got all of the gunge. The base – the beanbag part – was some sort of material, half-cotton, half-plastic. She wiped it down with a damp cloth. She turned it and saw the spider – Jesus Christ. It was long dead, curled up, wedged in between the cloth and the wood. She held the tray over the sink and shook it. The spider dropped into the sink, and she turned on the tap and watched as the water carried the spider, swept it along, to the plughole. Legs came away from the body. Paula turned the water to the max. She thought she'd have to go at the body with the knife. But the water did the job – the spider was gone. Her dressing gown was a bit wet, though, the front and one of the sleeves.

She went to the kitchen door. She listened.

Nothing from upstairs.

She was ahead. As long as she didn't let herself get sucked into the WhatsApping. The time would slip past her – Nicola would slip past her – if she allowed that to happen.

She was starving. She'd stick one of the slices of bread into the toaster now. Two birds, one stone – she'd eat the toast and the smell would climb up through the house. She'd bring it out to the hall and wave it about before she buttered the thing and ate it.

She was ahead – that was it. In charge of the day, in charge of the house. In charge of her child and herself. Giddy again – she'd have to be careful. Unfair to herself again – she *was* being careful.

The bread had seen better days but there was no mould on it. She'd got to it just in time. There were six or seven slices still in the wrapper. One for herself, six for madam. Two for herself, five for madam.

Her phone was hopping away on the kitchen table. She put the bread in the toaster and went back to the lounge. It looked okay – it looked fine. She'd folded the duvet but now she shoved it back where she'd always stored it, in the gap between the couch and the wall. It was a manky old thing in daylight.

She went back to the kitchen. The toast was done. The toaster had flung it out, onto the counter. The smell – it was like the smell of coffee, better than the thing itself. She brought it out to the hall and waved it. Like a priest with his incense. *In nomine Patris.* She could remember bits of the Latin mass, from when she was a little kid – before they moved it to English. *Et Filii, et Spiritus Sancti.* She brought the holy toast back into the kitchen. *Amen.* She'd check the phone while she ate it. That was how she'd measure the time that she'd give the phone. She'd sit facing the door in case Nicola came in. She wouldn't sit at all. She knew by the weight of the Dairy Manor tub as she took it from the fridge – there wasn't that much left. She got the lid off. There was enough.

Nicola's girls had WhatsApped her again. She'd answer them – their mammy just needed a rest. They weren't kids, though – they needed honesty. She'd ask Nicola before she answered.

Tony again.

ILL DROP BY LATER

Then another one.

OK?

She'd ask Nicola about this one too.

Then she remembered Nicola the night before, half-dead on

the couch – nearly comatose. She wouldn't be asking Nicola to make any decisions.

There was one from Mary.

NEED ANYTING XX BESIDES DE BLEEDIN OBVS X

She could answer this one. It was nice to be able to fire off one, at least. That would do her. She'd put the phone up in the press, beside the wine bottles.

GRAND FOR NOW THANKS X

She'd bring Nicola's toast up now on the tray, and a mug of tea – she thought Nicola preferred tea first thing. It was nine o'clock. She'd heard the little girls leaving the house next door – she'd heard their mother telling them to hurry up in Polish. She hadn't understood the words but she'd known exactly what the woman had been saying – on her way to work, the baby to drop off somewhere, the pair of little wagons dragging along behind her.

She wouldn't bring the toast up yet. She'd see if Nicola was awake first. Sleep was more important.

She could smell her own toast – Jesus, she'd forgotten to eat it. She could smell it on the landing as she opened the bedroom door.

The room was still dark. It was like stepping into a different house or a different time of day. She wouldn't be able to see Nicola's face, the way Nicola was lying, without climbing onto the bed or opening the curtains. She stood still – she listened. Nicola was still asleep. God love her, she must have been utterly exhausted.

—It was the way he was looking at her.

It took Paula a second to realise – to accept – that it was Nicola who'd spoken.

—Sorry, hon – I didn't hear you. What did you say?

She might have imagined it, one of those tricks her head played on her.

—I said –.

181

Paula had heard Nicola perfectly. Each and every word. But she needed to hear it again. The words were so like an echo – words from long ago.

—It was the way he was looking at her, said Nicola.

—Who, hon?

—Lily.

Lily was Nicola's youngest.

—Who was looking at her?

Paula was terrified – suddenly. Terrified. The name – the wrong name, the right name – was going to bring everything down.

—Keith, said Nicola.

Paula didn't know the name.

—Who's Keith, hon?

—Tony's brother.

She knew him now – she remembered. The younger brother. Married to the anti-vaxxer. With the dyslexic twins.

—What happened? said Paula.

She sat – she had to. The relief had gone down through her legs – it wasn't Tony. Relief and disgust. Shame. She could listen to Nicola – she'd be able to hear her.

—What happened? she asked again. —Love –? Nicola?

She half-hoped she'd hear Nicola crying – doing the thing she'd said she'd been unable to do. Paula would have been able to comfort her – to try, at least. She'd have been able to get onto the bed.

—Will I open the curtains? she said. —I'll open the curtains.

She leaned back on the chair. She grabbed hold of the nearest curtain, but she had to get up to do the job properly. She pulled the curtain back a bit – a bit more than a chink.

—There –, she said. —That's nice now.

Jesus – she was listening to herself. That's nice now. For fuck sake.

But it was okay – it was okay. She was filling the room with words. Gentle words. Meaningless words. And it was fine – it was good. She wasn't avoiding anything. The sun wasn't going to bleach the evil out of what she'd heard. The way he was looking at her. She could hear the words. She could hear the words in Nicola's voice. She could hear them in her own.

She sat again. She sat carefully. Her back was killing her again. Trying to distract her.

—When did this happen, Nicola?

Nicola hadn't budged. She was lying with her back to Paula. She was facing the wall.

—Funeral.

—At a funeral?

—Yeah.

—Whose funeral? I don't remember you going to a funeral.

—Does it matter?

—No, said Paula. —No, it doesn't.

—Tony's auntie. Connie.

—I don't think I knew she was after dying, said Paula. —Was it the Covid?

—And cancer.

—Okay, said Paula. —That's dreadful – poor woman. Are you hungry, by the way?

Nicola didn't answer.

—D'you want some tea – or coffee?

—Tea.

—Grand. No toast, no?

—No.

—You need to eat something, hon.

—No, I don't.

Paula stood. She was slow. The zip had gone out of her.

—I'll only be a minute, she said.

She went the three steps to the door.

—After the funeral.

Paula stopped. She looked at Nicola. She could only see the top of her head.

—Are they allowing funerals again? she said. —Proper funerals, like?

She saw Nicola shake her head slightly.

—No.

Nicola moved. She was sitting up. Paula sat on the end of the bed. But it wasn't good – she needed something behind her back. She went back to the chair and picked the throw up off the floor.

—Here, hon.

She leaned nearer to Nicola. She had a knee on the bed, so she could help Nicola to get the throw around her shoulders. Nicola didn't need any help. But she helped her, anyway. She put her hand on Nicola's arm – for just a second. Her back wasn't protesting too much. She was getting away with it.

—We weren't at the funeral, said Nicola.

—Right.

—There was only ten at it. Tony's uncle –

—That's Malcolm – am I right?

—Bernard.

—Who's Malcolm?

—I don't know, said Nicola. —You made him up.

—Probably.

—The four children and Auntie Connie's sisters and her brother.

—That was ten.

—Yeah.

—What happened after the funeral – sorry?

She pulled herself back. She was forgetting why they were there, what Nicola had been telling her.

—There was a get-together, said Nicola. —We shouldn't have gone.

—Where?

—Laura's garden – it was all outdoors.

—Who's that, hon? Who's Laura?

—Connie's daughter.

—Tony's cousin.

—Yeah.

—What happened? Paula asked again.

Nicola was looking at the open doorway.

—Why am I in this room? she asked.

—The other one – your old room. I haven't had a chance to tidy it up. It's full of Leanne's stuff – it's a bit of a mess, to be honest.

Nicola yawned.

—You slept, anyway, said Paula.

—What?

—You slept – I'm just saying. Cos you said you couldn't – last night.

—Yeah.

—That's good – at least, said Paula.

Jesus, this was hard.

—Sorry, she said. —I was interrupting you. You were saying about Laura – is that the girl's name?

—Yeah.

—The do in her garden.

—It wasn't a do.

—You know what I mean, said Paula. —The afters.

—Tony should've gone on his own, said Nicola.

—But you went.

—Yeah –. I kind of wanted to. Jesus –. I hardly knew Connie. And I don't think Tony was that mad about her. He wasn't exactly heartbroken.

Nicola was looking past Paula, at the bit of day she could see through the gap in the curtains.

—A day out, she said. —Simple as. An excuse to dress up. Jesus –.

Paula said it again.

—What happened?

—Lily came with us. Obviously.

Nicola was looking out at the landing again.

—It should've been a school day but there was some meeting on or something – I can't remember. Anyway, she said she'd come with us.

Nicola looked at Paula.

—It was nice.

—Must've been, said Paula. —We had great times together when you were Lily's age.

Picking Paula up, putting her to bed, washing the vomit off her face.

—D'you remember *Dirty Dancing*?

They'd gone to *Dirty Dancing* together – just the two of them.

—The girls know it off by heart, said Nicola. —Same as me.

—That's nice, said Paula.

Nicola had told her that before but, still, she wanted to cry. She'd got something right – one thing right, at least, with Nicola.

—We were laughing about it, said Nicola. —Going to a funeral as if it was a party. Lily said we should have had pre-drinks. She started making up names for funeral cocktails.

—She's a funny girl.

—Death and Tonic – that was one of the ones she came up with.

Paula laughed.

—I've had a few of them, myself.

—Tony got a bit annoyed. In the car, like – on the way there.

—Where?

—Laura's place – I told you.

—Where but?

—Clongriffin.

—Okay. Not far then.

—No. He couldn't find it, though – and he was getting a bit worked up. And Lily found it on Google Maps and she was telling Tony where to turn and –

—He didn't like it.

—He loved it.

The fuckin' faggot.

Charlo's voice, inside Paula – she swallowed it down.

—That's nice, she said. —That's – d'you know what? It's kind of wonderful.

Nicola nodded.

—Yeah, she said. —It was. I was a bit jealous. He was listening to her – you know.

Nicola was looking at her hands on her lap.

—D'you want that tea now, Nicola?

Nicola nodded.

—Yeah – thanks.

—Just ordinary, yeah? Not the mint or the chamomile?

—Yeah – ordinary.

—And a bit of toast?

Nicola nodded again.

—I'll only be a minute, said Paula.

She had to hold tight to the banister. She reminded herself – she wasn't escaping. There wasn't a fire – she didn't have to charge. The front door wasn't tempting her. She'd be making the breakfast and going back up.

She stopped at the bottom of the stairs, though. It was a nice day out there. She could see that through the pebbled glass. But it could have been bucketing – getting out of the house would still have been a joy. The rain on her face, the snow, the bullet-sized hailstones – it would have been just brilliant.

She went into the kitchen.

She went to the sink and vomited. She turned on the tap, so Nicola wouldn't hear her. She reached out for the radio. She couldn't see it – her eyes were burnt shut – but she knew exactly where it was. She turned it on. Fuckin' Tubridy – but it didn't matter. He'd mask whatever noise she was going to make. She didn't have to panic – she could get through this. She could be brand new going back up to Nicola.

Jesus, Jesus, Jesus – what was she going to hear then? What poison had she passed on to Nicola and her girls? The rotten scent that attracted badness – she was a filthy fuckin' bitch. She should have killed herself years ago.

She was okay – she was okay. Holding her face down, close to the cold water, was doing her good. She could open her eyes. She could stand up straight. She'd stopped spinning. She put her hands under the tap. She brought them up to her face. That was good. She bent – she was fine – and took hold of the corner of her dressing gown. She brought it up and wiped her face with it. The tea towel was too scratchy for the job. The dressing gown was soft, still new – a Christmas present from Nicola's girls. Jesus, Jesus, Jesus.

She was fine.

She filled the kettle. She turned off Tubridy. She filled a mug with water. She put two slices of bread into the toaster.

She drank the water – she gulped it. God, it was good.

She'd be fine.

She looked at her phone. There was a text from Mary.

HOWR THINGS X

She didn't know how to answer. She couldn't joke, she couldn't tell the truth.

TALK LATER X

She scrolled through the others, from last night to a few minutes before. She found the one she was looking for. Lily. A WhatsApp.

HOWS MAM NANNY? XXX

She went to the Contact Info, so she could look properly at the photo. Lily and the dog, Gilbert. The faces side by side – Lily trying to match the dog's expression. A miracle of a child. So – just so fuckin' marvellous. Nicola had had to spend months in bed at home, and weeks in the Rotunda, when she was pregnant with Lily. Paula had stopped drinking for good by then. She'd looked after the other two girls. They'd stayed here some nights. She'd got them to school. She'd fed them, she'd loved them. She'd demonstrated – she'd tried to prove to Nicola that she could be trusted. But she'd never felt it in herself, that she'd succeeded. The girls loved her – she knew that – but Nicola tolerated her.

The kettle clicked and the toaster threw out the toast, one machine right after the other – Ta-dah.

She sent one back to Lily.

SHES GRAND HON. JUST TIRED XXX

She put the kettle back down and grabbed the phone.

TALK LATER XXX

Another tattoo for her neck – Talk Later, in Greek. Or Irish.

She was done – she was ready. She'd two mugs of tea on the tray, the carton of milk, a hill of toast on a plate, cut into quarters, buttered, and a jar of marmalade for those that wanted it, and – she got one now from the cutlery drawer – a knife. She put the phone on the tray, then took it off and put it on the table. She picked up the tray, and put it back down. There was a mirror in the cutlery drawer – she'd just seen it. An old mirror from a compact – that would do her.

She looked. She'd pass – her eyes weren't too red. It was half-dark up in the bedroom, anyway.

The sugar bowl was too big for the tray. She got a cup from the press and poured some sugar into it. She picked up the tray.

She was grand going up the stairs, nothing in her fighting to turn back. She was absolutely starving – she was kind of glad she'd vomited. She felt ready.

But – God – she was terrified.

She could hear her phone buzz in the kitchen. It was the last thing she heard from the outside world before she walked back into Jack's bedroom.

Nicola was under the duvet again.

—There's loads of people worried about you, hon, said Paula. —My phone's doing the tango downstairs.

Nicola didn't answer.

—I have your tea here. And the toast. I'm starving – I don't know about you. Sit up there, hon.

Nicola wasn't moving.

—Nicola – come on. You have to eat.

The thought only occurred to Paula now – Nicola had gone back to sleep. What sort of an eejit was she, barging in? But she pushed that one away. She'd only been gone a few minutes. They had to talk. Nicola had to talk – Paula had to listen.

—Nicola – get up.

She put the tray on the chair. There was a bit of a clatter, the

189

mugs hitting each other, but nothing spilled. She put her right hand under the duvet and found one of Nicola's feet. She held it, squeezed lightly, stopped squeezing.

—Up, she said.

—I don't want to go to school, said Nicola.

Paula smiled. She couldn't believe it, really – she'd been puking a minute ago. She took a piece of the toast off the plate. She bit into it.

—Jesus, that's lovely.

Nicola was lifting herself.

Paula took one of the mugs off the tray and put it on the windowsill.

—Take the tray here – look it.

She lifted the tray off the chair.

—Straighten your legs there.

She had to put one knee on the bed, so she could get the tray across to Nicola. Nicola took it from her.

—Thanks, she said.

—No bother, said Paula.

She took another piece of the toast before she got off the bed.

She could reach her tea comfortably from the chair. She'd put the milk into her own mug down in the kitchen. The toast felt like wine going down through her – God, it was brilliant, especially the melted butter.

Nicola had gripped the mug by its handle but she hadn't lifted it off the tray.

—Don't forget the milk, hon, said Paula.

Nicola picked up the carton. It was a relief. Nicola had seemed a bit drugged, the way she was moving, and Paula had started to wonder if she was. She'd wondered if Nicola had been given something by her GP – antidepressants or something – and if she should even search for them, take control of them. Nicola hadn't brought her bag or a jacket. But Paula knew – when it came to hiding things, desperate people were geniuses.

Nicola took the little lid off the milk. It was one of the

half-litre cartons, so it was easy enough to manage. She poured the milk – the exact amount she wanted – into her mug. She screwed the lid back on the carton. She picked up a piece of toast and bit into it.

—You don't want marmalade, no?

Nicola shook her head.

—Grand, said Paula.

She held her mug in both hands. She watched Nicola put the rest of the toast into her mouth.

—So, she said.

Nicola picked up another piece of the toast.

—What happened then? said Paula. —When you got to Laura's.

Nicola took the lid off the marmalade and picked up the knife.

—I've changed my mind, she said.

—Fire away.

Nicola had put the toast back down on the plate. She held the jar, tilted it, and coaxed a dollop of the marmalade out with the knife, onto the toast.

—They were all in the back, she said. —We didn't have to go through the house or anything. There's a side passage, like. But even that was a bit dodge – there were way too many people. There must've been about forty. And the gardens are really small there – new houses, you know. There were people in the house too – coming and going. Keith's wife, Gemma – God, I hate her. She was in and out of the house – no mask or anything. Breathing all over Tony's aunties and uncles.

Paula put her mug on the windowsill. She leaned across and took a piece of the toast.

—When was this, Nicola? You didn't tell me about the funeral, I don't think.

—A couple of weeks ago, said Nicola.

—Oh, said Paula. —Right.

—I was with Hazel, said Nicola.

—Hazel?

—Tony's sister, Mammy – Jesus.

—Hazel – that Hazel. Grand.

—How many Hazels do you know?

—Dozens of them – feck off. Go on.

—And Hazel's kids and some of the other cousins – Lily's cousins – they were going out to the front and I said she could go with them.

Nicola looked at the tray.

—Will I get rid of that thing for you, hon?

Nicola didn't answer. Paula stood to get the tray.

—No, it's fine, said Nicola.

—Okay, said Paula.

She didn't want to sit down again. But she did.

—What happened? she said.

—It was where I was standing, said Nicola. —That's why –.

—Why what, hon?

—I was facing the garden, said Nicola. —My back was to the side gate, like.

—Where Lily's cousins were going through.

—And Lily.

—'Course, said Paula. —Lily as well.

—Keith, said Nicola. —The way he looked at Lily. He followed her when she was passing.

—Followed her?

—His eyes, said Nicola.

She looked at Paula.

—He was nearer to me than you are, she said. —I was looking straight at him. And I followed – his eyes, like. I knew already, though. I knew he was looking at Lily. But it was the way he was looking at her. She's fifteen.

—Yes.

—And she looks fifteen.

Paula nodded.

—He was – Keith was with one of Tony's cousins. Another fella – the same age. And he said –. Keith said. She's hot.

—God.

192

—I don't think he cared.

—That you heard him.

—No.

—The fuckin' bastard, said Paula.

—He didn't exactly shout it but he didn't whisper it either. He didn't care if anyone heard. He just said it like it was nothing – like he was talking about the weather. *It's* hot – you know.

—And there's no chance that he was –?

—No!

—Okay, said Paula. —Sorry.

Christ, she was stupid – trying to trip up Nicola. She'd jumped on it, though – she'd jumped at the chance to catch her out, make her seem hysterical. It wasn't what Paula wanted – it was the last thing she wanted.

—Go on, hon, she said. —Please.

—Well, said Nicola. —Other people must have heard him.

—Did – what's the girl's name, the girl that was with you – Hazel? Did she hear him?

—She must have.

—She didn't say anything?

—No.

—Or look at you when she heard it?

—No.

—Did Lily hear him?

—No. No. She was gone out to the front.

—With the others.

—Yeah.

—Jesus, Nicola – I'm so sorry. That's just fuckin' awful. It's evil.

Nicola looked at her tea. She tilted her mug and stared into it.

—Where was Tony? Paula asked.

—I'm not sure, said Nicola. —I didn't look. He was talking to his aunties and uncles, I think. They were kind of all together, in the chairs. The garden chairs, like.

—Did he hear what his brother said?

—No, said Nicola. —I don't think so.

—Did you tell him?

—What?

—Did you tell him about it – later, like – what you heard?

—No, said Nicola.

She was still looking into the mug.

—I didn't.

—Right –.

—I didn't tell anyone, said Nicola.

She put the mug back on the tray.

—No one.

—How come? Paula asked.

Nicola didn't answer.

Paula had seen Charlo looking at Nicola the way she'd imagined Nicola had seen Tony's brother looking at Lily. Paula had seen it – and she'd seen Nicola looking at her, her eyes pleading for help. And Paula had picked the frying pan up off the cooker and she'd hit him with it. She hadn't hesitated. She hadn't given herself time for doubt or consequences. She'd done what she'd needed to do. What came natural. She hadn't known if she was killing Charlo and she hadn't cared.

She said it again.

—How come?

This time, she thought, it sounded a bit like she was pecking at Nicola.

And maybe she was.

—How come what? said Nicola.

—I don't know, said Paula.

—It was a funeral, said Nicola.

—Yeah. 'Course.

—I didn't want to start anything.

—I know.

Paula sighed.

—I know, she said again. —After though, hon.

—What?

—You didn't say anything after?

—No.

—To Tony. Or to what's his name – Keith?

Nicola said nothing.

—Did – did you say anything to Lily? Paula asked.

—No, said Nicola.

—Okay.

—She didn't see him.

—Not that time, said Paula.

She was going too far – she was a bitch. The urge to dig at Nicola, to accuse her – it was almost joyful. She had her in the dock and she knew it wasn't fair – it wasn't what she wanted. But it was hard to push back the feeling – it was Paula's turn to be the prosecutor.

Nicola said nothing. She hadn't moved. Paula was hoping now that Nicola had missed what she'd said.

—You're a cunt.

Paula looked at the door to see who'd spoken.

It was Nicola – of course it was Nicola.

—Sorry, said Paula. —I'm sorry.

Neither of them spoke after that. For a minute. Two minutes. Paula fought the need to get out of there, to stand up, lean down and pick up the tray – drop the contents on Nicola or carry it back downstairs. The need to shout. The need to attack. To cry, to scream. To beg forgiveness. To roar abuse. To lie down, will herself out of life. What had she done? How had she done this?

She sat there – forever. She didn't take her eyes off Nicola. She wanted to speak – she was dying to say something, to mend it, to let them keep going or go back to where they'd been before she'd opened her stupid mouth. She hadn't a clue what, though – she had no idea what she'd say. There were no magic words, none that she'd ever known. The ones she'd tried had all been useless. I love you. Fuck me. Do anything you want to me. Don't – please, Charlo – don't. I'm sorry.

Ask me, ask me, ask me.

—Nicola –.

—What?

—Can I say something?

—You've said plenty.

—Not really. I haven't.

—What?

She wasn't going to say sorry again. It was useless. Nicola would hear it – Paula feeling sorry for herself.

—Don't blame yourself, said Paula.

—I don't.

—You do – if you're anything like me. And before you say you're nothing like me, you're right. In loads of ways – I wouldn't know where to start. But you're wrong as well.

Nicola said nothing. This was good, Paula decided. She could keep going. Nicola wanted to hear what she had to say.

—You're a woman, hon, said Paula. —You're to blame for everything – absolutely everything.

She wished her mug wasn't empty. It was good to have the thing to hold but – Christ – she was thirsty. Her head was pounding. She wouldn't stop now, though. She wouldn't allow herself the excuse, get downstairs and put the kettle on. She had to get this done. While she could trust herself. While she could trust the words.

—And the first person who's blaming you is yourself, she said. —Amn't I right?

Nicola glanced at her.

—You blame yourself for not doing something, said Paula. —And you'd be blaming yourself if you had done something. You're to blame for that dirtbird looking at Lily the way he did. That's what you think. That's what you feel. That's how I felt, anyway.

Nicola was looking at her now, not looking away.

—Do you still feel that way? she asked.

—No, said Paula. —No – I don't think I do. I'm too old, maybe. No – no, that's not right.

—What?

—I don't think like that now. Because of you.

—What d'you mean – because of me?

—Watching you, said Paula. —The way you live. The way you – what's the thing they say? Conduct yourself – the way you've always conducted yourself. And d'you know what, Nicola? I'm only thinking this now – putting it into words, like. You didn't lick it off a stone. And you definitely didn't get it off your father.

—What?

—Your resilience – is one thing. Your spirit – I can't think of another word. I don't mean like spooky. I mean your strength and your energy. And – Jesus, hon – your grace. The way you –. I'm glad I'm talking like this.

They were at her eyes – her head was suddenly full. The tears crept out of her – it wasn't a gush.

She put the mug back on the windowsill. She had to be careful – she couldn't see clearly. She needed to wipe her eyes. She couldn't see – and she wanted to see Nicola. She put her hands to her eyes. She stopped herself from apologising. Sorry – I'm an eejit here, crying. She used the pads of skin below her thumbs, to wipe the tears, to clear her vision. She dried her face with the sleeve of her dressing gown. It was a bit of a shock – she was still in her dressing gown.

—We're a right pair of sluts, she said. —Still in our jimjams.

She was disappointed. She'd been hoping to see Nicola crying alongside her. But Nicola wasn't crying.

Grand, though, Paula thought. It wasn't the point – not really. It wasn't about tears.

—You said. Earlier, like. You said it was the way that – I keep forgetting the fucker's name.

—Keith.

—That's right, said Paula. —It was the way that he was looking at Lily.

—Yeah.

—D'you want to say more?

Nicola didn't answer.

—Do we want more tea? said Paula. —That's probably an easier one to answer, is it?

—Yeah.

—Grand, said Paula. —A break for the ads. I don't think I've any biscuits.

—Doesn't matter.

—I could go and get some.

—And never come back.

Paula stood.

—I always came back, she said. —I never left in the first place.

—But I did – is that what you mean?

Jesus – what had Paula gone and said? Had she ruined everything that had just happened? She didn't let the panic grab at her.

—No, she said. —It's not what I mean.

She took the tray off the bed.

—Give that to me here, she said.

—I'm not going back, said Nicola.

—Grand, said Paula. —I won't be a minute. D'you want anything else to eat?

—No.

—Sure? While I'm down there?

—No.

—Grand.

She went into the bathroom and put the tray on the floor. She hadn't shut the bathroom door. If Nicola leaned out a bit, she'd see her mother sitting there, pissing. She pulled her bottoms back up. She washed her hands. She picked up the tray. Her back wasn't bothering her. Was that a good sign or a bad sign? It was no kind of a sign.

She half-filled the kettle.

She tapped her phone screen, to see if there were missed calls or messages. There was another one from Mary.

ALL GOOD? NEED ANYTING X

She couldn't let herself get distracted.

GRAND FOR NOW TALK LATER X

She took the mugs and the plate off the tray, and the

marmalade. She washed the mugs. These two were better than the other clean ones. It would give her something small to do, keep her away from the phone.

She dried the mugs. She didn't really want tea but she'd want it when she went back up. She'd want the mug in her hands. She'd want the activity, and the taste – to keep her conscious. Calm. Sane. It was something she often thought, or heard. Staying sane – keeping her sanity. Men didn't have to worry about their sanity. Men were never mad. Only the girls.

She heard the bathroom door being shut, upstairs. That was Nicola, out of the bed.

She poured the hot water in on top of the teabags.

There was another message from Tony, and two missed calls. Poor Tony.

Poor Tony, with the predator for a brother.

HOW IS SHE? IS HER PHONE OUT OF BATTERY?

Did he know?

SHES OK TALK LATER

Had he guessed? Had he seen the Keith fella ogling Lily? He'd have seen him in action before, any time they'd been out together. He might have joined in. She didn't know – she wasn't being fair. Maybe. She didn't know if they were close, Tony and Keith, if they got on or could even stand each other. It had been a funeral – that was why they'd been in the garden at the same time. She couldn't remember Tony ever mentioning Keith, or Nicola, except when Nicola had been giving out about Keith's wife – Paula had forgotten her name again.

She put her phone on the table. She picked up the tray.

Off again.

Nicola was back in the bed, exactly where she'd left her. She hadn't gone under the duvet.

—Here we are, said Paula.

She put the tray on the chair.

—What time is it, hon?

—Don't know, said Nicola.

Nicola had a nice watch on her wrist. Kind of a man's watch, with a big face on it. Paula couldn't remember the make. It wasn't a name she knew.

—Doesn't matter, she said. —D'you want the tray on your lap again or beside you?

—Beside.

—Grand, said Paula. —Scooch over a little bit there or it might fall off the bed.

She parked the tray on the duvet, and sat on the chair. She wished she was where the tray was, beside Nicola.

—Your work, though, she said.

—What?

—Did you phone in?

—No, said Nicola. —Why would I?

—It's only a question, Nicola, said Paula. —You're not working today. Do they know? That's all.

—There's no they, said Nicola. —I'm they.

—I didn't know that – I don't think I did. That's amazing – Jesus.

—I told you.

—Yeah – but. I didn't –. I don't think I understood it, fully. No boss at all?

Nicola sold gym equipment. She'd never been busier, she'd told Paula during the first lockdown. The gyms were all shut but people were making their own gyms in their homes. She'd offered Paula a rowing machine.

—There's no one I have to phone in sick to, said Nicola. —That's me.

—Brilliant, said Paula. —I could never do that.

—You did it for years, said Nicola.

—No, I didn't.

—You were your own boss.

—No, I wasn't – was I?

—Yeah, said Nicola. —A lot of the time.

—I was a cleaner, hon.

—You ran your own business.

Paula started to laugh.

—Now she tells me.

She took her mug off the windowsill.

—I don't care, said Nicola. —About work. I couldn't care less.

—Oh.

—Oh?

—Just – it's not like you.

—Are you worried?

—Of course, I'm worried, said Paula. —Yes, I'm worried.

—Worried you won't be getting any more freebies?

Paula looked down at the tea in her mug.

—I'm grateful, she said. —I always have been. But, Nicola. Fuck off.

She looked at Nicola just as Nicola looked up at her.

—Sorry.

—Okay, said Paula.

She stood. She put the mug on the windowsill first. She thought she'd need both hands to help push herself off the chair. But she was fine. Telling Nicola to fuck off had done her the world of good.

—I'm opening the curtains a bit more, she said. —It's too dark in here. It's making me drowsy.

—Okay.

—What about the window?

—What about it?

—Do we want some fresh air?

—Okay.

—Just a little bit – there.

She put her hand out, into the day.

—It's a nice day out there, she said.

There was training or something going on on the all-weather pitch. She hadn't seen that in ages. It was a gang of secondary schoolkids, boys and girls. They were running around cones. She could hear a teacher shouting some sort of instructions.

She could sit again. She leaned back and picked up the mug.

Nicola was lying back, against the pillows. There was no head-board, so her head was leaning against the wall. She didn't look comfortable. She looked dreadful. Paula couldn't remember ever seeing Nicola this way – pale, mottled, so unhappy. The room was too bright – she should have left the curtains alone.

—Nicola –. Nicola?

—Yeah.

—D'you want to talk?

—No.

—It was the way he was looking at her, said Paula. —The Keith fella. You said that.

—I know.

—What did you mean?

—I don't know.

—You said it, Nicola – it's what you said.

—I know – I heard you.

—And I heard you, said Paula.

—It reminded me, said Nicola.

Her voice sounded different, like her throat was being held, like she was being choked. Maybe it was because of the way she was lying back. But Paula knew – it had nothing to do with her physical position.

—Your father, she said.

Her own voice sounded different, she thought.

—His face reminded you of your father's. Am I right?

Cry, she thought – she pleaded. Cry now, love – please. And she could cry too. With Nicola.

—Yeah.

She could hear Nicola breathing. She could hear herself. She could hear the teacher outside. She could hear girls outside laughing.

—Okay, she said.

Nicola's hair was shorter than it used to be. She couldn't cover her face with it any more. But the way she was lying, that was what she would have been doing – hiding behind her hair.

—Jesus, hon –, said Paula.

—Stop calling me fuckin' hon.

—What?

—You usen't to call me hon, said Nicola. —Or anyone else. Now you call everyone hon. Just cos your bezzie for life Mary calls everyone hon – it's sad.

—D'you know what, Nicola? said Paula. —You're actually right. But fuck off anyway.

—You fuck off. Hon.

—Nicola –.

—I know. Yeah. When I saw him looking at Lily – his face. His expression. It reminded me –. I don't even know what to call him.

—You used to call him Daddy or Da.

—I'm not doing that.

—Okay.

—I can't.

—Call him what you like, said Paula.

She'd pulled herself back from defending Charlo, his status as Nicola's father. He *was* your father, Nicola – he wasn't the worst.

—Go on, hon – sorry – love. Is that okay?

—Yeah.

—I'm allowed to call you love?

—Yeah.

—Thank God for that. Go on.

Nicola moved. She groaned as she shifted herself in the bed.

—I thought –, she said, and stopped.

She moved again. The tray was shaking. The tea was slopping over the top of Nicola's mug. Paula stood, and lifted the tray and waited till Nicola had settled. But Nicola lay on her back, like she was going to sleep. Paula brought the tray out to the landing and left it on the floor. She came back into the room.

Nicola was looking at the ceiling.

—Jesus, said Paula. —I feel like a psychiatrist, with you lying there like that.

—She's lovely, said Nicola.

—Who, hon – love. Who? Lily?

—Beyoncé.

—What?

Paula looked at the ceiling, where Nicola was looking, and saw the poster. It wasn't a full-sized thing, like the ones on the walls. It was a page from a magazine, an ad for one of Beyoncé's CDs.

She laughed.

—D'you know what? she said. —I've never seen that before. Is that Beyoncé?

—Yeah, said Nicola. —*Dangerously in Love.*

—She's gorgeous, alright. I can't see her that well, though.

Paula laughed again.

—I sometimes wondered if Jack was gay, she said. —I wouldn't have minded if he was.

—Maybe he is, said Nicola.

—Not according to your woman up there on the ceiling, said Paula.

—She's a gay icon, said Nicola.

—Jesus now – as far as I can tell, every woman that ever sang is a gay icon. But I don't know – I haven't a clue.

She looked at the other pictures on the walls, and at the concert tickets Jack had Blu-tacked over his bed. Arctic Monkeys, Arcade Fire, Lupe Fiasco.

—How come you never saw it?

—I never looked, said Paula. —I never noticed.

As she spoke, she felt she'd been tricked into giving the answer to an entirely different question. I never looked – I never noticed.

—Too busy picking his clothes up off the floor, she said.

Another trap – she couldn't remember picking Nicola's clothes off the floor. Not once. She'd been a very different mother to Jack – a source of pride. And shame. She'd always been ashamed – she always would be. She wished it was Jack who was with her right now. It would have been so much easier.

But she was probably deluding herself there too. His time would come too. His day of reckoning.

—Anyway, she said. —You were starting to say something before you mentioned Beyoncé.

—I don't remember.

—You do, said Paula. —You said, I thought. That's what you said. I thought. And then you stopped.

—That's what I thought, said Nicola.

—What d'you mean?

—I thought I'd stopped it.

—Stopped what?

—You've stopped calling me hon.

—Stopped what, Nicola?

—I kind of miss it.

—Nicola –.

—Him.

It was like the name of a horror film.

—Your father, said Paula.

Nicola was staring up at Beyoncé.

—When you saw Keith –.

—I don't care about Keith, said Nicola. —He's only an eejit. The world is full of Keiths.

—It is. I know.

—He has daughters.

—Keith? Jesus.

—Yeah.

—D'you think –?

—No, said Nicola. —If you're asking me do I think did Keith ever do anything to them. Or would. No. I doubt it. I don't care.

—Nicola –.

—I don't. Care. I don't fuckin' care. I thought I'd done it.

—What?

—Got rid of him.

—Your father.

—No one will ever do that to my children, said Nicola.

Paula thought – she knew – she was going to hear something she wouldn't survive hearing.

—Do what, Nicola?

She was hoping Nicola wouldn't answer.

—What, Nicola? Did your father –?

Paula sat up.

—Do you remember the time – the morning I threw him out of the house?

—Yeah.

—I saw him looking at you, said Paula. —Inappropriately – is that word okay with you?

—Yeah.

Nicola was still staring at the ceiling.

—The minute I saw him, said Paula. —And I saw you. I grabbed the pan and I hit him. You remember?

—Yeah.

—That's what happened.

—Yeah.

—That's what you saw.

—Yeah.

—Now, said Paula. —What I have to say. Is. That's all I saw. It was enough – more than enough. The second I saw him. But, like I say, that's all I saw. That's –

She wasn't going to cry. She couldn't let herself become a distraction.

—That's what I remember seeing, she said. —It's all I saw.

Nicola said nothing and the silence was dreadful.

—Love –? Nicola?

Nicola moved her head so she was looking at Paula. She looked younger lying like that. Like a child, nearly. Like Paula's child.

—What? said Nicola.

—Was there more?

—More what?

A ring on the bell, a hammering on the door, a bird or a football hitting the window – anything would have been perfect, anything that would have let Paula jump up off the chair and escape.

—You know what I mean, Nicola, she said.

—Yeah.

—Was there more?

—Yeah.

—Jesus, love – God. I don't know what to say.

—Grand, said Nicola. —Whatever.

—What happened? said Paula.

She surprised herself that she'd said the words, that she could say them. She was still sitting there, looking straight at Nicola.

—He put his hand on my back, said Nicola. —And left it there. And rubbed me up and down.

—Jesus –.

—And he stood –. Too close, like.

—How long did that go on for – d'you remember?

—I'm not the one with the memory problems. Hon.

—Tell me.

—Not that long, said Nicola. —Like – a week. Three times.

—Then I saw him. Is that it – what happened?

—He said I'd make some man very happy, said Nicola.

—He said that –?

—Yeah.

—Was I there?

—Not really, said Nicola.

—What?

Nicola didn't answer.

—What d'you mean?

Nicola said nothing.

—Nicola – what d'you mean? When was this?

—The night before –.

—I saw him? The night before I hit him?

—Yeah.

—Okay, said Paula. —Nicola –?

—What?

—If I'd seen him – if I'd heard him. That time – the night before. I'd have killed him. Okay?

—Okay.

—I'd have fuckin' killed him.

—You were asleep.

—Sorry –?

—Passed out, said Nicola. —Downstairs. I was trying to wake you up.

—And he said that.

—Yeah.

—Sorry – where was I? On the couch –?

—Yeah.

—Excuse me.

Paula stood.

She was going to be sick. Again. She wanted to vomit. To pour it – hurl it out. Get rid of it. The evil. But she couldn't leave the room. She wouldn't come back if she did. She wouldn't be able to. Standing seemed to be enough, and the decision not to walk out. She was in control. She was doing okay. She could keep going.

—Why? said Nicola.

She was sitting up again. Paula hadn't noticed her moving.

—Why what?

—Why did you say excuse me there?

—I don't know.

—Liar.

—It doesn't matter, said Paula.

She sat.

—I thought I wanted to go to the toilet, she said. —Actually – being honest. I thought I was going to be sick.

—Okay.

—So –.

—Are you going to be?

—No, said Paula. —I'm not. I'm grand. Not grand. Dreadful. I don't know how to put it into words. What you just told me – how I feel about it – I don't know.

208

—Go on ahead if you want to puke.

—I don't –.

—I'm not stopping you.

—I don't.

—Fine.

—It's not fine.

—He stood right behind me.

—Stop –. No, don't. I didn't mean that.

—Against me. When I was trying to wake you.

Neither of them spoke for a minute, less – what felt like hours, what felt like outer space. Paula could hear every bit of herself, everything that was going on inside her.

She was ready to talk again, able to ask.

—Did anything else happen – did he do anything else? Jesus Christ –.

—No.

—Okay, said Paula. —Okay. But why didn't you tell me?

—You were unconscious.

Paula closed her eyes. This was as bad as it was going to get. It had to be. She slowly shook her head. And stopped – she didn't want Nicola thinking that she was denying what she'd told her.

She opened her eyes. The room was still there. Nicola was still there.

—Okay, she said.

—You were, said Nicola.

—I know, said Paula. —I know. But –.

—What?

—I did get rid of him.

—I was so frightened.

—God, love – I can imagine. The things he did to me – Jesus.

—I was frightened!

—So was I!

—I wasn't married to him!

—I know but –

—He was my father! He was my fuckin' dad! You stupid cunt!

She couldn't see Nicola. There was nothing of Nicola in the thing there on the bed.

—You were supposed to be my mother – you were supposed to protect me!

Paula was on the landing. She shut the door after her. Nicola had started to scream – really scream. Paula stepped on the tray. Thank Christ it had the cushion under it – it didn't slide. A miracle nothing spilled.

For fuck sake.

The screaming inside had stopped. *The Exorcist* was over. She opened the door. She didn't look in.

—D'you want your phone?

—No.

—D'you want tea?

—Yeah.

—Grand, said Paula. —I'll be back in a minute.

A few minutes away from her – she'd love her again by the time she came back up the stairs. You were supposed to be my mother! You were supposed to protect me! The ungrateful little bitch – the batterings Paula had taken, to keep the bastard from battering the children. He'd beaten her senseless, he'd raped her. Because she'd put herself between him and the kids – all the kids. Not just madam. Jesus, though – the way her head was going, nearly blaming Nicola, throwing the responsibility back on her. She had to get downstairs for a while, get herself back, have a breather. Become the mother again. With her daughter in the bed, not some other strange mother. She could live with this. She could get through it. The things she could endure. She'd heard what she'd just heard and here she was, filling the kettle. All set for round two, or three – Jesus Christ, she was looking forward to it. Something huge was happening – something fuckin' huge.

There was a text from Maisie, John Paul's daughter.

HI GRANNY NORTHSIDE. I'M IN RELIGION LEARNING HOW TO BE A NUN XOX

It was a joke between them. From one of their days out in

town – Maisie had looked a bit bewildered when Paula had mentioned that one of her mother's aunts had been a nun. Maisie hadn't really known what a nun was. They'd got hot chocolates in Starbucks and googled nuns for hours.

HI SISTER MAISIE. HOPE YOUR FEELIN HOLY! XOX

She'd made a cartoon of Charlo. Over the years – that was what she'd done. He'd become a pet, at her side when she wanted him there. He'd behaved like she'd wanted him to, in her head. She'd assembled the best parts of him – she'd put together the man who'd made her gasp the first time she'd seen him, the fella who'd made her laugh. She'd never forgotten the reality. Her body would never have let her. The reminders were all over the place. Every inch of the house was full of jolts. The Little Museum of Charlo – even if Nicola had tried to fill it with new things and fresh paint. It hadn't been for Paula's sake she'd done it, painted over the evidence – Paula knew that now.

She looked at the ceiling, at Nicola right over her. Through the plaster and the boards, the dust balls and the base of the bed, the mattress.

She thought of Joe. She missed him, suddenly. His dependability, his lessons – history, ornithology, every bloody subject – his books and his hearing aids on the little table beside his bed.

—I'll put them back in if I see you're asking me a question.

—There's nothing wrong with your hearing, Joe – they're only for show.

—Sorry, Paula – I missed that. Did you say something about snow?

—You're gas.

—Your skin – here, look. It's as white as snow.

—I'm Mary's little lamb now, am I?

—And I'm the shepherd.

—And you want to ride the sheep and not poor Mary, is that it?

—Nursery rhymes aren't my strong suit. I apologise.

—And Mary's the shepherd, by the way.

—I'll read it later.

—You do that, and then you can explain it to me.

She was smiling. She could feel it cracking her face. He'd laughed. He wasn't just the dry oul' shite she'd been making herself remember. She'd have liked a bit of his company now – a walk, a chat.

HI JOE. HOW ARE THINGS WITH YOU? X

All the right grammar went into her texts to Joe – like his to her – no shortcuts with the spellings. What the fuck was she doing, though, with Nicola upstairs? Nearly flirting with him, hoping to. She was distracting herself – it was okay, it was permitted. For a little while.

She'd two new mugs, teabags ready, trapped under two spoons. She poured the water into the mugs. She'd check the rest of the messages before she went back up.

She had the idea as she was picking up the phone again. Brilliant, brilliant – she was a genius.

TONY NICOLAS AFTER TESTING POSITIVE. BOTH OF US. SHES OK TALK LATER

She read it again and sent it.

And a different one for Lily.

LILY YOUR MAM IS AFTER TESTING POSITIVE SHES FINE SENDS HER LOVE AND SO DO I XX

She sent it.

She half-expected the bed to be empty, the bedroom window wide open. But Nicola was propped up where she'd left her.

—I'm back, she said.

Nicola said nothing.

—As you can probably see, said Paula.

She heard herself yapping – she was a fuckin' eejit. *Spot on, Paula.* Charlo was in the room. The bastard had slid in past her. He was leaning against the windowsill. Smirking.

Nicola made room – she shifted herself a bit nearer the wall as Paula brought the tray to the bed.

—Problem's solved, anyway, said Paula.

Nicola was looking at her.

—What problem? she said.

—I told Tony we're after testing positive, said Paula.

—Why?

—He'll leave us alone, said Paula. —And he'll tell the girls.

Nicola was looking out the open door.

—Okay, she said.

—It makes sense, said Paula. —When you think about it.

Agree with me, you bitch, or praise me – just fuckin' agree,
at least.

—Okay, Nicola said again.

—It'll make things a bit easier, said Paula.

She looked out the window before she sat. The all-weather
pitch was empty again. There were seagulls nesting on the flat
roof of the clubhouse – it was definitely a nest, in against what
might have been the water tank. They were herring gulls – Joe
lesson No. 247. They were huge, the pair of them – central
defenders. She was smiling. She liked herself when she thought
up things like that.

She heard Nicola move in the bed, she heard the spoon in
the mug, before Nicola spoke.

—How?

Paula turned.

—How what, Nicola?

Nicola was holding her mug close to her face. She looked
like she'd just woken up. She looked curious.

—How did I get tested? she asked.

—The test centre, said Paula. —Croke Park – I think it is.

—How did I get there?

—You drove, said Paula. —Your car's outside.

—Is it?

—It must be. It's how you got here last night. Isn't it?

Nicola put her mug on the tray. She lifted herself a bit,
careful not to shake the tray too much – she was looking at it
as she hoisted herself.

—I don't know, she said. —I haven't a clue.

—Jesus, said Paula. —I kind of took it for granted. I think I saw you with your key – your car key. When you came into the house. Hang on.

She put her mug on the windowsill. There wasn't a sniff of Charlo in the room. There was just the two of them, Paula and Nicola. She went to the door.

—D'you really not remember how you got here? she asked.

Nicola shook her head, once, after a second.

—No.

—Back in a tick, said Paula.

She went out, and into her bedroom. It felt like she hadn't been in here in ages – she was back home after a holiday. The curtains were shut. That was weird too – she'd opened them the day before, before she'd gone with Mary and Mandy for her Covid jab. That was only a day ago – Jesus, less than twenty-four hours. She pulled open one of the curtains and there, outside the Polish family's house next door, was Nicola's car. Her Hyundai Accent – properly parked, as far as Paula could see. Pomegranate red – a red that needed another word beside it to do it justice. Paula had written the names – the car and the colour – on a piece of paper after Nicola had brought her for a drive in it. It must have been two years ago. She'd written the names down after she'd got home, so she could tell everyone – Mary, Jack, Joe. The smell of a brand-new car – if she ever smelt one again she'd think of Nicola, no one else.

She remembered now why the curtains had been closed. She'd come in quickly last night and changed into her pyjamas and dressing gown. Her clothes were on the bed – Exhibit A. Exhibits A, B, C and D. The knickers have seen better days, your honour.

—You drove, she said just before she got to the door of Jack's room. —Your car's outside.

She was hoping she'd see Nicola smiling.

She wasn't.

She shrugged, and slipped a little in the bed. A funny moment, Paula thought, but Nicola still wasn't smiling.

—Okay, she said.

—Still not remember?

—I'm not sure, said Nicola.

—Not to worry, said Paula. —It'll come back.

That was a load of shite. Paula had forgotten big chunks of her life and they'd never be coming back. She'd read that book, *The Girl on the Train*, and the description of the main girl in it, the alcoholic girl, not being able to remember things and being told that she wouldn't be remembering them because there was no memory after you blacked out, because blacking out was a form of death – it had all made sense to Paula. She remembered feeling grateful when she finished reading that book.

The wine – the wine last night.

That was why she'd half-expected to find the bed empty a few minutes ago, the window open, a sheet hanging out the window where Nicola had climbed down to the garden – and Nicola in the kitchen screwing the top off the bottle. But that wasn't Nicola – it was herself that Paula had been imagining.

—What about you? said Nicola.

—What about me? said Paula.

—How did you get tested?

—Same as you – did I not come with you?

—Is that even allowed?

—What?

—Are you not supposed to go on your own?

This was good – it was fun.

—I don't know, said Paula. —Will I look it up? My phone's downstairs. Like – what if you can't drive or you don't have a car? Like me.

—Okay.

—There's no way a taxi would take me, said Paula. —Is there?

—Don't know.

—Come here, but, said Paula. —You're the one that matters. The girls don't need to know if I was tested.

—You don't get the results there, said Nicola. —In the place – the centre. They're sent off to Germany or America first.

215

—Shit, said Paula. —Shit. Shit. Damn.

Nicola laughed.

—You've been caught out. Hon.

—Fuck.

Paula had never been happier – she thought that was true.

—Will he know?

—What?

—Tony – will he know that the tests go off to Germany and that?

—Oh yeah, he will, said Nicola. —Half of his side have had it.

—Okay.

—They love their super-spreaders.

—Ah, fuck it, said Paula.

She sat. She leaned back and took the mug off the window-sill. It didn't seem to matter now, results or no results. Nicola would get up soon and go home. She was fine there, in the bed.

—What'll you say, though? said Paula. —After me telling him you have the Covid.

—I don't get you, said Nicola.

—When you go home, said Paula.

—I'm not, said Nicola. —You didn't hear me.

—I did, said Paula. —I did.

—I'm not going home, said Nicola. —I told you that.

—I know, said Paula. —I did hear you.

—I don't have to stay here –.

—'Course you have to stay here, Nicola, said Paula. —I told you. You can stay as long as you like. I told you.

—I went and got tested, said Nicola. —I have all the symptoms, so the results will be a formality.

—Perfect.

—And you're the same, said Nicola.

—Brilliant.

Nicola had hijacked Paula's plan. Nicola was the adult again, Paula the eejit who needed looking after. What had happened? Who'd done the swap?

Nicola was still in the bed. Paula was still the nurse.

—D'you want some water?

—No.

—Sure?

—Yeah.

—Nicola.

—What?

—I'm sorry.

She waited for Nicola to say something. She felt herself leaning forward. But she stopped. Nicola didn't have to say anything. Paula had said her bit – that was what mattered. She wondered what time it was. She was hungry.

Nothing. Not a word. Neither of them moved. It was okay. It wasn't too bad. It felt like work, though – hard work, real effort – just sitting there. But that was okay as well. It was right and proper. Who was going to speak first, though? They couldn't stay like this forever. Paula's eyes felt raw – or, boiled. The wrong size for their sockets.

—D'you want anything? she asked.

—No, said Nicola.

—You're not a bit hungry, no?

—No.

—Grand.

—Are you?

—No, said Paula. —No.

—You are.

—I'm not, said Paula. —What you told me there –.

Nicola looked at her. Straight at her.

—What you said, said Paula. —About me being passed out and – like – everything. I'm sorry.

—Okay.

—Thank you.

Paula smiled at Nicola. Nicola wasn't looking at her.

—I don't think –, said Paula.

—What?

—Well, said Paula. —Like – back then. I don't think –.

Shut up – shut up, for fuck sake!

—I don't think we knew as much, she said. —As we do now. We weren't as alert – I don't think.

Jesus Christ, she was a fuckin' fool. She couldn't keep her stupid mouth shut. *Spot on, Paula.* She'd just taken back her apology. And she didn't believe a word of what she'd just said.

—Sorry, Nicola – sorry – I didn't say that. I did – obviously, but –. It's shite.

—I know it is.

—It's a bag of lies – a pack of lies, I mean. It was just automatic – making excuses. And there aren't any. I'm sorry.

—Okay, said Nicola.

—End of.

—Yeah.

—I knew girls, said Paula.

She wondered what she was going to say – she actually wondered. Even as she was speaking. What trap was she walking herself into now? But this time it felt right. Her throat was tight. Her eyes were even bigger, fuller – sorer. She was telling Nicola the truth.

—When I was a young one, she said. —Girls in school and around. And Jesus, Nicola – we used to joke about it. Like – uncles pawing them when their mas and das weren't looking. And even brothers. But like I said – we joked about it. Christ knows what went on.

She sat back.

—No, she said. —We knew.

She looked at Nicola.

—We knew. We knew it happened – it could happen.

She stopped. She thought she was going to cry – she thought she might even have been trying to make herself cry. But she didn't want to. It wasn't her right.

—Your grandda was harsh, she said.

—Harsh?

—Yeah, said Paula. —Tough. Severe.

—Did he ever –?

218

—No, said Paula. —No. Never. But your Aunt Carmel hinted that he'd – done things to her. But – d'you know what, Nicola?

She sat up straight again. She was stiff – a bit cold. Frightened.

—I wouldn't let her, she said.

—What?

—I wouldn't let her speak, said Paula. —I wasn't having it. I colluded – is that the word? It is. I colluded with them – the church and them. I wouldn't let her tell me what she wanted to tell me. I think that's what happened everywhere.

She looked straight at Nicola.

—That's my opinion, she said. —That's my tuppence worth. We hid behind the jokes. We're fuckin' gas – the Irish. I have to go for a wee – sorry.

—So do I.

—Me first. Age before beauty, hon.

She leaned against the bathroom door. Just for a second. She wasn't going to vomit – she felt like she already had. She had, but that time – downstairs, at the sink – felt so long ago, or something she'd imagined.

She didn't delay or overthink. She did her business, washed her hands and went back to Nicola – who was on the landing right in front of the bathroom door, waiting for Paula to come out.

—Jesus –!

Nicola slipped past her and shut the door. Paula hesitated. Would she go back into Jack's room or downstairs for a bit? She went into Jack's room and she was looking out at the seagulls when Nicola came back in.

—Come here, she said.

—What?

—Just come here and look.

Nicola stood beside Paula.

—See? said Paula. —Over there – on the roof. The herring gulls.

Nicola turned away and got back into the bed.

Paula felt foolish now, and she resented it. It was hard to read

219

what was happening. Outside, on the landing – one woman going into the bathroom, the other one coming out – it had been comical, something they'd been sharing. Now, she just felt like an eejit – her and her fuckin' herring gulls. With her second-hand knowledge. She wasn't even positive they were herring gulls.

She stayed at the window. She didn't know what to do. She was exhausted – and wired. And frightened. And wretched. The momentum was gone. They were back where they'd started. But that wasn't true. Everything was different. Nicola had said things and Paula had said things. And they were still in the same room.

—What did Tony say? she said.

Her voice – she nearly surprised herself. It was like she hadn't expected to hear herself speak – she didn't think she'd be up to it. She sat down as she spoke. She was pleased – nervous. Happy – sick. She wondered if she actually had spoken – Nicola didn't seem to have heard her. She was lying down again. Paula thought about slipping out quietly. She'd go into her room and lie down for a while.

—I didn't tell him, said Nicola. —I told you.

—Not at all, though? said Paula. —Not afterwards, no?

—No, said Nicola. —What would I have told him?

—That his brother's a dirtbird, said Paula.

—What would the point of that be? said Nicola.

—I don't know.

—Yeah – well.

Paula waited. Were they finished?

—I couldn't, said Nicola. —Yeah –. I couldn't.

—Okay, said Paula. —It couldn't have been easy.

—It didn't happen, said Nicola. —So it wasn't anything.

—Okay, said Paula.

Jesus, Jesus, Jesus.

—What d'you want to do, Nicola?

—Honestly?

—Yes.

—I want to die.

It sounded different this time. Flatter – more sincere. Paula pulled herself back – she didn't rush in. She said nothing. She hoped she'd hear Nicola crying. But Nicola didn't cry.

Paula stood up. Pain shot through her – up, from the base of her spine, right through her. She sat on the bed. She put her back against the wall – she pushed herself back against it. She pulled her legs, her feet, up onto the bed. She waited till her back calmed down – it wasn't too bad. She put her right hand out and rested it on Nicola's head.

—Love, she said.

Nicola didn't speak. She didn't move.

—Love, said Paula again.

She left her hand on Nicola's head. She'd done it when Nicola was a child – when they were all children. When they were in bed. When she remembered.

The way she was sitting – it wasn't doing her any good. It was torture, it was agony. She let herself slide. *Not for the first time, Paula.* She lay flat on her back. She put her hand on Nicola's head again but it was awkward now, the way she was lying. So she gave it up. She looked up at Beyoncé. She loved the idea of Jack gazing up at that woman. She loved the fact that she'd never noticed her up there before. She loved that it was Nicola who'd pointed her out to Paula.

She listened, but she couldn't make out if Nicola was sleeping.

—I could get used to this, she said softly.

She turned her head a bit to the left, so she could look out the window. There was a gull out there – one of the neighbours – hovering, floating. Then it seemed to sway, effortlessly. One flap of the wings – Paula thought she heard it. Gone.

The day had moved. The light was different. She didn't know the time but she knew she'd slept for an hour. She just knew. She was hungry. Seriously hungry. But it was lovely, lying like

221

this. She'd have happily stayed this way till she faded away – Nicola asleep, herself half-asleep. But she'd have to get up. She'd have to cook, check her phone. She'd have to keep the world outside away.

It was livelier out there, and next door. The little girls were home from school – they were bombing up and down the stairs. She could hear traffic even though she was in the back of the house. Cars and people on the other streets – the engines felt further away, like she was on a raft off the coast.

She was on a raft, herself and Nicola. They could stay out here – up here, in here – as long as they wanted. As long as they stayed asleep or half-asleep. As long as they could drift. As long as they didn't have to talk. Didn't have to deny or apologise, or accuse or beg. They were floating on the sea, on salt water – tears. The tears that Nicola wouldn't cry. That was it, though – the sea was made of tears that had already been cried. Paula's, her mother's – every woman who'd ever lived. Their tears were keeping Nicola afloat. And Paula. As long as they said nothing. Beyoncé was the sun up there. Or the moon, pulling them along, like the moon did to the tides. This could go on forever, as long as they were just friends on the raft, side by side and silent, not mother and daughter. Not addict and victim. She could hear the gulls out there, having a row or a laugh – or warning her. They were drifting towards the shore – the shore was drifting towards them.

She was too hungry to keep this going. She wasn't going to be able to drift again, to wake up further along the day, in different light and sounds. This was the quiet bit in the horror film, just before the shock. But she'd already had the shocks. This was the calm after the storm. She hoped. The calm between the storms. Probably. Whatever it was, it was great.

But she was hungry and as far as she remembered there was nothing to eat in the house. It felt like years since she'd stood in front of the fridge.

She'd have to sort something.

Grabbing the man's leg – that was the best thing about

watching a horror film. She'd always loved it, with Charlo and boys before Charlo. And Joe. Grabbing their legs and making them jump. Manhandling them. When the head burst through the door or the hand came up out of the toilet or the little girl in the red coat was actually a knife-wielding little oul' one in a red coat – she'd make the men jump. The sex was always great after a horror.

Enough.

She had to get up. She had to catch up. She had to be a mother. I want to die. That was what Nicola had said. The last thing she'd said to Paula. A few hours' kip in her little brother's bed wasn't going to make that wish go away.

Feet out from under the duvet, then she turned on her side and slid off the bed. She was fine, her back was grand. The rest – the break – had done her good. Nicola had the Covid, and so did Paula – she reminded herself of that as she went down the stairs. It was brilliant, though – the story, the big fib. She loved it. They'd be living the lie, the pair of them.

It was darker at the front of the house. She was in the hall and – like that – she'd come back down to earth. They could pretend they had the plague but Nicola was probably suicidal. And Paula – she was devastated. And angry. She shouldn't have climbed off the raft. Fuck the raft – there was no raft.

She went into the kitchen and it was brighter – earlier again.

—Fridge or phone, fridge or phone?

She was muttering to herself. There was still a bit of life in her.

She went for the phone. There was a text from Mary.

LOOK OUT YR DOOR XX

That would be food. Mary had left a bag for her on the step. Two bags, probably. Opening the fridge would be easier now. Guilt wouldn't get a look-in.

TANX X BADLY NEEDED!! WE HAVE THE COVID BTW WERE GRAND JST FEELIN A BIT SHTE X

She'd tell Mary, eventually, that their Covid was a lie, a spoof. Mary would love it. Paula was tempted to send her a text now, tell her the truth, get the crack going between them. But she didn't give in to it. She wasn't doing this for the crack.

There was a text from Tony – just the one.

OK. HOW IS SHE?

She thought about this one. She wanted to worry and to reassure him – both.

NOT GREAT BUT NOT 2 BAD

I'm not too bad either, thanks for asking – prick. She'd never thought of Tony in that way before – the possibility that he could be a prick. Grand was the word she'd always have attached to Tony. Dependable, steady, handsome, soft, a bit dull, but – most importantly – grand. She'd seen him changing nappies. She'd seen him cooking – he cooked more often than Nicola. She'd seen him watching *The Devil Wears Prada* with the girls, giving it and them all of his attention, laughing at them laughing. He'd helped Nicola carry Paula up the stairs. And after – after the drinking stopped – he always made sure he was looking straight at her when he asked her how she was.

But maybe he was a prick. Maybe he was a prick too.

All would be revealed.

Jesus.

She finished the text.

BIT OF A TEMP AND COUGHING A BIT BUT OK

She sent it to Tony and put the phone on the table. She couldn't wait any longer. She was dying to see what Mary had left her. Nothing too healthy, she hoped. She'd have eaten a Swiss roll. She'd have demolished the thing, then pushed the wrapper to the bottom of the bin. She was a bit giddy, maddened by the hunger. No, she wasn't – she was entertaining herself, distracting herself.

It was funny – not so long ago, they'd never have left anything on their steps. Not around here. Whatever it was – food, drink, old clothes, videos, a kitten – it would have been gone in seconds. Charlo would never have passed a bag on a step.

She was worried again, a bit low – cold. There was something about the hall. She never got to the door without memories – the bad stuff – grabbing at her, trying to stop her, slapping her hand as it reached for the latch. And opening the door – it was never good, never only good. It didn't matter why she was opening it, where she was going or how excited she was – the dread was always with her. In her. And now, she was still in her dressing gown. She hated that, the lazy slut – there'd be people passing. The bag would be out of reach, too far to get at without letting go of the door. She'd be on the step, locked out – in this state. Banging on the glass, hoping Nicola was awake, her phone on the table in the kitchen. A shadow always crept up to her when she went too near the front door. *Going anywhere?*

She opened it. She'd forgotten to double-lock it the night before.

She saw nothing. The bag she'd been anticipating – Centra, or Lidl, a big supermarket bag – wasn't there. Maybe the old days weren't quite over and someone had robbed it, seen Mary hauling it through the gate and waited till she'd texted Paula and left. Some bitch was shovelling Paula's Swiss roll into her gob, looking at Paula from one of the houses across the way.

She saw the bag – a bag. At her feet. A paper bag, folded up, almost flat. She bent down and picked it up. It wasn't food – it was nearly weightless. A Dunnes bag. She knew what it was before she looked. And she was right. It was a cardigan – a pink cardigan. Mary had said she'd get her one. Fuckin' pink as well. And she'd have to wear it – Mary would have to see it on her. She wanted to laugh. She wanted to bring it upstairs and show it to Nicola, explain what had happened, what she thought she'd be finding on the step and what she'd got instead.

She didn't feel as hungry now, as desperate.

She had her hand on the fridge when the bell rang. She thought she'd been electrocuted. She jumped – she did. She groaned.

She wasn't going to answer it – she wasn't going back to the door.

Her phone buzzed, on the table.

It was Tony.

LEFT SOME STUFF OUTSIDE. X

A bag of food – it had to be. It wouldn't be another cardigan.

He'd be outside, at the gate. He'd be nervous about leaving the bag unguarded. He'd be worried that they'd both slipped into unconsciousness or were coughing themselves to death. She'd go out and wave. Where was her mask? Upstairs – it was up in the back pocket of her jeans. It was just as well she hadn't got showered and dressed. She was guessing she looked the part, like something diseased.

She opened the door. She grabbed the bottom of her dressing gown and brought it up, over her face. She pulled the door open and got her foot in front of it, to make sure it didn't close on her. She saw the bags before she saw Tony. Two SuperValu bags, leaning against each other. She could see a net of oranges, carrots, a thin bar of chocolate.

She saw Tony. She was right – he was at the gate.

—Ah, thanks, Tony, she called out.

She sounded too healthy – she nearly laughed.

—I don't have a mask, hon, she said – weaker.

—How is she? he asked.

He looked worried. He looked tired.

—She's sleeping, she said. —Can you hear me?

—Yeah.

—Yeah – she's sleeping. She's fine – she'll be grand. Thanks for this, Tony, though – you're a star.

—Go on back in, he said.

—I will, yeah.

She grabbed a handle and pulled a bag towards her, and behind her, into the hall. She did the same with the other bag.

—How are you feeling, Paula? she heard him.

—Grand, she said. —Not too bad. Considering. It hasn't really hit me yet, I don't think.

—Give her my love, yeah?

She was closing the door as she spoke.

—'Course I will, she said. —And I'll keep you posted – don't worry.

She had the door nearly shut when she heard Tony.

—How come you got the results so quickly?

—What?

—How come yis got the test results so quickly?

She'd opened the door a bit more, so she could see him as he spoke. He wasn't trying to catch her out – that wasn't on his face.

—They just knew, said Paula. —By the state of us. They told us to get home and isolate, the results aren't going to be a surprise.

She thought she was getting away with it. She opened the door a bit more.

—And anyway, sure, we have to keep isolated till we get the results, she said. —Regardless.

—Yeah, said Tony. —Yeah – I was just wondering.

—Grand, said Paula. —Seeyeh.

She waved and shut the door. She pushed it, to make sure it was properly locked. She was parched – lying always made her thirsty. She hadn't thought the thing out properly, though – the path, the consequences. Was there anything else that could trip her up? She'd think about it later – she'd talk it through with Nicola, if Nicola was talking.

She looked down at the bags. She knew – they were heavy and she'd already been stupid pulling them. Jesus, though – the excitement. She carried the stuff, four or five things at a time, from the hall to the kitchen table.

She opened the chocolate and broke off three cubes. She could feel it melting, crawling all around her mouth, flowing into her blood. She had to sit down, to get over the shock. It was the only way to eat chocolate – when you were starving. She wouldn't be greedy, though. Tony hadn't been thinking of her when he'd picked this chocolate off the shelf. Dark, with chilli in it. Grown-up chocolate. It was the best thing she'd tasted since the last time she'd had a drink.

Jesus – where had that thought come from?

From her heart, from her blood. From every cell of her.

It was fine, though. It wasn't gin or heroin. It was only fuckin' chocolate.

And this – the growing pile on the table. It was a relief, an old feeling. There'd be food in the fridge – there'd be treats for the child.

She got up and went back out to the hall. There were no demons this time, no shadows. She stood at the foot of the stairs. She heard nothing from up there. Nicola was asleep. Or resting. She might have heard Tony's voice, and Paula's. She'd be listening to Paula now coming and going. She'd know that she was being looked after.

Charlo had often given her chocolate. A Toblerone after a hiding. She'd always eaten it. Shared it with the kids. Or hidden it till they were all out of the house or asleep.

Tony wasn't Charlo.

She hadn't opened the fridge yet. She was still piling the stuff on the table. Getting her exercise. She'd one bag empty. The difference between what she normally bought for herself and what Tony and Nicola bought – it wasn't just money. Broccoli stems – they looked like the bits she'd have thrown out, the bits you cut off to get to the broccoli. Corn on the cob – the whole yoke. Happy Pear sun-dried tomato pesto. It wasn't all bad, though – she smiled at the thought – it wasn't all healthy. There was a tub of Ben and Jerry's ice cream – some stupid name on it but it looked like vanilla. There was a big pack of Keogh's crisps – lightly salted.

Nicola had made a middle-class woman out of herself. Paula looked at what Tony had delivered and she realised that she'd seen it all before, in the kitchens of the houses she used to clean. Did Nicola have a cleaner? Paula didn't know. The thought made her giddy, a bit sick. An Irish one, or a foreigner? Someone from around here, even a woman she knew? It was mental.

She'd always known that Nicola had been making more of herself, right from the get-go, from the day she'd come home from the sewing factory, the day they'd closed it down – Nicola had been seventeen – and told Paula that she wanted to do something with her life. Paula had known she would and she'd cheered her every step of the way. But the food here – it was the proof that she'd never really noticed before. It wasn't like the food – the quality of it, the packaging – that Nicola had brought for Paula, when Paula had needed it.

It was gas.

But there wasn't the makings of a stew. There was a bag of carrots but no spuds, and no meat – no stewing steak or chicken thighs or sausages. There'd be no stew smell – the aroma crawling up the stairs to Nicola.

She'd emptied the first bag. The second one was full of ready-made meals. It surprised her – it didn't disappoint her. Puncture the lid and throw it in the microwave. Happy days, but it still shocked her a bit. She was putting at least a week's worth of processed grub on the table. She was shoving other things aside to make room for the chicken kormas and lasagnes. She was catching another glimpse of Nicola's life, a laziness she'd never have shown to Paula. Then it struck her – they were sick, they had the Covid. Tony had bought convenience food, effortless food, stuff they could eat without using every pot and knife in the house.

Then, at the bottom of the bag, she found a white paper chemist's bag. She ripped it open – paracetamol, Lemsip – apple and cinnamon. And there was Lypsyl – two of them. One for Nicola and one for Paula. She held hers and sat again.

Tony wasn't Charlo. It was official.

What was Nicola doing up there? Why wasn't she at home? She had a man who brought her pesto and Lypsyl, who clearly knew his way around a supermarket. She hadn't married her father, that was for sure.

She took the wrapping off her Lypsyl, and the top, and put it to her bottom lip.

Nicola was at the door.

—Hiyeh, hon – love.

—Where did all this come from?

—Tony.

—Was Tony here – was he in here?

—No, said Paula.

She felt caught out but she didn't know how, or why.

—He left it all outside, she said. —And he texted me.

—Oh –.

—He sends his love, by the way.

—You were talking to him?

—At the door only, said Paula. —He was at the gate. I made myself sound feeble – don't worry.

—What?

—We've both got the Covid, remember?

—Oh –, said Nicola. —Yeah.

It wasn't a joke, a bit of fun. Paula could see that on Nicola's face. They were sharing nothing. Nicola looked drugged, half-alive. Maybe she actually did have the Covid.

—Are you hungry, love?

Nicola looked cold.

—Nicola?

—What?

—Are you hungry?

—No, said Nicola. —I mean – I might be. What is there?

—It's all here, look it. There's everything – it looks like. He's spoiling us. Lasagne, chicken korma – looks delish, that one. Cottage pie, chicken tikka masala. Or maybe plain pasta – would you like that?

—Any cornflakes?

—Ah, shite, hon, said Paula. —I don't think so.

She looked at the table, everything on it, and hoped to see the cornflakes she knew weren't there.

—No.

She even looked around the kitchen, as if she was visiting, in someone else's house.

—No – sorry.

She could run down to the Centra. No one would see her, no one who mattered. Someone would see her – everyone would see her. She'd blow their cover. She'd never get this chance back.

230

She found her phone under the chicken tikka masala. Mary had texted her.

A JEEZUS DATS SHITE NEED ANTING? XX

Paula brought the phone up to her face. It seemed to be getting darker in the kitchen.

CORNFLAKES. THANKS FOR CARDY BTW LUV IT XX

She took off her dressing gown and picked the cardigan up off the floor, where she'd shoved it when she was making room for the food on the table. She held it by the shoulders and gave it a shake.

—What's that? said Nicola.

—An elephant, Nicola, said Paula. —What's it look like?

—It looks like it would fit one, anyway.

—Feck off, said Paula.

She was thrilled, relieved – the real Nicola was lurking behind the dummy. Jesus, though – the ups and downs.

Her phone buzzed.

NO BOTHER. ANTING ELSE? XX

Paula opened the fridge, finally. She took out the carton of milk and held it, weighed it. She put it back.

MILK.

—Is ordinary milk okay with you, Nicola?

Nicola nodded, once.

Paula thought about bread. She'd ask Mary to get her a large sliced pan. But she saw something that she hadn't taken much notice of when she was piling the stuff on the table. A nice-looking old-fashioned pan of white bread, in a clear plastic bag.

BUTTER STEWING STEAK A FEW SPUDS XX

She sent it off.

—You'll have your cornflakes in twenty minutes, madame, she said.

—How come?

—Mary's getting them, said Paula. —She gave me this.

She was putting the cardigan on over her pyjama top. She

didn't like pink but she knew it suited her. So she'd been told. More than once. Joe had told her. It might have been the only time he'd said something like that, about how she looked. That wasn't true either – he'd often complimented her and she'd often liked his compliments and sometimes – only a few times – they'd given her the creeps. But she remembered now – she'd gone shopping with Joe. She'd forgotten that – she'd forgotten a lot. Artaine Castle – they'd gone to the Tesco's there. And she'd made him come into Penneys with her. He hadn't objected – he hadn't said he'd wait outside. He'd followed her in, he'd stood beside her, he hadn't sighed or looked at his watch, or taken out his phone. And he'd told her that the pink jacket she'd tried on – she remembered now, it had been too tight under the arms – he'd told her it was lovely on her, and that pink – all those jackets had been pink – was her colour.

She'd texted him earlier. Had she texted him? She was sure she had. She'd check in a minute to see if he'd answered, or if she'd texted him in the first place.

—I hate the sleeves of these things, she said now. —They're always too tight.

She'd been talking to Nicola but Nicola wasn't there.

Panic dropped through Paula. She looked at the press where she'd put the wine earlier. It was shut, but that didn't mean anything. Too busy being sexy in pink – she hadn't noticed Nicola. She opened the press. She saw the bottles where she'd left them – it was herself she was checking up on. Paula was tracking Paula. Nicola was probably up in the toilet. Or back in Jack's bed.

Paula turned on the cold water. She filled a mug. She drank it in one go. It always helped. It washed out the jitters, it dampened the nerve ends.

She went to the kitchen door.

—Nicola?

—What?

Nicola was in the lounge.

—Are you in there?

—Yeah.

—D'you want anything?

Paula didn't know why she was lingering at the kitchen door. She did know – she was nervous. She couldn't help it. She kept anticipating what she, herself, would have done – how she'd have escaped or got what she needed. She went to the lounge door. Nicola's face was lit by her phone.

—I'll leave you to it, said Paula.

—Leave me to what?

—Whatever you're doing.

—I'm not doing anything, said Nicola.

—Grand, said Paula. —Would you like anything else, while you're waiting for your cornflakes?

—I don't care, said Nicola. —Whatever you're having.

—Nothing you crave, no?

—Crave?

—Want.

—I'm not pregnant, Mammy.

Paula laughed.

—Will I open the curtains?

—It's your house – do what you want.

Paula went to the window and took hold of the curtains. She wanted to pull them off the rail and fling them over Nicola. There, yeh bitch – that's what I want. Abracadabra – fuck off. She half-expected to see faces on the other side of the glass – Tony, the girls, Joe. But it was just the garden and the wall and the gate, and the houses across the way.

—Nothing to report out there, she said.

She glanced at Nicola. She looked pale, wrecked – uncared for. Being Nicola had always been work – Paula knew that. The woman who stepped out of her house every day was a brand. She'd told Paula that, herself. She'd been joking, smiling, and looking like a million dollars.

Whoever it was on the couch now, she wasn't a brand.

She was Nicola.

—What about a toastie? said Paula.

The toasted sandwich maker – another present from madam – was in the same press as the wine. She'd seen it, pushed to the back, when she'd opened the press a few minutes ago. It was still in the box, and Paula had never used it. It wasn't new. It was an old one of Nicola's, although it wasn't old.

Nicola looked up from the phone screen.

—Yeah, she said.

—You wouldn't say no to a toastie?

—Yeah –. No.

—Grand, said Paula. —Leave it with me.

She nearly skipped out of the lounge. There were tomatoes on the table, and she'd seen cheese. There was the lovely bread. She was sure there was enough butter left in the tub to scrape across the bread – she wouldn't have to wait for Mary.

She needed a chair to reach the sandwich maker.

She wondered now why she'd put it so out of reach.

Because she'd hated the thing. The handout, the charity – fuck her.

She took it out of the box and put the box back in the press. She didn't want Nicola seeing it, and wondering why Paula still had it. Mind you, it had been in the stupid box when Nicola had brought it into the house. Nicola had kept the box, so she'd probably always intended passing it on to Paula.

She was down off the chair and she'd plugged in the sand-wich maker. She'd two slices of the bread cut, buttered. She'd been right – there'd been just enough. She'd had to be careful spreading it, the bread was so fresh. The tomatoes were those little ones – cherry tomatoes. She popped one into her mouth, and bit. God, it was lovely – she'd always liked tomatoes. There was a packet of cheese – flat slices – Emmental. Mental cheese – you've come to the right place, hon. She tore a bit off a slice and put it into her mouth. It was nice – a bit bland, maybe. That was one of Joe's words – bland. He was a bit of that, himself. That wasn't fair. But it kind of was.

The butter was supposed to go on the outside. She'd never really understood why and she didn't give much of a shite – the home economics lesson could wait. In her mind, in her hands, on her skin – she was being watched. She looked at the kitchen door – Nicola wasn't there. She felt like she was on the telly, in a programme. *Now I take the mental cheese – its blandness brings out the flavour of the tomatoes, I always think.* One slice was enough, she reckoned. *We don't want to overdo it.*

She was losing it. She could see it – her hands were shaking. Her head was skipping all over the place. She had four of the cherry tomatoes and she'd forgotten what she was supposed to be doing with them. She knew, but her mind kept running on ahead, or back. She was nervous of the knife.

She sliced the tomatoes. Mission accomplished, she rewarded herself with another one for herself. She put the tomato halves on top of the cheese. *Like four sets of red eyes staring back at me, I always think. My kids – ha ha.* She lifted the sandwich off the plate. She was in luck – the bottom slice of bread wasn't sticking. *We're poxed today, ladies.* She lowered the sandwich onto the hotplate – she supposed that was what it was called – then brought down the top, the lid, and pressed until she could lock it into place. She heard the hiss – she could already smell the cheese.

She found her phone.

Joe had answered her.

PHONE ME, PLEASE. JOE

What sort of an answer was that? She looked at the text she'd sent him.

HI JOE. HOW ARE THINGS WITH YOU? X

What was going on? *He's found someone else, Paula. Fuck off. A younger model. Fuck off. Sixty or so – some bird who appreciates him. Fuck off. Another pink bird, wha'.*

Nicola was at the kitchen door.

—Did you say something there?

—No, said Paula. —At least – I hope not. Joe wants me to phone him, she said.

Nicola knew Joe – of course, she did. They'd met a few times. She didn't like him. Paula was pretty sure of that. She'd smiled whenever she saw him but there'd never been warmth in the smile. But, Paula thought now – only now – she'd never seen Nicola's face light up for anyone. Except her girls.

Jesus, this was dreadful. It was unbearable.

—I'd better phone him, I suppose, she said.

She lifted the lid of the toastie maker. It was easier than looking at Nicola.

—This looks ready, she said.

Nicola was right behind her.

Checking on her. The old Nicola.

But she wasn't. She was looking at the things Tony had brought them and that meant squeezing in between Paula and the table.

Paula got the knife in under the toastie. She slid it onto the plate.

—There now.

There now. Enjoy. See yis all next week.

There wasn't room for both of them in the kitchen. Paula couldn't cope. She held the plate out and grabbed her phone.

—Back in a minute, she said.

She stopped at the door – she didn't even know where she was going.

—I just have to phone him, she said. —He'd never have texted me like that if it wasn't urgent.

Urgent.

For fuck sake – unlike what was facing her, her suicidal daughter.

Nicola sat – dropped herself onto one of the chairs. She made room for the plate on the table. She stared at the toastie. She looked around. She stood. She took the knife off the breadboard.

Paula should have hidden the knife. It was what Nicola would have done – *had* done. The knives, the corkscrew, the bottles. Hide and seek with the Spencers – the crack had been ninety.

She watched Nicola sit again.

236

—Back in a bit, hon.

Nicola didn't answer – Paula heard nothing as she went into the lounge, across to the window. Talking to Joe would be easier if she had something to look at. She had Favourites open on her screen. Joe's name was under the children and the grandchildren, and her sister, and Mary.

She'd forgotten about Mary. Paula would be standing at the window when Mary came through the gate with the cornflakes. She stepped back a bit. She sat on the arm of the couch. It wasn't comfortable – her back was giving out, ordering her to get up and back into the kitchen to Nicola. She stood. She tapped Joe's number. She put the phone to her ear. Did he have the Covid? She'd tell him she had it too, in case he wanted her to bring him anything. But he had his kids for that. Whatever he was going to tell her, she'd make sure it was a short call.

—Joe?

—Yes.

—It's Paula.

—Yes.

—You said to phone you, she said.

—Yes, he said. —Yes, I did.

She was frightened now, afraid she was going to hear something bad – he was going to say something horrible.

—Mary died, he said.

—What?

—My wife.

A different Mary – not her Mary. His ex-wife – he was divorced.

—Ah, Joe, she said. —I'm sorry.

—Yes.

—Was it the Covid?

—Yes, he said. —Complications.

—I'm sorry.

—Thank you.

—It's rough.

—Yes, it is.

—When?

—What?

—When did she die, Joe?

—Last week, he said.

—Oh.

—Ten days now.

—Just – when you asked me to phone you –.

—I didn't want to put it in a text, he said.

—No.

—It would have been wrong.

—I know, said Paula. —And listen – I'm really sorry.

She could hardly remember a thing about his Mary. She'd been a teacher – a secondary teacher, English and history, Paula thought. They hadn't slept in the same bed for years before they'd separated. They'd been separated for a long time before they'd divorced. They'd had four kids. Paula had never met them and that – now – annoyed her.

—What age was she, Joe?

—Seventy-one, he said.

—Young enough, said Paula.

That sounded bad, like she was accusing the woman of dying too easily, on purpose.

—Yes, said Joe. —We met in college.

—Yeah.

—She had an underlying condition.

That was typical Joe – underlying condition instead of asthma or cancer or something specific. Maybe he'd been the underlying condition. Charlo definitely had been.

—Ah – it's rough, said Paula. —Did you get to the funeral?

—No.

—Did you not?

—I wasn't one of the ten.

—You didn't sneak in, no?

She could tell – he hadn't understood her. Her gentle joke – she thought it was gentle – had gone straight into one of his hearing aids and out the other. But, really, it hadn't been a joke. She'd have sneaked into a funeral if she'd wanted to pay her respects, if it had been someone she'd once been close to. She'd have marched right in. That was the difference – a difference – between them. Joe couldn't eat a piece of cake without a fork – Paula didn't even need her hands. It was the way they'd been reared, the way they'd grown up. She'd liked it. So had he, she'd thought.

—I'm your bit of rough, she'd said, once. —Amn't I?

—Paula, he'd said. —You are so not rough – as the young people might say.

—Around the edges, but, she'd said. —I am – go on, admit it.

—No.

—I don't mind, she'd said. —I like it – go on.

—Alright, he'd said. —But it's an attractive roughness.

—That's nice, she'd said.

—Very attractive.

There were definitely times when being Joe's friend had been more than going to concerts and learning the names of birds.

—Is anyone there with you, Joe? she asked him now.

—Who?

—Well – one of your kids.

—No, he said. —No.

—D'you want me to come over?

What was she saying? She'd Nicola in the kitchen – she wasn't going anywhere. She just wanted to hear him saying yes. She wanted the option.

—You can't, he said.

—No, she said. —No – I just thought –. The circumstances and that –.

—I'm fine, he said. —But thank you.

—No, she said. —You're right.

She thought of something.

—And anyway, she said. —I have the Covid, myself.

—Do you?

—I do, yeah, she said. —Not too bad, though.

—Good –.

—I'm over the worst of it, I think.

—Paula, he said. —Be careful.

This was terrible. She was terrifying the man – another woman was about to die on him.

—I will, she said. —Don't worry.

—You sound fine.

—Ah, I am. You should've heard me a few days ago, though. I sounded like a duck with asthma.

—I wish you were here with me, Paula, he said.

—I wish I was there too, Joe, said Paula.

Her lie – her coronavirus porky – was having an amazing effect.

—You make me laugh, he said.

—You're not laughing, Joe, she said.

He laughed, and she really wished she was there with him.

—Listen, Joe, she said. —Look it – I've to go, sorry. I've Nicola here with me and she's not great.

—There? he said. —In the house?

—Yeah, said Paula. —She tested positive as well and it made sense for her to come here, away from her kids and the rest of it.

—And she infected you? Is that what happened?

—No, she said. —I'd tested positive already.

She should have just told him to fuck off, the way he was talking.

—It's been great, actually, she said. —Having the company. And listen, our kids don't infect us. Others – yeah, maybe. But not the kids.

—You're right, he said. —How is she?

She'd always had the feeling that Joe wasn't that mad about Nicola. He looked at Nicola and saw what he thought Paula had been like years before – a woman who wouldn't have looked sideways at him.

—Not great, she said quietly.

She was at the door out to the hall, and she closed it over, although she didn't close it completely. She held on to the handle.

240

—She'll be grand, she said. —But she's in bits, God love her.

—I'm sorry to hear that, said Joe. —I'll be thinking of her.

—Thanks.

—And you, he said. —I'll be thinking of you, Paula.

—That's nice, she said. —And I'm really sorry about Mary. It was weird, all the same – the two Marys.

—And you're all alone there, she said. —I'm sorry.

—It won't go on forever.

—If you say so.

—I do, he said. —I'll phone you again – if I may.

—You may, she said.

Somehow, she knew – he was smiling. He'd said that – if I may – so he'd hear her response. Here – now – she really, really missed him.

—Do you need anything, Paula? he asked. —Is there anything you want?

—George Clooney would be nice, Joe.

She heard him laughing.

—I'm fine, she said. —Tony is looking after us.

—Tony?

—Nicola's husband, she said. —You've met him.

—Yes, he said. —Tony.

He hadn't a clue who Tony was.

—He's been dropping stuff in for us, she said.

—That's good, he said. —And really – if you need –.

He'd stopped talking. She heard something, like choking.

—Joe –?

She heard it again.

—Joe – are you crying?

He was crying. It was obvious now – she'd said the word and he'd let her hear him.

—Ah, Joe –.

—I'm sorry.

—There's no need – don't say that.

—I'm sorry –.

Her own eyes were filling.

—You've got me started now, she said.

He tried to laugh – she could hear him.

—I'm very lonely, he said.

—So am I.

She waited. He said nothing else. She wasn't sure if he was still crying. She wasn't sure if he was still there. She heard him sniff.

—I've to go, she said.

—Yes, he said.

—I need to check on Nicola.

—Of course, he said. —Goodbye, Paula.

—Bye bye – phone me tomorrow.

—I will.

—If you want.

—I will.

She took the phone from her ear before he hung up. She put the phone on the arm of the couch and wiped under her eyes with the corner of her dressing gown. She was starting to hate the dressing gown. She sniffed it – it smelt alright. She put her fingers under her eyes. The skin didn't feel too hot. She'd be okay. She *was* okay.

There was another thing she remembered now – about Joe's Mary. She'd left Joe for a woman. How had she forgotten that? It had been – when they'd started going out with each other – by far the most interesting thing about him.

Nicola had put all the stuff away while Paula was talking to Joe.

Half the toastie was still on the plate.

—That for me?

—If you want it, said Nicola.

She was sitting at the table.

Paula sat. Nicola stood.

—What's wrong?

—Nothing.

—Sit down, said Paula. —Unless you're in a hurry, are you? We're isolating, remember.

—That was clever, by the way, said Nicola.

She sat. She slumped, like a big kid pretending to slump. She was wearing a grey hoodie. It must have been an old one of Jack's – it was too big to be Leanne's.

—Thanks, said Paula. —It gives us time, like.

—For what?

—It gives you time.

—I don't need time, said Nicola. —I'm not thinking like that any more.

—Like what, hon?

Nicola didn't answer.

Paula bit into the toastie. It was lovely – the tomatoes were just right, soft but not too hot, the way they sometimes got.

She held up the rest of it.

—Not bad, she said. —If I say so myself.

—I knew you were going to say that.

—Feck off now, said Paula. —I made it, I'm entitled to like it.

—Self-praise is no praise, said Nicola.

She was coming out of her slump, a bit. She was sitting up.

—D'you ever wonder where we learn those things? said Paula.

—What things?

—Like what you just said – self-praise is no praise. Says who? D'you know what I mean? Why shouldn't we praise ourselves? Is it school?

—What?

—Where they teach us these sayings. Self-praise is no praise, flattery will get you nowhere. Excuse me – hello. Flattery will get you fuckin' everywhere. And what's wrong with praising yourself now and again?

—What for?

—Jesus, love – anything. Anything you can. This.

She put the last of the toastie into her mouth.

—It's lovely, she said. —There now – what's wrong with that?

Her phone buzzed – it was beside the plate. She looked at it.

—Mary, she said. —Your cornflakes are at the door.

Nicola started to get up.

—No, said Paula. —Hang on. I told them all you were in a bad way.

—Why?

—To keep them away, said Paula. —And I'll be honest with you, Nicola – I enjoyed it.

She stood up.

—Enjoyed what? said Nicola.

—Making it up, said Paula.

She was at the kitchen door. She stopped. She went back to the table.

—We're up and down, the pair of us. Like a pair of yo-yos. You up, me down, me up and you down.

She was dying to see Mary, even just to wave at her. But what she'd actually been doing was walking away from Nicola, again.

She sat.

—And, Nicola, she said.

—What?

—You are in a bad way.

Nicola said nothing.

—Maybe we both are, said Paula. —What d'you think?

Nicola was looking at the table.

—Nicola?

—What?

—D'you agree?

—With what?

—That we're both in a bad way, said Paula.

—Well, Mammy, said Nicola. —I'll tell you. That sounds like shite.

—Okay –.

—Sentimental shite – that's all that is. That's my diagnosis.

—I'm trying to get us to talk, said Paula. —That's all. D'you want them cornflakes?

Nicola shrugged.

—They can wait, so, said Paula.

She reached for her phone, to thank Mary. But she stopped. She pushed the phone away, to the end of the table. She couldn't see Nicola's phone anywhere. The satsumas Nicola had brought with her the night before were the only things left on the table, besides Paula's phone, and the plate.

—D'you want one of your satsumas? she asked Nicola.

—No.

—I'm having one, anyway, said Paula. —Haven't had one of these in a long time.

She pulled at the orange net till there was a hole big enough to let her take one out. What was she going to do? What was she going to say? The satsuma was helping – something to do, something in her hands.

—D'you want tea?

—No.

—Coffee?

—No.

—Sure?

—No.

—Nicola.

—What?

—I can't believe sometimes – that I still live here.

Nicola looked at her properly now, straight at her – interested, listening.

—You were here, said Paula. —You saw everything. Not everything, but more than any kid should see. And here we are.

She made herself smile. The phone buzzed. She made sure she didn't look at it.

—I think, she said. —I think I thought – that everything that happened then happened to me. Happened to me, just. Only to me.

She looked up.

—I don't think there was ever blood on the ceiling. But maybe I don't remember.

—There wasn't, said Nicola.

—I think that's what I love about Beyoncé upstairs?

—What?

—It's so innocent, said Paula. —So lovely. When I think of everything else that happened.

—Jack was too young.

—Was he?

—Yeah.

—Well, said Paula. —I hope so. But I can remember –.

She'd peeled the satsuma and put her thumb into its centre, to halve it. She put two segments into her mouth.

—Oh, that's lovely.

She leaned over and placed half the peeled satsuma on the table, in front of Nicola.

—There you go, she said.

Nicola picked it up.

—But – yeah – I can remember, said Paula. —I had Jack in my arms. I was sitting – Jesus, Nicola, I was sitting here, exactly here. And he was bleeding – there was blood all over him. His head and his face and on his top. And I couldn't figure it out – I couldn't see where it was coming from.

—You.

—Yeah, said Paula. —Yeah. Me.

—I'm not playing this game, said Nicola.

—What –? What game?

—You Think That's Bad.

—There is no game, Nicola, said Paula.

—I'm not playing it, said Nicola. —I'm not having it.

—Sorry, Nicola, said Paula. —I don't know what you're on about. Honestly. Like – I don't know what you mean.

She wanted to get up and go – gone, down to Mary's house, anywhere, just out of the house.

—You were going to tell me that you know exactly what I'm going through, said Nicola. —You've already more or less told me that you had it worse – because I never bled on top of one of my children. An experience I've been deprived of, thank Christ. But you're going to tell me that it'll be grand because you've been through far worse and you're still sitting in the same fuckin' chair that you sat in when you bled on your blue-eyed boy and – sure, look at you – you're grand.

—Jesus, said Paula. —You really hate me, don't you?

—Yeah.

—Okay, said Paula. —Thanks for your honesty – much appreciated.

—Am I supposed to thank you?

—Nicola – I was hoping I could thank you.

She wasn't going to cry. She wasn't going to fly across the table and grab Nicola's hair.

—I'll be honest, she said. —I want to tell you to fuck off out of here if that's how you feel. And I don't doubt you, by the way. And I don't blame you either. But – I don't know what I was going to say. I was hoping this would be easier – that's all.

—Easier?

Paula shrugged.

—Yeah.

She got another satsuma out of the net. She started to peel it.

—I know, she said. —No. I don't know. I don't know. Anything I say – Nicola. Anything I say – I don't know what you're going through or have – already gone through, like. I don't know. I've no problem saying that. I know you hate me.

She hoped for the interruption, the contradiction – but Nicola stayed silent, looking over Paula's shoulder at the sink and the window.

—I do know that much, she said. —I know it's mixed up with other things – feelings. Can I say one thing? One thing that might annoy you?

She smiled – she couldn't help it. She was dancing through a fuckin' minefield.

—Go on, said Nicola.

—I hated my mother, said Paula. —I loved her but I hated her as well.

She waited – she hoped.

—Why? said Nicola.

—Because she never warned me, said Paula. —She never warned me about what I was letting myself in for. And she knew. Believe me. I don't like talking bad about the dead – and I loved her as well. But – Nicola. My father was a horrible man. He was just horrible. He wasn't in the same league as your father but – Jesus. And one of the reasons I married Charlo was to get away from my own father. He never did anything to me – or, like your father did with you. But my mother sat back and said nothing. If she was sitting where you are I'd scream at her.

She stood up and went to the sink. She turned on the cold tap. It surprised her how easy it was – she felt light.

—D'you want water? she asked – she shouted over the noise of the tap and the water hitting the sink.

—No. Yeah – okay.

—Anything else?

—No.

—Sure? There's all that food.

Nicola didn't say more. Paula found two clean mugs and filled them, and brought them back to the table. She sat, and put one of the mugs in front of Nicola.

—Thanks.

—No bother.

She drank. She put the mug down. She examined her hands. She wasn't shaking.

—I know, she said. —The situations are different. You didn't marry your father.

Nicola was holding the mug, although it was still on the table.

—Did you?

—No, said Nicola. —No, I didn't.

—The girls, Nicola, said Paula. —They're not going to do what I did. Because of you.

Nicola glanced at Paula, then away, then back.

—Why d'you think you know all this? she said. —What makes you think you can sit there and – like – persuade yourself

248

that what you're saying is true? Even a bit true, or even worth listening to.

—I'm old, hon, said Paula.

—Stop calling me hon – please. And everyone else. It's embarrassing.

—I'm old. Nicola. And – yeah. I'm a bit wiser.

—Wiser than what? The fridge? Me?

—Not you, no, said Paula. —But I am your mother –

—Don't even –

—And I'm talking to you and – let me finish, Nicola, just let me speak, then you can do what you want. I know it's late in the day but it's better than never. I'm talking to you now and I'm listening to you. As your mother.

Paula could feel sweat on her forehead, in her hair, already turning cold.

—And I know, she said. —Even if my mother, God rest her, had tried to warn me off Charlo I'd have ignored her. It would've made me more determined. So – I'm not blaming my mother for my life. I was in love with your father, believe it or not. He wasn't always a monster.

—Is that true? said Nicola.

—True? said Paula. —The truth? He hit me the first time when I was pregnant.

—With me.

—Yeah, said Paula. —With you. Exactly. I'm sorry.

—Jesus.

Nicola wasn't crying, and she didn't look like she was going to.

—Would you do it any different? Nicola asked.

—If I could go back?

—Yeah.

—D'you know what? said Paula. —It's a horrible question. She laughed.

—Sorry, she said. —Jesus. I think –. I don't know what I fuckin' think. No – I do. I'd have left him sooner – I'd have thrown him out sooner. Much sooner. If I went all the way back

249

to when he asked me up to dance and if I'd done the sensible thing and said no –.

She laughed again. She wiped her eyes.

—We wouldn't be sitting here, she said. —I wouldn't have had you. I might have had other children but they wouldn't have been you and you're the best thing that –.

She couldn't talk. She couldn't see. She reached out, her hand across the table. Nothing. Nothing. Nothing. Then she felt it – Nicola's hand.

She wiped her face, her eyes, with her free hand.

—I think I'm after getting the satsuma juice into me eyes.

She laughed – she had to. Although she thought she was going to be sick again. She couldn't keep her hand in Nicola's. She couldn't stay sitting. Nicola let go first. Paula stood and went the couple of blind steps to the sink. She didn't need to see. She knew exactly where to put herself. She filled her hands with cold water and brought her face down to meet them. She did it again.

Nicola was beside her.

—Are you alright?

—I'm grand, said Paula.

She'd turned off the tap. Her face was wet. She gathered up the dressing gown – again – and dried her face.

Nicola was still there, beside her.

—I want tea, said Paula.

—I'll make it.

—You won't, said Paula. —You want a cuppa, yourself, yeah?

—Yeah – go on.

Paula filled the kettle and heard Nicola sitting down behind her. She put the kettle on its base and pushed the switch down. She waited till she could hear the kettle kicking into action. Then she turned and sat down.

—Are my eyes red? she asked.

—Not really.

—Not really?

Nicola shrugged.

—You look fine, she said.

—If I could do anything, said Paula. —Nicola. Anything at all. I would. I would.

Nicola nodded, once – again.

—Okay.

—And Nicola, said Paula. —As well –.

—What?

—You're here, said Paula. —Here. You came here – yourself.

—I'd nowhere else, said Nicola.

—You could've gone anywhere. Anywhere you wanted. But you came here.

Paula stood up. The kettle had clicked itself off.

—You might hate me, hon – and I'll call you hon if I like, by the way. But like I said, you might hate me but I'm your mother. I can take it.

She didn't know if that was true. She hadn't a clue.

—Were there any biscuits in Tony's bags? she asked.

—No.

—No?

—No.

—Jesus, he's fuckin' useless.

Mary might have left them a packet or two on the step, with the cornflakes. A family pack of Club Milks – Paula would have eaten half of them.

She brought the mugs to the table.

—Here we go – the Rosie Lee.

She sat.

Nicola stood and got the sugar off the counter, then opened the fridge and took out the milk. She put the carton in front of Paula.

—I don't know what to do, she said.

—Do nothing, said Paula. —Do exactly what you want.

—Did you?

—Did I what?

—Do exactly what you wanted, said Nicola. —Ever.

—Jesus, said Paula. —Well –. I married your father.

—Is that it?

—And I threw him out, said Paula.

She smiled.

—So there you go, she said. —The beginning and the end – kind of.

—Okay.

—It's only the years in between that are crap, said Paula. —But I had you. And the other three. And Nicola –.

—What?

—I wouldn't be here if it wasn't for you, said Paula. —That's literally true. That's what I wanted to say earlier. So, there you go. You can take the credit or the blame.

She wanted to go to the toilet again, badly, but she had to keep going.

—But come here, she said. —You have to let me be your mother now. You've been mine for long enough. It's my turn.

She meant it. She could feel it, almost like her body was changing – she was becoming something else. The fridge, her phone, the bills, the telly, her favourite shirt upstairs, anything that ever had to be changed or mended – Nicola had given them all to her. But it wasn't about money, or that kind of independence.

—Do what you want, she said again.

—I'm not going back, said Nicola.

—Well, you're stuck here for ten days, anyway, said Paula. —Isn't that the amount of time we're supposed to isolate? I think it is.

—No, said Nicola. —I mean – I'm not going back.

—Okay, said Paula. —That's a big one to take in. Is that because you think you let Lily down? Because –

—It's because I don't want them, said Nicola.

—Okay.

—I wish I'd never had them, said Nicola.

It was like Nicola had stabbed herself, right in front of Paula. Or, she'd got the knife and run the blade down the side of her

252

face and opened it to the bone, and Paula was only allowed to watch.

She'd say nothing – she was going to say nothing. This was the test – she knew. She remembered hating her children, hating their bodies that kept getting in her way, their cries and questions, their silence, their eyes.

—I want nothing to do with them, said Nicola.

—Okay, said Paula.

—Or him.

—Have you told him? Paula asked.

—No, said Nicola. —I haven't told him anything. Why should I?

—I don't know, said Paula. —Peace of mind?

—Whose? said Nicola.

—Honestly? said Paula. —Mine.

—You want me gone.

—No, said Paula. —No, I don't. You're great crack, sure.

Nicola didn't smile.

—No, said Paula. —I don't want you gone – seriously. I said it already, you can stay as long as you want.

—But –.

—But nothing, said Paula. —No ifs or buts. Stay.

Get up, you spoilt menopausal bitch, and go home to your husband. Paula could hear herself saying that – it was her voice. This cranky yoke in front of her – she'd run away because her perfectly arranged life had been knocked sideways a bit, because of something some slack-jawed cunt had said at a funeral. Fuck her.

That was the thing, though – the perfectly arranged life. That was how Nicola had managed it, how she'd kept Charlo away – and Paula. It was how she'd coped. For thirty years. She must have been exhausted – she *was* exhausted.

—D'you want to go back up to bed? said Paula.

Nicola didn't answer.

—Are you hungry?

—No!

—Well, I am, said Paula. —And I'm bursting for the toilet.
She stood.

—I was hoping we'd have everything sorted before I went up
but that's looking a bit unrealistic now, I suppose.

Nicola smiled – Paula saw it.

—It smiles, she said.

She resisted the temptation to grab her phone off the table
as she went. She knew – Nicola would take a couple of the
ready-made meals out of the fridge while Paula was gone.
They'd be in the microwave by the time she got back. Nicola
would never let herself be looked after. She'd never submit.
Even putting something in the microwave – she'd do it herself,
and she'd do it for Paula.

Paula washed her hands, and had a quick look in the bathroom mirror. She'd do. Jack's door was wide open. The sun
was shining directly into the room. They were well into the
afternoon. And not a child in the house washed. One of her
mother's sayings – Paula's head was full of them.

Nicola was sitting where she'd left her – there were no lasagnes doing the conga in the microwave.

Paula grabbed the net of satsumas.

—We'll have another of these fellas, will we? D'you want
one, Nicola?

—No.

—The vitamin C, said Paula. —You can't get enough of it.
She took an orange from the net. She started to peel it.

—So, she said. —You're staying.

—If I'm let.

—You are, said Paula.

—Only for a while.

—Grand.

—I'll find somewhere.

—Okay.

—You don't believe me, said Nicola.

—I do.

—You don't.

—Listen, hon, said Paula. —I believe you. But I can hardly believe it. Does that make sense?

—Yeah – okay.

—I have to catch up, said Paula.

—Same here, said Nicola.

—What d'you mean? Paula asked her.

She put some of the satsuma into her mouth, and bit.

—I don't know, said Nicola.

—Don't know?

Paula opened her mouth and let two, three, four pips drop onto her hand.

—This one has pips, she said. —How does that happen? It looked exactly like the other ones and they didn't have any.

She was looking at the pips.

—I don't like the pips, she said. —D'you know what I think of when I see them?

Nicola said nothing.

—Balls, said Paula. —Little balls. Like a pup would have or something. After it's been neutered.

Nicola laughed.

Paula dropped the pips onto the table.

Nicola put a finger to one of the pips and nudged it.

—You're mad, she said.

—Mind you, said Paula. —They're all the same. The fruit and veg – full of little balls.

It was a conversation – a riot – she'd had with Mary, after Mary brought an avocado to work, and cut it open. Oh, fuck, she'd said, Bruce Willis got here ahead of me. She remembered telling Leanne about it later, the two of them clutching each other, in tears.

—I don't know what I'm doing, said Nicola. —I *do* – but I only thought of that now, really.

—Leaving?

—Yeah.

—A big decision.

—I'm aware of that, thanks.

—I'm just saying, said Paula. —I couldn't do it.

—You're a saint.

—I didn't mean it like that, said Paula. —It's a fact – I couldn't. I tried.

—I remember.

—Do you?

—You told us to put clothes into our schoolbags, said Nicola. —We stood at the door, waiting for you to open it. You told us we were going to Carmel's.

—But I didn't open the door, said Paula.

—No.

—I was too frightened.

—I went to do it, said Nicola. —And you slapped my hand.

—Did I?

—Yeah.

—Jesus – Nicola, said Paula. —I'm –. I was terrified. I did it – I mean, I stood at the door – sometimes on my own, all set to go. Did you know that?

—I saw you at the door sometimes, said Nicola. —Just standing.

—Did you know?

—I didn't know, said Nicola. —But I remember it scared me.

Paula wiped her eyes.

—I need something to blow my nose, she said.

She looked around.

—Tony never thought of toilet paper, she said.

—Here, said Nicola.

She was holding a wad of toilet paper out to Paula.

—Where did that come from?

—It was in the pocket of this, said Nicola.

Paula blew her nose, and wiped it. She put the tissue in her dressing-gown pocket. She looked across at Nicola. Her eyes were dry. The paper hadn't been for herself, to wipe her own eyes. She'd found it in the hoodie pocket. Paula got the tissue from her pocket and wiped her nose again.

—How can you be so cold? she said.

—I don't know.

—I'm sorry I said that, said Paula. —Sorry.

—I don't care, said Nicola.

—It was wrong.

—I honestly don't care, said Nicola.

—Jesus – Nicola.

—I've had it.

—That I can understand, said Paula.

—Well, I don't, said Nicola. —Understand. So don't dare start telling me that you do.

—Can I ask you something? said Paula.

—What?

—Lily –.

—That's not a question.

—Lily being gawked at by that dirtbird –.

—Keith.

—Lily didn't see him.

—No.

—She will, though, said Paula. —She'll see him – and the other Keiths. We both know that.

—Okay, said Nicola.

—I'm not trying to catch you out.

Nicola nodded.

—Okay.

—You're not going to be there, said Paula. —So –. Who'll teach her?

—Who taught me? said Nicola.

—I did, said Paula.

She'd said it before she'd thought about it. It shocked her – it was true.

—I did, she said again. —I got a frying pan and I brained him with it.

—That's true, said Nicola.

She sat back.

—After how many years of watching you being dragged around by the hair?

That was true too.

There was no noise, anywhere. Not from outside, or next door. The kids in there, and their mother – they had their ears to the wall.

—Have you ever been?

—What?

—Dragged by the hair.

—That's it, said Nicola.

—What?

—It's what you think, said Nicola. —If I haven't been beaten or dragged around or burnt with a cigarette – I saw that too, remember. I haven't lived – I don't have anything to complain about. I've a good husband because he doesn't hit me.

—It's a start.

—Shut up.

—Sorry, said Paula.

She wanted to slap Nicola. Again.

—It's some measurement, said Nicola. —Some gauge. Isn't it? Does he batter you?

—I know –.

—What about does he bore you? Or does he annoy you? Does the prospect of spending the rest of your life with him fill you with dread?

—Is that what you feel?

—I don't know what I feel, said Nicola. —I don't know if I feel. I don't know. And I don't know why it's all about Tony. What's wrong with Tony, what's right about Tony. There's nothing wrong or right. I don't want to be a wife. I think I know that much.

—Have you spoken to Tony about –?

—I'm not talking about Tony, said Nicola. —I told you. It's not about Tony and – come here as well – it's not about you either.

—It's about you.

—Yes!

—I hear you.

—Oh, great! That's fuckin' great!

—Right, said Paula. —You're upsetting yourself, I'm upsetting you. Enough.

She grabbed the mug and hoped there was some water left in it. There was – she could feel its weight before she looked in and brought it to her mouth.

She drank.

She put the mug down.

—I'll tell you what I thought, she said. —What I thought was going to happen. What I hoped. Okay? Nicola?

Nicola nodded.

—Okay, said Paula. —Good. I thought you'd stay here for a while till you calmed down and felt better –.

—Stopped being a woman.

—Okay, said Paula. —Stopped being a woman – hysterical and menopausal and the rest of it, yeah. I thought you were right to be upset, by the way – about what you saw. I don't honestly know what I'd have done if I'd seen the Keith cunt. I don't know – maybe nothing. God knows, I did nothing for years. But – I'll be honest. I felt a bit superior – just a little bit. I felt one up on you, because I'd got rid of your father the minute I saw him looking at you. But – anyway.

She was talking normally, calmly, word followed by word – saying things that surprised her as she spoke.

—I thought you'd have a bit of a rest here with me. I thought we might even have a nice time. And I thought you'd be grand. You'd stay for a bit and then you'd go home. I couldn't imagine that you'd want anything different. You have the perfect life. All you've done – all you've managed. Jesus, Nicola, you're amazing – I'm not trying to get you to see different, I'm just telling you what I thought. What I think.

There was still some water in the mug. She drank the last of it. Her stomach growled.

—Listen to that, she said.

—What?

—Nothing, said Paula. —It doesn't matter – my stomach.

She reached for the bananas on the counter.

—Come here to me.

She pulled one from the bunch.

—I haven't had a banana in a long time, she said. —Tony must've known we'd be too busy to cook anything.

—Just stop it, will you.

—What?

—Making it about Tony, said Nicola.

—I wasn't, said Paula. —Was I –?

—I like bananas, said Nicola. —Tony knows I like bananas. So what?

—Nothing.

—I should run back into his arms because he knows I like bananas, said Nicola. —Jesus.

Paula had peeled the banana.

—I'm afraid to eat it now, she said.

—Eat it, said Nicola. —Go on. Just leave Tony out of it – it's only a fuckin' banana.

—I have your permission, yeah?

—When I nearly lost Lily, said Nicola. —The only things I could eat – that I could keep down – were bananas. And toast.

—I remember that, said Paula.

—For months, said Nicola. —You'd think it would have put me off them, but it didn't.

—That's kind of nice, though, said Paula. —It is. He remembered. They're kind of a love letter.

—They're a threat, said Nicola.

—Ah, Jesus – Nicola. They're only bananas.

—They were love letters a minute ago.

—This is mad, said Paula. —We should both be laughing. Why aren't we laughing?

Nicola took a banana. She wasn't smiling. She peeled it.

Paula bit into hers.

—Vanessa and Gillian, said Nicola. —They're grown up – they're adults.

—The little one, though –.

—What little one? said Nicola. —Lily? She's taller than me.

—She's still a child.

—I don't care, said Nicola.

—You do, hon, said Paula. —You're only saying that. You do care.

The scream tore flesh from Paula's bones. It wasn't human. Nicola's mouth was open, gaping, but it wasn't a noise that could have come from Nicola. Nothing had readied Paula for this. She wasn't looking at Nicola. It wasn't even a replacement – an imposter, some creature that looked like Nicola. Nicola wasn't there – nothing was there.

The silence was worse. It wasn't silence. It was something unbearable – agony.

This was the test.

—Okay, said Paula.

Nicola screamed again.

Paula stayed where she was. Her phone was near her. She could grab it, call for help or scream, herself.

She didn't.

She didn't look at it.

She looked at Nicola. It was Nicola again. Just Nicola.

—I don't know, said Nicola. —I don't know.

—Okay.

—I don't know, said Nicola. —I'm frightened.

—You're here, said Paula.

—I'm frightened, Nicola said again.

—I know you are, said Paula.

—I don't know what to do.

—Whatever you do, said Paula. —Whatever you decide. Will be right. Nicola –? Nicola?

She wasn't sure, but she thought Nicola was looking at her.

—I believe that, said Paula.

She did. She could feel its truth seep through her, colouring her.

—What I just said, said Paula. —I believe it. You decide – you'll be right.

Nicola nodded.

Paula watched as she pulled one of the sleeves of the hoodie so that it covered her fist, and she brought it up to her face and wiped her cheeks and eyes with it.

—Nicola?

—What?

—It'll be grand, said Paula. —Whatever you do. It'll be fine.

—I don't know.

—It will.

—I feel so bad, said Nicola.

—I know, said Paula.

Nicola wiped her face again.

—How long are we supposed to isolate? she asked. —Is it ten days?

—Yeah, said Paula. —I think so. Or eight.

—We're stuck with each other, said Nicola.

Paula smiled – she thought she did.

—We are.

Acknowledgements

My thanks to Lucy Luck, Dan Franklin, Nick Skidmore, Deirdre Molina, Paul Slovak, Lynda Myles, Sarah-Jane Forder, Graeme Hall, and thanks to Jay Green for the cat and the Springsteen ticket.